HOME BEFORE MIDNIGHT

VIRGINIA KANTRA

BERKLEY SENSATION, NEW YORK

THE BERKLEY PUBLISHING GROUP
Published by the Penguin Group
Penguin Group (USA) Inc.
375 Hudson Street, New York, New York 10014, USA
Penguin Group (Canada), 90 Eglinton Avenue East, Suite 700, Toronto, Ontario M4P 2Y3, Canada
(a division of Pearson Penguin Canada Inc.)
Penguin Books Ltd., 80 Strand, London WC2R 0RL, England
Penguin Books Ireland, 25 St. Stephen's Green, Dublin 2, Ireland (a division of Penguin Books Ltd.)
Penguin Group (Australia), 250 Camberwell Road, Camberwell, Victoria 3124, Australia
(a division of Pearson Australia Group Pty. Ltd.)
Penguin Books India Pvt. Ltd., 11 Community Centre, Panchsheel Park, New Delhi—110 017, India
Penguin Group (NZ), Cnr. Airborne and Rosedale Roads, Albany, Auckland 1310, New Zealand
(a division of Pearson New Zealand Ltd.)
Penguin Books (South Africa) (Pty.) Ltd., 24 Sturdee Avenue, Rosebank, Johannesburg 2196,
South Africa

Penguin Books Ltd., Registered Offices: 80 Strand, London WC2R 0RL, England

HOME BEFORE MIDNIGHT

A Berkley Sensation Book / published by arrangement with the author

PRINTING HISTORY
Berkley Sensation mass-market edition / August 2006

Copyright © 2006 by Virginia Kantra
Cover design by Pyrographx
Book design by Kristin del Rosario

ISBN: 0-425-21108-8

BERKLEY SENSATION®
Berkley Sensation Books are published by The Berkley Publishing Group,
a division of Penguin Group (USA) Inc.,
375 Hudson Street, New York, New York 10014.
BERKLEY SENSATION and the "B" design are registered trademarks of Penguin Group (USA) Inc.

PRINTED IN THE UNITED STATES OF AMERICA

10 9 8 7 6 5 4 3 2 1

For Michael

*I always say I couldn't do it without you, darling.
Now you know it's true.*

ACKNOWLEDGMENTS

Special thanks to all the people who took time from their important jobs and busy lives to answer my questions patiently and correctly, especially Lt. A.J. Carter (Ret.), criminal investigation, Durham Police Department; my sister-in-law, retired corrections officer Virginia Grisez (how would I have come up with that plot point without you?); my sister, nurse extraordinaire, Pamela Archbold; financial adviser Fred D. Gunther; estate attorney Kevin Stroud; and the Office of the Chief Medical Examiner in Chapel Hill. Everything I got right is because of their generous help. Everything I got wrong is my own fault.

Thanks to Judith Stanton and all the members of Heart of Carolina—you know who you are!—for your ongoing support.

Thank you, Jean, Drew, and Mark, for living through my deadlines with me.

And deepest thanks to Cindy Hwang, to Damaris Rowland, and to Melissa McClone for helping me make this book the best it could be.

ONE

Stokesville, NC—A seventeen-year-old denied admittance to his high school dance stabbed his mother, grandmother, and sister to death on Friday night, authorities said.

The youth, identified Sunday as Billy Ray Dawler, is a sophomore at Jefferson High School. School officials and police said the teen was apparently under the influence of alcohol.

Police were informed of the stabbings early Saturday morning by an anonymous caller. Detectives discovered the bodies of Shirley Dawler, 49, Tammy Dawler, 33, and Tanya Dawler, 15, at the family's home at 543 White Pine Road. Neighbors report frequent late-night visitors to the modest brick bungalow, but no witnesses for that evening have come forward.

* * *

BAILEY Wells shivered. And she thought *she* had issues in high school.

Dropping the microfiche printout on her bed, Bailey lifted her heavy brown hair off her neck. Outside her window, a willow drooped, pale in the moonlight, listless in the heat.

For better or worse, there was no place like home. And nothing hotter or lonelier than a Carolina summer night.

Even with the windows locked and the thermostat lowered to sixty-five degrees, the air gripped the house like a warm, damp fist. The grinding whine of the cicadas swelled the night and buzzed in her blood. She had to be crazy to leave New York—the exciting career opportunities, the sophisticated nightlife, her cozy studio apartment—for this.

Not crazy. The thought slipped in like a breeze under the windowsill, stirring her mood. *In love*.

Bailey flushed and dropped her hair. No, that wasn't right, either.

Anyway, she could admit—to herself and the cicadas, at least—the career thing hadn't gone exactly as planned. She had hoped her job as personal assistant to a bestselling crime writer would give her a break from tweaking other people's manuscripts and the time and motivation to work on her own. But after two years of working for Paul Ellis, she was no closer to submitting her own novel. Oh, admit it. She wasn't even writing.

As for her nightlife . . . She had burned out on bars and blind dates. She was sick of guys who were never as young or as tall, as emotionally available or financially stable as their on-line profiles promised. She was tired of drinking bad wine and cheap beer to blur the edges of her evenings, thankful she didn't generally wake up with anything worse than a headache. Most nights she chose to spend alone in her fourth-floor East Village walk-up, watching *Friends* reruns and throwing shoes at whatever scuttled from beneath the minifridge.

At least the cicadas made a change from cockroaches.

She stared out at the moon-dappled lawn and the fancy new streetlights of the town where she'd once been voted Most Likely to Leave. She hadn't given up, she told herself. Not yet. She'd just . . . grown up.

Enough to come home.

Paul had broken the news. "I would never insist that you come with us," he had said, with one of his special looks. "But this new book is a wonderful opportunity for you. And you're from around there, aren't you? Stokesville, North Carolina? You probably even remember the Dawler killings. It was quite a scandal at the time."

Nineteen years ago.

"I was seven," Bailey said. "Maybe your wife—"

His wife of five years was Helen Stokes Ellis, a wealthy Magnolia-in-exile who preferred her bourbon on the rocks and her relatives at a distance.

Paul shrugged dismissively. "You know Helen never reads the paper. Or pays attention to the news, if she can help it."

Bailey squashed the satisfaction she felt at his small disloyalty. "But she's from the area. I mean, the town is named after her family. She knows people."

"But she doesn't understand my work. I want you, Bailey."

Bailey's heart beat a little faster.

"We both want you," he had added. "Helen will be glad for the company, and I need your help with this book."

Bailey doubted Helen would deign to notice her existence. But it was irresistible to be needed. To be valued for something other than her ability to attract and keep the right man. The "right man," as defined by Bailey's mother, being any white, single, thirty-year-old, Methodist, Southern professional.

Maybe Paul didn't meet her mama's specifications.

Maybe he didn't feel Bailey's writing was ready to show anyone else yet.

But he needed her. He'd said so.

After the move, he'd even insisted she make her home with them, with Paul and Helen, in Helen's house. God knew, he had said with a droll look, there was enough room.

The old Stokes place had been built in the 1930s for a large and prosperous family. The sweeping verandas and imposing columns in front were balanced by two thoroughly modern additions in back, the master suite and a kitchen-and-dining wing, flanking an artfully landscaped swimming pool.

Bailey had her own room and bathroom in the original part of the house, with high ceilings and heavy wood trim that more than made up for the uneven floors and cramped shower. Maybe she didn't have a view of the pool, but she was welcome to use it whenever Helen wasn't entertaining or sunbathing or, well, there.

She wouldn't be there now, Bailey thought, glancing at the clock. It was almost midnight. On her "at home" nights, Helen went to bed early and fell asleep with the television on. No one would notice, no one would care, if Bailey snuck down to the kitchen and fixed a snack to eat by the pool.

Unless Paul was up, working.

Bailey pushed the thought away.

She made her way downstairs in the dark, refusing even to look in the direction of his study to see if his lights were on. All she wanted was to sit by the pool and watch the cool gleam of the water and the bugs committing suicide in the patio lights while she smothered her restlessness in ice cream. *Stress eating,* Dr. Phil called it. *Ask yourself what you really want.*

She knew what she wanted.

And what she couldn't have.

Ice cream was better. Safer.

In the kitchen, she dug deep into a round carton of Edy's butter pecan. The heaped ice cream looked lonely in the bowl, so she added sliced strawberries and then a squeeze of chocolate syrup and then—on impulse—a second spoon.

Two-fisted eater? her conscience mocked.

She ignored it. Carrying her spoils, she slid open the patio door, flipped on the lights . . . and froze. Apprehension squeezed her chest. Something big drifted below the surface of the water, dark against the submerged lights. Something big and dark, with floating hair.

Bailey took a step forward, dread backing up in her lungs.

Helen was not in her room.

She was in the pool. Facedown, at the bottom. Faint, dark swirls curled upward through the luminous blue water.

Bailey's bowl slipped from her hands and shattered against the Mexican tile.

LIEUTENANT Steve Burke hadn't worked the graveyard shift since he was a wet-behind-the-ears detective. Most investigative work took place during the day, when folks were awake and around to talk to. But in a small department, rank was no protection against a shit assignment. Somebody had to be on call through the midnight hours, and it was usually the new guy. Steve didn't mind. It meant flextime, some time to spend with Gabrielle.

Of course, Gabby wouldn't be happy if she woke and found him gone, but he'd left a note. With any luck, he'd be back before breakfast.

He pulled up the long drive and parked his truck behind an ambulance and a pair of black-and-whites. The big house was lit up like the folks inside were giving a party, which, from what he'd heard, wouldn't have been unusual. Not that he'd ever been invited. He grimaced and got out of the truck, grabbing his kit from the passenger seat. Helen Stokes Ellis might have married a man who was Not From Around Here, as folks delicately and pointedly referred to Yankees. But now that she was back home, she didn't socialize with people who were Not Her Kind.

Steve had never met Paul Ellis, the husband, but he'd heard stories about him, too. The briefing room was thicker with gossip than the barbershop or his mother's Wednesday morning Bible group. Ellis was a real pain in the ass. He'd recently pissed off the chief of police by implying that his department had railroaded a murder investigation twenty years ago.

It was all before Steve's time, but his sympathies were with the department. He had no patience with self-styled experts. And no reason to believe Ellis wouldn't be equally critical of the police's handling of his wife's death.

No wonder the patrol officer on duty tonight had been anxious to pass the buck to Steve.

Steve prowled up the walk, carrying his kit. Yellow crime scene tape was strung around the house like bizarre party decorations. *That* would get the neighbors' attention in the morning. How long, he wondered, before the press showed up? Not just the local press, either, the papers from Raleigh and Durham and even Charlotte. Paul Ellis was a bestselling true crime writer. His wife was a wealthy older woman who'd spent years maneuvering on the social pages. This case had the potential to blow up in Steve's face. And the explosion could attract national media attention.

His lucky night. There were guys already grumbling over Steve's hiring, detectives with more seniority who'd be only too happy to accuse him of hogging the limelight . . . or point their fingers if he screwed up.

Raising the yellow tape over his head, he walked in through the open front door.

Uniforms clustered at the other end of the long hallway. Beyond them, an arch opened up on some big room walled with glass. He'd get sketches and photographs of the layout later. For now, he focused on Wayne Lewis, the responding officer. Lewis, a fresh-faced rookie, was young enough not to resent him, and hadn't known him long enough to dislike him.

"What happened?" Steve asked quietly.

Lewis cleared his throat. "The homeowner—Helen Stokes?—was found drowned in the pool."

The majority of drownings were accidental. Most involved the use or abuse of alcohol.

"And you called me because . . . ?"

Lewis turned red to the tips of his big ears. "The victim was fully clothed and has swelling and a slight laceration on the back of her head. She could have slipped and hit her head on the side of the pool as she fell. Or . . ."

Or she could have gotten an assist into the water.

Steve nodded. "Okay. Who's the R.P.?" Reporting party.

"The husband," Lewis said. "Paul Ellis."

"He find the body?"

"Negative. The deceased was discovered just after midnight by Bailey Wells, Mr. Ellis's personal assistant. She lives with the family," Lewis explained.

Steve followed the patrolman's gaze across the room,

where a skinny brunette knelt beside a handsome, haggard man in a leather armchair. Her dark hair hung in lank strands around her pale face. Her plain black blouse clung to her narrow rib cage, revealing the lines of her bra and the shape of her breasts. Steve felt an unwelcome twinge of compassion. There was something vulnerable and appealing about her, even though she wouldn't win any wet T-shirt contests, for sure.

"Why is she wet?" he asked.

And why the hell hadn't anybody thought to bring her a towel?

"She pulled Mrs. Ellis out of the pool," one of the other cops volunteered.

Steve looked to Lewis for confirmation.

Lewis nodded. "Apparently she was trying to resuscitate her when Mr. Ellis called 911."

Well, that was natural, Steve conceded. Competent. Even heroic. It was just too bad the brunette's intervention had further fucked up an already compromised crime scene.

Despite her bedraggled appearance, she was talking soothingly to the man in the chair, patting his arm.

Steve narrowed his eyes. "Who's the guy?"

"That's Paul Ellis." Lewis sounded surprised he hadn't known. "The writer."

Like he was supposed to recognize him from his book jacket or something.

"Get her away from him," Steve ordered.

"She's comforting him," the second cop said. "The man just lost his wife."

Steve should sympathize. He'd lost his own wife thirty-one months ago. But however much he had railed against Teresa's cause of death, at least he'd known what killed her. He didn't know what had killed Helen Ellis yet. And he didn't like the fact that the two major witnesses at the scene had had ample opportunity to coordinate their stories.

He glanced again at the bereaved widower and the stringy-haired brunette, assessing their reactions. Ellis looked suitably distraught, like a man confounded by the accidental drowning death of his wife. Or like a man who had committed murder.

Beside Ellis's red-eyed display of grief, his assistant, Wells, looked pale but composed. Maybe too composed?

Steve admired self-control. He had no use for hysterics. But Bailey Wells had known the dead woman. Lived in her house. Discovered her body. He expected her to demonstrate some emotion at her death.

He studied Wells's white face, her dilated pupils. The result of shock, maybe. It definitely wasn't grief.

"She lives here, you said?" he asked Lewis.

"Yes, sir."

He watched Wells lean forward to murmur to Ellis and wondered. Just how personal an assistant was she?

"Have you notified the medical examiner yet?"

"No, I . . . the paramedics responded first and I—"

"Do it now," Steve ordered. He was too late to preserve the scene, but at least the ME could view the body. "I'm going to get consent from Ellis before I do a walk-through. Lewis, I want you to take pictures. We need to record the scene before the body's moved. In the meantime, separate those two until I can take their statements. And somebody bring that woman a towel."

BAILEY was barely holding it together. She huddled on a kitchen chair, listening to the low voices and slow footsteps outside, feeling as if her head had disconnected from her neck and was floating somewhere above her body.

Her body. Floating.

Bailey shuddered.

"You want another towel?" asked the female officer who had been banished with her to the kitchen. Like Bailey needed a baby-sitter.

Or a guard.

She shuddered again. She couldn't seem to stop shaking, bone-deep tremors neither the warm night or her now-damp towel were doing a damn thing to dispel.

"No, thank you," she said politely, because her mama had raised her children to be respectful to the law. Anyway, it wasn't the officer's fault Bailey was stuck in here while poor Paul wrestled his grief and guilt alone.

She'd felt better when she could comfort him. She'd felt useful. Valued. *Glad.*

And then she had despised herself because it was wrong to rejoice in being needed when he was hurting so and Helen was . . .

God, she couldn't believe it. Helen was *dead.*

Bailey hugged the towel around her shoulders as if it could shield her from the memory of Helen's flaccid face and vacant eyes. She had put her mouth on Helen's cold, slack mouth. She had blown her breath into Helen's unresponsive lungs. She'd done everything she knew how to do, over and over until she was dizzy, and it hadn't been enough.

Now she couldn't do anything. She couldn't see anything. The police had closed the kitchen blinds, leaving her to worry. And to wait. She sat, stunned. Numb. Her hands twisted in the towel. Her mind tumbled and spun like a double-load dryer at the laundromat.

Maybe she should call her parents? Or a lawyer. But she felt too guilty to face her mother's eyes, and she wasn't guilty enough to need a lawyer.

There had to be something she could do.

Bailey stirred on the hard wooden chair. "Do you want some tea? Sweet tea?" she added, in case the cop thought in this house of death and Yankees she might not be served the proper syrupy beverage that lubricated the South.

The woman—OFFICER M. CONNER, read the nametag on her uniform—looked surprised, as if the chair had spoken.

Bailey saw the "no" forming in her eyes and offered, "Or I could make coffee."

"I guess I could drink coffee," the other woman conceded.

Relieved, Bailey stood, forcing her knees to support her, her hands to uncurl, her mind to focus on the mundane task of spooning grounds into a paper filter. She had just put the pot under the drip when the door slid open and the tall, plainclothes detective came in from the flood-lit patio.

Bailey remembered him because he stuck out—older than the officers who had first appeared on the scene, younger than Paul, and confident in a macho way that raised her hackles. Beneath his loose sport coat and heat-wilted shirt, his body was solid. Muscled. His eyes were black and bold, his features harsh and so aggressively masculine he was almost homely.

She thought at first, stupidly, he had been attracted by the smell of the brewing coffee.

He nodded once to Conner before his hard, cop's eyes sought Bailey. "Miz Wells? I'm Lieutenant Burke." His deep-timbred twang plucked her nerves. "I'd like to ask you a few questions."

Bailey nodded, her teeth chattering. She couldn't think. She needed time. She snagged a mug down from the cabinet, unable to control the trembling of her hand. "Coffee?"

"No, thank you, ma'am." He didn't smile.

Her head still felt light. Her heart was racing. "Do you mind if I get some for myself and Officer Conner?"

"You all go right ahead," he said, just as polite, but with a rasp in his voice.

She poured two coffees, added milk to her own, and put the cream and sugar within easy reach of the female officer. The whole time, Lieutenant Burke watched her, a glint in the back of those eyes, like he wasn't used to being put off.

Bailey sat back down, leaving her coffee untouched on the table. Burke had taken the chair opposite hers, his bulk cutting her off, hemming her in, creating an island of privacy in the brightly lit kitchen. His knees were large and square. And too close, she thought, but she didn't know how to scoot back her chair without offending him.

She folded her hands to hide their shaking and waited.

"All comfortable now?" Burke asked.

Bailey flushed. "Yes, thank you."

He pulled a notebook from his breast pocket. She braced herself to relive the horrible moments with Helen in the pool. "Where are you from, Miz Wells?"

She gaped at him. Shouldn't he be asking about Helen? About the accident? But she pulled herself together to answer. "I've spent the past four years in New York."

Lieutenant Burke didn't look impressed. She wasn't trying to impress him, she reminded herself.

"And you moved here . . ."

"Over three weeks ago." Her throat relaxed as she swallowed. Maybe his questions were intended to put her at ease.

"Why?"

Why did it matter? "Because Helen wanted to," she answered evenly.

And Helen always got what she wanted. With her children grown and flown and her prize-winning husband receiving the lion's share of attention in New York, Helen wanted to go home.

Burke made a sound, a masculine grunt that could have

been challenge or acknowledgment. "Helen. That's the deceased."

A statement, not a question. Bailey nodded anyway.

"What was your relationship with her?"

Bailey tightened her hands in her lap. "I work for her husband."

"And what is it you do, Bailey? May I call you Bailey?"

Despite the drawled intimacy, she didn't think he liked her. Her sister would have known how to make him like her. Maybe they even knew each other. He looked about her sister's age.

Bailey nodded again. She felt like one of those plastic dogs in the rear window of a car, her head bobbing with every bump in the road. She stiffened her neck. "I'm his research and editorial assistant."

Burke didn't look impressed by that, either. "For how long?"

"Two years."

"So you've known Helen Ellis . . ."

"Two years," Bailey repeated, bewildered. Uneasy.

Those hard, dark eyes met hers. Bailey felt the jolt in her stomach. "Did you like her?"

Bailey's heart pounded. Nobody liked Helen, not even her children. She was like a wasp, shiny and dangerous, with an annoying buzz and a painful sting.

Bailey moistened her lips. "I'm sorry she's dead."

Burke was silent, his gaze still narrowed on her face. She stared back like a possum caught in the headlights of an oncoming car.

"All right." He flipped a page in his notebook. "Tell me what happened here tonight."

Relieved, she did her best to cooperate. Prompted by his questions, she told him about dinner—just the three of them, cold chicken and a salad she had picked up earlier in the day from the natural foods market—everything as usual, everything fine.

She wasn't stupid. She knew he was trying to establish whether Helen's death was an accident, just as she knew that over sixty percent of the time, female homicide victims were killed by a spouse. But even the indignation she felt on Paul's behalf—poor Paul, what must he be feeling?—was muted and blurred, as if she were still struggling underwater. She clung to facts as if they were lifelines tossed to her by the grim-faced, deep-voiced detective.

After dinner, they had followed their regular routines. Paul had gone to his study to work. Helen had gone to bed.

"Did you see her go to her room?"

Bailey forced herself to remember. "No. I took a walk. I usually take a walk."

"Anybody see you on your walk?"

Dazed, it took her a moment to realize he was asking if she had an alibi. "I don't . . . No."

"You don't know?"

She was so tired. "I didn't see anybody."

"How about when you got back?" he asked. Casual. Relentless. "Did you see anybody then?"

"No."

"Mrs. Ellis? Mr. Ellis?"

"No."

"Wasn't that unusual?"

"Not really," she said, adding with weary humor. "It's a big house."

He didn't smile.

She tried another answer to satisfy him. "I don't like to intrude on the Ellises in the evening."

"But they weren't together, you said."

"No." She didn't think so.

"Do you remember what time it was?"

"Late. After nine."

Burke glanced at his notes. "And Mr. Ellis was still working?"

"Yes." She was pretty sure.

"Why didn't you go to his study? To see if he needed you?"

Her mouth went dry. She reached for her coffee, but it was cold. She took one sip and put it down. She never sought out Paul at night. It was one of her rules, painfully arrived at and scrupulously adhered to.

"You're his assistant," Burke said in that deceptively laid-back voice. "It would be only natural for you to check in with him."

"I went to my room," she said firmly. Too firmly. "To read."

Burke sighed. "And where is your room?"

She told him. She was used to organizing facts. Good at remembering details. She told him the layout of the house and the view from her window and the exact time she had left her room to get ice cream.

"Butter pecan," she said before he could ask. "It's my favorite flavor."

His mouth didn't so much as twitch, but there was a gleam in those dark, dark eyes. Humor, maybe. Respect? Or suspicion. Bailey didn't know him well enough to guess. She didn't want to know him.

"Why two spoons?" he asked.

Bailey felt faint. Her pulse pounded in her head. "Excuse me?"

Burke's face was like a rock. His voice grated. "We found two spoons by your broken bowl. Who was the second spoon for?"

TWO

THE brunette's pale lips parted. Her deep brown eyes widened in distress.

Gotcha, sugar, Steve thought, but there was no satisfaction in it. Not much satisfaction in anything anymore.

He pushed the thought away. And waited.

She closed her mouth.

"The spoons?" he prompted.

"I thought . . . If anyone joined me . . ." She fell silent.

"Anyone?"

Her thin face flushed.

"Mrs. Ellis?" Steve asked, though he knew damn well her employer's wife hadn't brought that blush to her cheeks.

Bailey Wells shook her head, avoiding his eyes.

"Then . . . ?" He wanted her to say it. He wasn't going to lead her.

Her flush deepened. "Sometimes, when he's working late, sometimes Paul will take a break. I thought . . . It was so hot. . . . Not that I would interrupt him or anything," she added hastily.

Sure you wouldn't, Steve thought. *It's late at night, the wife's out of the picture for the evening. . . .* It was the perfect opportunity for a poolside rendezvous.

The perfect setup for murder.

"So the second spoon was for Mr. Ellis," he said without expression.

"Not really. Maybe. I just wanted to be prepared." Bailey Wells met his gaze with defiant humor. "Like the Boy Scouts."

Something in her eyes, wry and honest, pricked Steve's weary resignation. A little of his suspicion leaked away.

Possible. Not every conveniently dead spouse was dispatched by an unfaithful husband, a too-eager girlfriend.

He made a note. "So you got your ice cream. And then?"

"And then I saw her. Helen." Bailey's slim throat moved as she swallowed. "In the pool."

Steve squelched his instinctive, protective response, the conditioned reflex of male hormones and Southern upbringing to a Woman in Distress. Teresa had known just how to play that big-eyes-and-trembling-lip routine to get him to do what she wanted. So did Gabrielle. But he was tougher on the job. He'd trained himself to be.

"Let's go back a minute. You saw her from here? The kitchen?"

"No. I suppose I could have, but . . ." Bailey frowned with the effort of remembering. "No."

"So you came outside."

She nodded.

"Were the lights on?"

"I think the pool lights—the underwater ones?—may have been. I turned on the patio lights myself."

He took her step-by-step through her story, aware of Officer Margie Conner listening silently from her post by the coffeepot. Even though she didn't contribute a question, he needed her there. For his own protection: a male detective never interviewed a woman without a female witness present.

Bailey Wells was a good interview subject, observant, coherent, and intelligent. He wondered again if she were guilty or just remarkably self-possessed. Cold.

Steve didn't like cold women.

On the other hand, hysterics wouldn't have saved Helen Ellis.

"Why did you jump in the pool?" he asked.

"Wouldn't you? I didn't know how long Helen had been . . ." She stopped, her hands clenching on the towel.

Dead, Steve supplied silently. *Unconscious.*

Bailey's knuckles were white. Maybe she wasn't so cold, so unaffected by the death, after all. She could be exerting control to keep from falling apart.

He could understand that.

"I didn't know how long she was underwater," she said. "Recovery drops to twenty-five percent after four minutes without oxygen. I needed to start rescue breathing as soon as possible."

"How do you know that?"

She blinked. Around the dilated pupils, her eyes were the color of the dark Jamaican rum he drank on his honeymoon, her lashes thick and straight. "I took a life-saving class in high school."

He wasn't talking about her life-saving skills. And he didn't care about the color of her eyes. Annoyed with his momentary distraction, he asked, "Where did you learn how long somebody can go without oxygen?"

"Breathing space," she said.

She didn't make sense. Steve grunted noncommittally.

"Breathing Space," she repeated. "The Nelson Crockett story?" When he still didn't respond, she leaned forward in her chair. "It's Paul's latest book. Nelson Crockett was the Tennessee serial killer who strangled his victims. He liked to bring them back several times and . . ." She broke eye contact, looking down at her hands. "He liked to bring them back."

Jesus. Steve stifled a jolt of revulsion. He made another sound, inviting her to continue.

Bailey raised her head. "Unconsciousness usually occurs after the first minute, but if you begin artificial ventilation right away, the victim has a ninety percent chance of response. Of course, repeated assaults on the airway cause tissue damage, so the victim's ability to breathe on her own once recovered is compromised."

Steve made a grab for his slipping detachment. The last thing he expected when he was pulled from bed in the middle of the night was a lecture on deviant sexual strangulation by a woman who looked like an elementary school librarian.

"Did Mrs. Ellis give any sign of breathing on her own?"

"What? Oh. No." Bailey shivered. "I kept trying until the paramedics came, but . . ."

Steve glanced at his notes. "How long?"

"I don't know. I was trying to save her. I didn't look at my watch."

Steve raised his eyebrows. He wasn't expecting sarcasm, either.

"It felt like forever," she said.

Seven minutes, Lewis had told him.

"I tried," Bailey said again. Her voice cracked.

Steve didn't need her assurances. He had already interviewed the EMS workers on the scene. She'd done everything right. The paramedics had praised her presence of mind. Her technique. Her persistence. If she had wanted Helen Ellis dead, she would have fumbled. She could have quit.

Or she could have delayed just long enough to make her best efforts useless.

Recovery drops to twenty-five percent after four minutes without oxygen.

"And Mr. Ellis?" he asked quietly.

"I don't understand."

"Where was he?"

"He was there. He came as soon as I called."

"Before or after you entered the pool?"

"Right before. I called—well, I screamed—and then I jumped in the water."

"Did he help you recover Mrs. Ellis from the water?"

Her lashes fluttered. "I . . . No. I wasn't really paying attention. I had to get her up on the side, and then I started rescue breathing right away."

"And what did he do?"

"He called the ambulance."

"Anything else?"

Her hands twisted in the towel. "He was very upset."

Steve nodded.

"She was his *wife*," Bailey said, as if men were responsible for their wives' dying every day.

Memories rattled like leaves down an empty street. Deliberately, Steve let them go.

"How would you describe the Ellises' relationship?" he asked.

"What do you mean?"

"Would you say they had a happy marriage?"

Bailey jerked. "Of course."

Of course. His mouth twisted cynically. Of course she would *say* it.

He took her through her story one more time, distilling

it to the essential facts he needed to write her statement. Twenty minutes later, the interview was over. He wasn't getting anything else from her tonight, unless she decided to make his job easier by copping to murder. Which she wouldn't. She wasn't stupid. He even doubted she was guilty, though he was keeping an open mind about that.

He stood. "You'll want out of those wet clothes. Officer Conner will take them for you."

And catalog them as evidence, although Steve didn't have much hope of finding anything useful. He hadn't found any blood on the pool deck, and Bailey's jump into the contaminated water would account for any traces on her clothes.

Had she thought of that?

He waited for her to object. When she didn't, he nodded and continued. "I'll have a statement prepared for you to read over in the morning. If you don't mind coming by the station to sign it—"

"It was an accident," Bailey blurted.

Well, hell. Slowly Steve surveyed her thin, intense face, her dark-as-rum eyes. He was going to get his confession after all. His faint disappointment surprised him.

He sat back down, nodding at her to continue.

Bailey expelled a shaky breath. "I'm not quite sure how to say this."

Tension thrummed through him. "Take your time," he drawled.

"Helen is . . . was . . . Helen usually mixed herself a nightcap at bedtime. I don't want to make too much of this, but she probably wasn't very steady when she came downstairs." She fixed her gaze on his face, willing him to believe her. "She must have slipped and fallen."

No confession. Just a simple explanation designed to get them all off the hook. Isn't that what he wanted? Nothing sensational, nothing involved that would set off tremors in his own life or in the department. He didn't do high-profile, high-intensity cases anymore.

He did his job.

"Thank you, Miz Wells," he said dryly.

"You could check for blood-alcohol levels."

"We certainly could," he agreed.

Realization darkened her eyes. "You were going to anyway."

He didn't say anything.

The flush returned, warming her cheeks. With her darkened eyes and messy hair, Bailey Wells looked less like a librarian and more like she'd just crawled out of bed. Or, with the right persuasion, could be tumbled onto one. The observation disturbed him.

"I'm sorry," she said, clearly mortified. "I didn't mean to tell you how to do your job."

"Occupational hazard," he said.

She nodded. "Because you're a police officer."

Detective, he thought.

"Because your boss is a crime writer." Steve smiled thinly. "Goodnight, Miz Wells."

MIZ Wells. Not Bailey.

Bailey watched the big-bodied detective saunter from the kitchen, looking tough and rumpled and suspicious. Misgiving churned in her stomach.

He didn't like her. He didn't believe her.

She huddled in her drying clothes on the hard kitchen chair, stinking of chlorine, hugging her stomach. That was okay. Lots of men didn't like her. Her sister Leann was the pretty one, the popular one, the one with boobs and boyfriends and a date to the prom. By the time Bailey figured out her invisibility to the opposite sex was at least partly a function of age—what seven-year-old could compete with a high school cheerleader?—her identity was set. Brainy Bailey, flat-chested, hardworking, and reliable. The kind of student teachers trusted to run errands in the hall. The kind of daughter parents trusted home alone on a Saturday night.

But Steve Burke didn't trust her.

He wanted her *clothes*. She knew what that meant. She felt violated. Scared.

She tightened her grip on the towel as the room wavered around her. That was so wrong. It was unfair. *Helen*—clammy skin, *don't think about it,* slack mouth, *don't,* empty, gleaming eyes—*was dead*. Bailey's breath came faster. Paul had enough to deal with right now without some macho cop with a prejudice against crime writers turning a painful personal tragedy into a terrible public spectacle.

Would you say they had a happy marriage?

Oh, God. Her stomach heaved with a terrible mix of guilt, fear and sympathy. Maybe he was right not to trust her.

A hand touched her shoulder.

"You all right?" Officer Conner's face, creased with concern, swam before her.

Bailey blinked; forced herself to smile. "Fine. Thank you," she added even as her insides rebelled.

"You sure?"

"Yes, if you'll just . . . I need to . . . Excuse me," she mumbled, and hurried to the powder room off the kitchen, where she was violently, wretchedly sick.

PAUL Ellis ran a shaking hand over his hair. The evening had *not* gone as planned.

Now he had some hulking detective in his study asking

him questions in a flat, deep drawl. "Do you have friends you can stay with tonight, sir? Family?"

He couldn't think. "I'll be fine."

"You shouldn't be alone," the detective said.

Paul exhaled noisily. "I won't be. Bailey is here."

Thank God for Bailey. She had surprised him, jumping into the pool like that. But her presence, her devotion, provided an invaluable backup.

"It might be better for you both if you found someplace else to spend the night," Burke said, stolid as a rock. "We're likely to be tied up here for some time."

"Why? It was an accident."

"That's certainly what it looks like. But your wife did hit her head. I'd just like the chance to look around, rule out the possibility of an intruder."

Paul didn't believe the intruder theory for one minute. And neither, he bet, did the detective. The implication was unbearable. Intolerable. *God*.

"I didn't sign that damn consent form so you could force me from my own home."

"I can't force you to do anything, sir. I want all this to be over as much as you do. But it sure would speed things along if my team didn't have to worry about disturbing you tonight."

Paul's indignation faded. Maybe this Sheriff Andy wannabe imagined he was doing his job. In which case, an appearance of cooperation would serve Paul better than threats.

"I'll need a change of clothes."

"Yes, sir. Officer Lewis can help you pack a bag. He'll take those clothes you have on and then drive you anywhere you want to go."

Paul flung up his head. "Are you people offering laundry service now?"

The detective was silent.

Paul sighed. "I'm sorry, Lieutenant. I want to cooperate. I really do. But this is my *home*."

"Yes, sir. I'm sorry for the inconvenience."

"She was my *wife*."

"Yes, sir," Lieutenant Burke repeated in his flat, deep drawl. "I'm sorry for your loss."

At least he didn't say he understood. No one could understand what Paul was thinking and feeling right now. Least of all some thick-necked redneck with a badge.

He had to tell Regan.

The realization broke through the numbness that gripped Paul like a stone through pond ice. Despite their estrangement, Helen's daughter would be devastated by her mother's death. And furious she hadn't been contacted immediately.

Should he make the call himself? Or have Bailey do it?

The detective said something, his words lost in the roaring inside Paul's head. Something about the coroner's office and releasing the body. Helen's body.

Paul held up his hand. He didn't want to think about the autopsy right now, about Helen's body photographed and measured, weighed and dissected.

"I can't deal with that now," he said. "Bailey will call your office tomorrow."

On cue, he heard a swift knock, and Bailey entered the room. Relief rolled through him. She'd changed her clothes and tied back her hair, but she hadn't bothered with makeup. Militant spots of color flew in her cheeks like battle flags. Her eyes were bright.

The detective's hulking body shifted in a play for her attention, but she never glanced at him. All her concern was for Paul.

"I came as soon as they let me," she said, crossing the room with uncertain steps. "Are you all right?"

He couldn't speak. He was overcome. He stared at her dumbly.

She put her hand on his arm, even that tentative touch a breach in the employer/employee distance she was so careful to preserve between them.

It wasn't enough, Paul realized. He wanted—needed—more from her than that. He pulled her to him, feeling her involuntary recoil, her quick stiffening against his body.

But she wouldn't reject his claim on her comfort. Not tender-hearted, loyal Bailey. He held her close, his heart pounding as he breathed in the bromine scent of her hair.

And at last, as he hoped, as he expected she would, Bailey put her arms around him and patted him awkwardly on the back.

From the other side of the room, the detective watched impassively.

THREE

GABRIELLE scowled from the front porch steps as Steve pulled into the driveway at nine-thirty in the morning.

Busted.

The headache building behind his eyes ratcheted up a notch. He wanted to spend more time with her. That's why he'd moved back to Stokesville. But not after he'd been up all night with a dead woman and three officers more used to drunk-and-disorderlies and traffic stops than crime scene investigation. And not before he'd had a chance to wash away the taste of station house sludge with a fresh pot of coffee.

Slowly, he climbed from the car, slinging his jacket over his shoulder.

Gabrielle narrowed her eyes as he approached the porch. "You missed breakfast."

At least she was speaking to him this morning.

Stooping, he dropped a kiss on top of his nine-year-old daughter's smooth, dark head, feeling his reality, his responsibilities, shift and grip around him. "Did you save me any?"

"Grandma did." Gabrielle scrambled to her feet, leaning briefly against his side in what passed these days for a hug. "You didn't call this morning, either."

Guilt scraped him. Steve opened the door to his mother's house. "I didn't want to wake you."

"Huh." Gabrielle snorted. "That's what I'm going to say when I'm a teenager."

Four more years, he thought. *They could make it.*

"When you're a teenager, I'm going to lock you in your room and sit on the front porch all night with a shotgun," he said mildly. "So it won't be an issue."

Gabrielle tossed her braid in a gesture so reminiscent of her dead mother that his chest squeezed. "That's police brutality."

"Good parenting," he corrected.

She flounced into the house.

The interior was cool and dim and smelled of bacon. Steve stopped in the entryway, rubbing the tension from the back of his neck.

"Gabby?" His mother's voice carried from the kitchen. "Who is it?"

Steve took a deep breath and followed his daughter down the hall. "It's me, Mom. I'm home."

"About time, too," his mother said.

Eugenia Burke was one of those Southern women who would look the same at seventy as she did at fifty-five, her body kept toned by exercise and her mind kept sharp by an interest in everything and everybody. As far back as Steve could remember, her hair was sleek and dark, her complexion moisturized, and her toenail polish pink. The death of Steve's father five years ago had hit her hard, but her life since then had settled into a routine of book club, Bible study, and volunteer work at the hospital.

At the time, Steve had figured Eugenia was filling the void left by her husband's death. Now he knew some chasms could never be filled. Eugenia had simply stepped back from the edge.

She slid a plate into the microwave and turned to face him. "I suppose it's too much to hope you were out all night on a date."

Steve crossed the sunlit kitchen to the coffeepot, refusing to rise to her bait. She knew where he'd been. He'd left a note. But he and Gabby had barely moved in when Mom took it into her head it was time he started dating agin, and now she never lost an opportunity to remind him he wasn't getting any younger and there were plenty of nice girls in Stokesville. "I was out on a call."

Eugenia nodded, momentarily distracted from her campaign to mend his broken heart and secure more grandchildren. "Helen Stokes. Bless her heart."

Steve raised his eyebrows, arrested in the act of pouring. "How did you hear about that?"

"Judith Griggs—you remember Judith, from the book club?—lives right down the street from the Stokes place. She saw the lights last night, and then the yellow tape this morning. She went over with a pan of her monkey bread, because that Paul Ellis is supposed to speak to the book club next month, and she was afraid maybe something had happened to him. But it was Helen." Eugenia took a plate of French toast and bacon out of the microwave and set it on the counter in front of Steve. "So, what happened?"

Steve looked down at the plate and then up at his mother. "Attempting to bribe a law enforcement officer, Ma?" he asked dryly.

"Certainly not," Eugenia said, blushing.

"Good." All he wanted was hot coffee, a cold shower, and a couple of extra strength Tylenol. But he went through the motions. You had to go through the motions. He dumped syrup over his plate. "Thanks for breakfast."

"Is somebody dead?" Gabrielle asked.

Shit. If he'd had any appetite, that would have killed it.

"A neighbor lady, honey," his mother replied. "Nobody you know."

Gabrielle's dark gaze fixed on her father's face. "Was she sick?"

Teresa had been sick. Ovarian cancer. Two short months, while Steve begged and threatened and cajoled and raged, and then she died.

"Not sick," he said.

"An accident?" Eugenia asked.

"Looks like it."

It looked like . . . trouble.

Steve had no witness, no weapon, no visible bloodstains, nothing to suggest homicide. Only a prickling under his skin, like a numb leg twitching to painful life, and a memory of skinny Bailey Wells with her arms around Paul Ellis.

Something stirred in Steve's belly. Anger, maybe.

He scowled into his cup. He wasn't emotionally involved. He didn't want to be emotionally involved. *Compartmentalize. Depersonalize. Detach.*

Eugenia ran water over the frying pan in the sink. "Dotty's going to want Bailey out of there now, you mark my words."

Steve set down his mug. There was a daughter in Atlanta who needed to be notified—Regan. And an estranged son, Richard, in Chicago. "Who's Dotty?"

"Dorothy Wells. Her daughter Bailey works for Helen's husband."

Well, hell.

"She told me she was from New York," Steve said slowly.

"She may be. But her family's right here in Stokesville."

"Why don't I remember her?"

"She's a whole lot younger than you," Eugenia said frankly. "Ten years at least. I'll bet you remember her sister, though. Leann Wells?"

"Nope."

"Beautiful girl," his mother said. "But she's married now. To Bryce Edwards. He sells insurance, I think."

He let her talk. He needed to know his territory, to relearn the fabric of town life so he could see the patterns and the pieces out of place. You never knew when some tidbit dropped in friendly conversation, in the checkout line or over coffee, could become the connecting thread in a crime.

Eugenia glanced over her shoulder. "So you talked to her? Bailey?"

He remembered Bailey's thin, pale face, her shock-dilated pupils, her unnatural composure. Her hands on the back of Ellis's shirt. He hadn't missed her initial stiffness when her boss grabbed her . . . or her awkward softening. He just didn't know what to make of it yet.

"She was at the scene. Of course I talked to her."

"How is she taking it?"

"I'd say pretty well." He watched Eugenia dry her hands on a towel, his mind turning over. "So, Dorothy Wells doesn't approve of her daughter's living arrangements?"

"Steven Burke." Eugenia pursed her mouth. "Are you attempting to pump your own mama for information?"

He lifted his eyebrows. The question was payback, he knew, for his earlier crack about bribing him with breakfast. "What are you talking about?"

"Yeah, what *are* you talking about?" Gabrielle asked from beside him.

She was growing, he realized with a pang, pierced ears, ragged nails and all. Her head was level with his shoulder.

He put an arm around her. "Nothing important. What are you up to today?"

Her shoulders hunched, dislodging his arm. "I don't know."

He watched her slide away along the counter. "You want to go to the movies, invite a friend?"

"I don't have any friends here," she said. Not sulky, but with the exaggerated patience she'd adopted recently.

Eugenia turned away, busying herself arranging the towel over the bar on the oven door. Letting him deal with it.

Steve's pulse banged behind his eyeballs. "Well," he said cautiously. "It's summer. You'll make new friends when school starts."

Gabrielle looked down. "Yeah. Sure."

She didn't say what he knew she was thinking, that she missed her old friends.

Neither one of them was any good at talking about their feelings, a shared trait that hadn't mattered much when Teresa had been alive to bridge their silences with her exclamations, explanations, and laughter. Now they managed as best they could without her. Going through the motions.

Adjusting well, the grief counselor had told him, smiling. Lying.

And he, God help them, had smiled and lied right back, desperate to be left alone to get on with it.

For a while he'd even convinced himself they were doing okay. But then Rosa, the nanny who had been with them since Gabrielle's birth, announced she was going home. To Brazil, a world away.

She loved Gabrielle, Rosa had insisted, tears in her eyes. Like a daughter. But it had been two years since the *senhora*'s death. Rosa missed her country, she missed her family, her own daughter was expecting another child. Teresa's parents had offered to find her part-time work close to their home.

Perhaps *a menina pequena* would like to make a visit to her grandparents? Rosa had suggested with a sidelong look.

Steve had recognized and rejected his wealthy in-laws' well-meant interference. Gabrielle had lost her mother. He'd be damned before he deprived her of her father, too.

"We could still go to the movies," he said.

"Dad, I'm not, like, five. You don't have to entertain me."

Maybe the full-time fathering gig was new, but he'd been married long enough not to agree with everything a woman said when she was in a Mood. He waited.

Gabrielle drew patterns on the countertop with her finger. "I guess a movie would be okay," she conceded finally.

And long enough not to make too much of his victories.

"You look at the paper, pick something out," he said. "I've got to wrap up some work stuff today, but we could catch an afternoon show. Three, four o'clock?"

She looked at him from under her lashes, her mother's trick. "The new Orlando Bloom?"

He almost said yes. "What's it rated?"

"R," Eugenia said darkly from beside the stove.

"But it's *Orlando Bloom*," Gabrielle repeated.

"Nice try, kid," Steve said. "Pick something else."

She threw him a tragic look.

Hell, they didn't need the movies. Plenty of drama here at home.

"Check the listings," he said. "See what's playing around four o'clock."

"If you go so late in the afternoon, you'll ruin your appetites for dinner," Eugenia objected.

"I'll take Gabby out for dinner." Steve smiled at his mother. "You can have a night off, too."

"Well, if you're sure . . ." she said doubtfully.

"Just the two of us?" Gabrielle asked.

The eagerness in her voice caught his heart and riveted his attention. He needed to spend more time with her, one-on-one.

Finding a Rosa replacement in D.C. had proved impossible. Even reducing his hours and juggling shifts, Steve was aware of too many missed dinners, too many late-night calls. They stuck it out until the end of the school year. And then, over Gabrielle's tearful protests and despite his own regrets, Steve put the Georgetown brownstone on the market and brought his daughter home.

"Just the two of us," he promised.

He loaded his plate into the dishwasher before heading upstairs to shave and change his shirt, taking his coffee with him. Gabby was on her knees on the floor of the living room, hunched over the newspaper, as he headed out the door.

SUNLIGHT thick as honey poured from the blue bowl of the sky. Heat beat on the black roof of the truck and shimmered from patched roads and dusty sidewalks. Steve's headache pulsed as he drove.

Twenty-four years ago he'd ridden this same route to Perry Middle School, sitting with the acknowledged jocks in the back of the bus, his sneakers stuck out in the aisle. This morning, the familiar streets looked as rundown and worn out as he felt. The shoe store was boarded up. The white steeple of the Baptist church needed a fresh coat of paint. The flyers in the barbershop window were curled and faded.

But like Steve himself, Stokesville was hanging on. The low property values attracted commuters working in larger towns and the research park nearby. The newcomers' wealth seeped in, replacing old tobacco money, nourishing new business: a local coffee house, a natural foods market, an independent bookseller. Attempts had been made to spruce up Main Street with a new bench in front of the hardware store, new flower beds around the memorial to the town's war dead, even fancy new streetlights.

Steve thought the lights, a pet project of the mayor's, made the downtown look like freaking Busch Gardens. The money would have been better spent resurfacing the roads or buying camcorders for the town's four police cruisers. But he'd been hired too late to argue the point, and he wasn't spoiling for a fight any more than he was looking for a challenge.

He just wanted to get through the days, and the nights, alone.

He bumped into the municipal lot that connected the squat brick police building with the town hall and the library. Somebody had taken his parking spot again.

Wonderful.

No point in getting pissed off. This wasn't his regular shift. Maybe the cop who had swiped his spot expected— hoped—he'd just stay home.

Maybe he should have.

He parked at the end of the lane by the dumpster, careful not to block the black-and-white waiting at the curb or the unmarked, four-door blue sedan. Inside the police entrance, the air-conditioning labored, recycling a compound of sweat, floor polish, and stale coffee.

Nodding to the desk sergeant, Steve strolled through the empty briefing room toward the office he shared with the other two detectives. Second shift wouldn't start for another couple of hours. Plenty of time to write up a progress report. Let the chief decide whether to continue the investigation into Helen Ellis's death or turn a potential public relations nightmare over to the big boys at SBI.

He was conscious of a small, indigestible lump under his ribs, like heartburn or discontent. He didn't mind letting the State Bureau boys handle the labwork. Stokesville didn't have their resources. But Steve had the training, he had the experience, he had the instincts to run this case.

It wasn't his call, he reminded himself.

He couldn't let it become his problem.

"Lieutenant! Lieutenant Burke?"

Sarah Creech, one of the department's three civilian employees, rolled through the door. The woman was built like a Humvee, with a pinup's face over full body armor. She ran the communications center like her personal command.

"Somebody to see you," she announced.

Steve raised his eyebrows, waiting.

But apparently the clerk had said all she'd come to say. Pivoting on her pointed heels, she marched back to her desk, trailing clouds of perfume like exhaust.

So, okay, he wasn't the most popular guy in the department. Also not a problem.

Shrugging back into his jacket—*Jesus,* it was hot—he walked down the gray hallway and opened the door to the public waiting room.

Bailey Wells sat rigidly on a chrome-and-tweed chair, her narrow shoulders straight under a padded black jacket and her hands clasped tightly in her lap. The sight of her clear brown eyes in her smooth, pale face knocked holes in his detachment and punched him in the gut.

His heart pounded. His blood rushed.

He stopped, stunned, as his dead libido roared to life.

Now *this* was a problem.

BAILEY'S research had never required a visit to the police station. She'd never even gotten a speeding ticket. Which was too bad, because if her police knowledge were based on more than statistics and court reports, maybe she wouldn't feel so intimidated now. So anxious.

So guilty.

Bailey remembered the look on the detective's face as she'd disengaged herself gently from Paul's arms, and a hot twist of shame and dread coiled in her belly.

Okay. She couldn't change her circumstances. All she could control was her feelings.

She gripped her hands together in her lap. She was pretty sure the department had been expanded and probably remodeled since that night nineteen years ago when Billy Ray Dawler had been arrested for his family's murders, but maybe Paul could use her observations. Anyway, looking around helped her stop thinking about the reason for her visit.

She noted a flag, some plaques on the wall, a square, smoked glass window like the ticket counter at the multiplex. Beside her chair, a spindly poinsettia dropped leaves onto the blue industrial carpet.

A door on the opposite wall opened, and the detective came out. In this small, stark space, he looked big and dark and not at all reassuring. There were tired pouches under his deep-set eyes and weary lines bracketing his mouth. Smile lines? He sure wasn't smiling now.

"Miz Wells," he drawled.

She stood like a student summoned to the principal's office. "Lieutenant . . ." Oh, God, what was his name?

A corner of that hard mouth twitched. Not a smile, but the slippery knots in her stomach eased. "Burke," he supplied. "Steve Burke."

"Bailey," she said automatically, and then flushed. He knew her name.

He didn't acknowledge her gaffe by so much as the

flicker of an eyelash. Maybe he was being nice. Or maybe Lieutenant Stoneface was used to suspects who stammered and fell over themselves whenever he spoke.

"What can I do for you?" he asked politely.

"You . . . Uh, I . . ." *Get a grip, Bailey.* She took a deep breath. "You asked me to stop by. To sign my statement?"

"That's right. This way, please."

Bailey walked through the door he held open, careful not to brush against his outstetched arm. But as she scooted past, she couldn't escape noticing his jacket hung open in the heat, revealing a white, wilted shirt and broad, muscled chest. He smelled of warm wool, clean cotton, and adult male.

She shivered. Fear? Or attraction? Either one put her at a disadvantage.

"Nervous?" he asked in his deep twang.

"Cold," she lied. "It's the air-conditioning. I mean, it's not like you're escorting me down death row."

"Not yet, anyway," he agreed blandly.

She gaped at him.

Humor gleamed in his dark eyes, but his expression never wavered. "My office," he said, nodding down the hall.

She hurried ahead toward another open door.

Three gray metal desks occupied the center of a room lined with shelves and corkboard. A fourth, aloof from the others, jammed in the corner behind a barricade of filing cabinets. The office looked like the computer lab of a financially strapped middle school. Stacks of books and papers jostled for space on the shelves. Fluorescent lights hummed and flickered overhead.

Burke prowled to the far desk and pulled up a chair for Bailey.

Cautiously, she sat, wary of the unfamiliar courtesy. Paul respected her too much as a colleague to open her door or hold her chair. "Thank you."

Burke propped against the edge of the desk, his knee by her shoulder. Too close. Again. The man had no concept of personal space. Or else he was deliberately intimidating her.

"How did you sleep last night?" he asked.

She didn't think he really cared. Unless he wanted to know if guilt had kept her tossing and turning all night.

Well, forget him. She'd already endured her mother's interrogation and her father's unspoken concern this morning. No way was she embarking on another round of explanations and excuses with a suspicious detective.

"Fine." Politeness prompted her to add, "And you?"

"I haven't been to bed yet." From his perch on the desk, he loomed over her. "I hear the Do Drop's comfortable."

Bailey's stomach sank. At least now she understood his interest in how she slept. Last night, one of the uniformed officers had driven Paul to the Do Drop Inn, a bed-and-breakfast in the center of town. Burke wanted to know if she had spent the night with her boss.

"I didn't stay at the inn," she said stiffly. "I was at my parents' house."

Burke regarded her without expression. The silence sucked at her like quicksand.

"Frank and Dorothy Wells, eight hundred and eleven Cardinal Street. I got in about three." Bailey stuck out her chin. "Way past curfew."

He regarded her, that gleam still in his eyes. "I'm not going to charge you."

"Well, that's a relief."

"Not for being out late, anyway."

Resentment smoldered, a welcome, warming lump under her ribs. "Look, I didn't come here to play games. Do you want me to sign a statement or not?"

Wordlessly, he handed her two closely typed pages of plain office paper.

"It's short," she said, surprised.

"You got anything you want to add? Any details you left out?"

Was he kidding? She couldn't tell.

"I won't know until I read it," she said.

Despite the lightness in her head, the twisting in her gut, Bailey forced herself to read critically, carefully, searching for inaccuracies or bias. She was used to organizing and summarizing facts. She was good at it.

So was he.

When she finished reading the statement through the second time, she looked up and found Burke watching her with heavy-lidded eyes.

"Well?" he asked.

She wet her lips, struggling to be objective. "It's very thorough," she said. "Concise. A little dry."

Like Burke himself, she realized.

His lips curled. "I wasn't asking for a critique of my writing skills. Not that I don't appreciate it, given your line of work. Was there anything you wanted to add?"

"Oh." She flushed furiously. He was almost good-looking when he smiled. If you liked that ex-football player, muscle-bound type. Which she, thankfully, did not. "No."

He leaned forward. "Then if you'll just sign and date this here . . ."

She snatched the pen from him and signed, stabbing the pen at the paper.

"You sure there wasn't something else?" he asked almost gently.

She squared her shoulders. "There was, actually."

Burke didn't stir from his perch on the desk. But his attention sharpened on her like a hound dog's spotting a squirrel. "What's that?"

She met his gaze straight-on. "I have to plan a funeral today, and I don't have a body."

He nodded. "Autopsy's scheduled for this afternoon. The body should be released then. Give me the name of the funeral home, and we'll see it gets there."

Well. That had gone better than she expected.

"And I need to get into the house," she added.

He rubbed his jaw. "That's going to take a little longer. I can't let you all in until we've completely processed the scene."

"I understand you have a job to do," Bailey said carefully. "But so do I."

"Unfortunately for your boss, my job comes first. I won't compromise this investigation for his convenience."

Frustration bubbled inside her. She couldn't fault him for being conscientious, but it was all so *unnecessary*. "What investigation? This was an accident. Even your chief says so."

His eyes narrowed. "You talked to the chief?"

"Well . . . yes. That is, Paul did. This morning."

He didn't say anything, but she felt the tension roll off him in waves like cold from a refrigerator.

She shivered. It was stupid to feel nervous. Even more stupid to feel guilty. Paul had been perfectly within his rights to talk with Chief Clegg. And if that made problems for the chief's lead investigator . . . Well, too bad.

She offered him a conciliatory smile anyway. "So, you see, there's really no reason to delay. And it would make my job a lot easier if I could count on the house being available. Helen's daughter will be here. She shouldn't have to stay in a hotel. Not to mention everyone who attends the funeral will stop by the house afterward, and I have to feed them. People are already coming by with food, and there's no one to accept it and no place to store it."

"I hear they do a nice brunch buffet at the Town Diner," Burke said, straight-faced.

He was joking. He had to be joking. She must have imagined that instant of stillness when he tensed and collected himself like an old dog who knows the limits of his chain.

"Unless Charlene is serving pecan tassies and tomato aspic, I'm afraid the Saint Andrew's Ladies Guild won't consider brunch at the diner an acceptable send-off," Bailey said. "But thank you for that thought."

This time she was almost sure he smiled.

Relieved, she stood, bringing herself to the same level, careful not to bump his knee or brush his thigh. "You'll be in touch? After the autopsy, I mean."

"Count on it," Burke said.

Her smile faltered. It was the assurance she came for.

So why did it feel like a threat?

FOUR

WALTER Clegg propped his regulation size elevens on his desk.

The chief's shoes and collar brass were polished and his uniform neatly pressed. After seventeen years managing the resources of his understaffed and underfunded department, Walt believed in the importance of police presence . . . and the appearance of his police. On days when tourists swelled the town—Founders Day, the Fourth of July—even the detectives turned out in uniform.

Steve understood the chief's reasoning, but buttoning on that blue uniform made him feel like he'd been busted back to traffic cop.

Which, in a sense, he had.

"Steve, you ever wonder why our jail is so small?" the police chief asked.

Steve raised both eyebrows. "Because county lockup is only five miles down the road?"

Walt ignored him. He was good at ignoring things that

didn't suit his purpose. "It's not that we don't have crime in this town. We just don't have as much of it as maybe you're used to. You've got to understand how things work here."

Steve's headache tightened its grip on his neck. "I know how things work here. I was born here."

"And your mother is a lovely woman," Walt said smoothly. "We'll never need to pay police informants as long as your mama is around. But you've been gone awhile. You need to remember folks count on us to preserve the peace, not stir up trouble."

Steve inhaled. He wasn't stirring up trouble, damn it. All he wanted was to put in his hours and go home. But . . .

"You said when you hired me that there's no such thing as small town crime," he reminded Walt.

"Well, that's true. Human nature is human nature wherever you are. We've got our share of bad apples. Bad asses, too, what with the gangs moving in from Durham and Raleigh and all. That's why I thought somebody with your experience would be such an asset to the department. But you know as well as I do that in a community this size, half the job is public relations. We've all got to get along."

Steve knew all about the importance of getting along. He had almost five months left of his six-month review period before his hiring became permanent. The last thing he wanted was to argue with his boss. But he'd be damned before he'd let concern for his job keep him from doing it.

"Somebody wasn't getting along with Helen Ellis," he pointed out.

Walt eyed him reproachfully. "Now, you don't know that."

"I haven't proved it." *Yet.* "But it's my job to keep an open mind."

"And it's my job to keep things from getting out of hand."

Steve waited. The thin stream of air from the vent overhead spent itself in the thickness of the room. Sweat dampened the back of his shirt.

"I heard from Paul Ellis this morning," Walt said.

Here it comes, Steve thought. "Did he retract consent?"

"Not yet. But he should. What were you thinking, placing the house in lockdown?"

"I was searching for signs of an intruder," Steve said evenly.

"That's bullshit. You know it, I know it, and if Ellis hasn't figured it out yet, he's dumber than I thought."

"Has he lawyered up?"

"Naw, he's just shooting off his mouth about how we're all against him on account of he's questioning our handling of the old Dawler case."

"Not me," Steve said. "The Dawler case was before my time."

"Yeah, I guess it would be. We only had seven officers back then. Biggest case we ever saw. I was lead detective. You must have been, what, in high school?"

It was an attempt to put him in his place.

"Just out," Steve said. "And in the army."

"Well, it doesn't matter. Point is, Ellis is threatening to talk to the press."

"What's he going to tell them? His wife died. We're investigating."

"He doesn't think we should be."

Steve didn't give a damn what Paul Ellis thought. "The ME doesn't agree with him."

"But the media might. He's one of them—a writer. *Police Bungle Death of True Crime Writer's Wife* makes a mighty interesting headline."

"I don't bungle," Steve said. "He signed a written consent to search."

"Which he can withdraw at any time."

"Then I'll get a warrant."

"Not without probable cause, you won't."

Steve's jaw clenched. "Which is why I haven't gone to the judge yet. I'm waiting on the autopsy."

Walt frowned and switched lines of attack.

"Ellis claims the responding officers contaminated the crime scene."

"Why would he say that if he doesn't think a crime has been committed?"

But Walt wasn't interested in speculating on Paul Ellis's motives. "Did they?"

Steve barely knew Wayne Lewis. But he wasn't sacrificing the earnest rookie to some egotistical writer.

"Look, the EMTs were already there. Lewis called me, and I took appropriate steps to preserve the scene." After it had been tromped through by a team of paramedics and all four officers on duty that night. "I don't need Ellis or anybody else to tell me how to conduct an investigation."

"Except me," Walt said.

Shit.

"Yeah," Steve said slowly. "Except you."

"As long as we both understand that." Walt held his gaze a moment longer before he sighed and shifted a folder on his desk. "Autopsy's this afternoon?"

Steve nodded.

"Good. Wrap this up as quick as you can. The media is already circling. Let's not give the buzzards anything to feed on."

"I'll do my best."

"Just do your job," Walt said.

Easy enough for him to say, Steve thought as he got into his truck to make the forty-minute drive to the Medical Examiner's office.

Do the job.

Get through the day.

Go through the motions.

Easy enough to do. Hell, he'd been operating on autopilot for almost three years. He ought to be relieved the chief didn't want any more from him than the standard minimum requirement.

But he wasn't. Dissatisfaction rode with him all the way to Chapel Hill like a sullen drunk in the back seat.

REGAN Poole had thought her day couldn't possibly get worse. How could it get worse? It started with a fucking phone call at fucking four o'clock in the morning that shattered her sleep and her psyche.

It wasn't fair. Children weren't supposed to have to deal with bolt-out-of-bed calls in the night. That was a parent's job. She remembering fumbling with her cell phone, heart pounding as she waited for her father's tired voice on the other end of the line.

Can you come pick me up?

. . . bail me out?

. . . send me money?

. . . tell me everything will be all right?

But it wouldn't be all right, Regan thought with a sting at her heart, whatever Paul said. He wasn't really her father. Her real father was dead.

And now her mother was, too.

Regan's hand tightened on the receiver. Count on Helen to make it all about her, even if she had to die to do it.

The telephone on the other end of the line rang mindlessly. Endlessly. *Pick up, pick up, damn you, pick up . . .*

Paul hadn't been able to get hold of Richard. That's what he'd said. Maybe it was even true. Maybe Richard had caller

ID. God knew her brother was smart enough, selfish enough, to ignore a call in the middle of the night from their drunk and incoherent mother or the stepfather they both despised.

She jiggled the phone. More likely Richard had been out last night. Or he was wasted. Or stoned. Son of a bitch.

Which was why she was stuck calling him now.

Grievance built under her breastbone, pushing out the pain. She didn't like to make personal calls at work. Someone might see and feel they had to make allowances for her. Regan never made allowances for herself. At twenty-three years old, she was the youngest account manager at the Buckhead bank branch, and she had to be better than any of them.

She jabbed her brother's number into the phone again. *Pick up, please pick up . . .*

"'Lo?" Richard's voice slurred.

Relief, grief, and worry flooded her eyes and spilled out. Not in tears. She would not let herself cry. In anger.

"Christ, Richard, it's two in the afternoon. Did you just wake up?"

"Regan?" She pictured him blinking and unshaven, trying to focus. To cope. "What's up?"

She pulled herself together. She could do this, she assured herself, shaking. She could do a better job of breaking the news than Paul had done.

"It's Mom," she said, reduced to mouthing her stepfather's words after all. Because in the end, what else was there to say? "There's been an accident."

WITNESSES lied.

Bodies didn't.

Not as long as the medical examiner knew his stuff.

Or in this case, her stuff, Steve thought, watching as Dr.

Elizabeth Nguyen bent over the body of Helen Stokes Ellis. The ME was small, dark, and decisive, with black-rimmed glasses above her blue surgical mask and slender, gloved hands. She'd appeared surprised by Steve's presence in her autopsy room. But when he didn't badger her with questions or puke on his shoes, she seemed to warm to him.

Or maybe she just warmed to her work.

She examined the body clothed and then naked, photographing and cataloging it with reassuring thoroughness: hair color, eye color, weight, scars, moles, dental work, age and general condition. The damp hair streaming over the table's edge gleamed with expensive highlights. The legs were waxed and tanned, the eyebrows plucked, the manicured hands scrupulously maintained. Delicate scars from cosmetic surgery traced the jaw and hairline.

Looking at the pale, crepey skin of the body's naked belly and upper arms, Steve felt a stab of profound pity. A flood of regret. Helen Ellis had been able to cheat age, but not death.

You could never cheat death. All you could do was make the most of the time you had.

Teresa had tried to show him that, but he'd learned it too late.

Nguyen paused and clicked off her mike. "I'll want an X ray of the skull," she told her assistant. She glanced at Steve. "You have a witness who claims the victim was drinking?"

The specter of Bailey's white, determined face and anxious eyes joined Steve's personal ghost gallery. *Helen usually fixed herself a nightcap at bedtime.*

He nodded.

"Well, I won't have the tox screen results for a couple of days," Nguyen said. "But based on the head laceration, I can tell you now that the victim didn't slip and fall."

The back of Steve's neck prickled.

It was an accident, Bailey had insisted.

Wrap this up as quick as you can, the chief had said.

Bodies didn't lie.

"What does the head laceration tell you?"

"In the crime scene photos, all the pool surfaces are rounded. If your victim slipped and struck her head against the side, the steps, even the railing, I'd expect to see a single impact site with non-specific bruising. No laceration and, obviously, very little blood."

Nguyen positioned the head on the table and then gestured for Steve to join her behind a screen. The X ray hummed.

So far she hadn't told him anything the responding officer hadn't seen. He waited until the ME resumed her position beside the table before he asked, "So what do you see?"

"Single impact site. Linear laceration." She traced it for him with the instrument in her hand. "The scalp is split. Your victim was struck with a heavy blunt object with at least one sharp edge and sufficient force to break the skin."

Fine. That accounted for the blood. But did it account for the death?

"Enough force to kill?" Steve asked.

"Probably not," Nguyen admitted. "I'll examine the lungs, of course, but my guess is she was still conscious, or at least alive, when she entered the water."

"Signs of struggle?"

Nguyen shook her head, continuing her deliberate examination of the body. "There are no defensive wounds on her arms or hands. No residue under the fingernails. She could have been unconscious, although there's no sign the body's been dragged. She may simply have been dazed by the blow. Disoriented. Possibly drunk, as well."

So she *was* nightcapped. Literally.

"Any chance the injury was sustained after drowning?" Steve asked without much hope.

"Unlikely. X ray will tell us more, but from the angle of the laceration, I'd say she was struck from above and behind. She probably never knew what hit her." The ME switched her mike back on, signaling the end of their conversation.

Steve didn't mind. He already had the information he came for. Now he needed to decide what to do with it.

Water hissed from the tap and drummed in the deep metal sink. The air was cold. Steve thrust his hands into his pockets as the medical examiner made the first shocking cut from shoulder to shoulder across the breasts and then the midline incision, chest to pubis. The body sighed open. The cavity yawned, slick and red.

He could leave now.

The internal exam wasn't likely to tell him anything Nguyen hadn't already divulged.

But he stayed, driven less by his detective's need to know than by an impulse to be there for the plucked and pampered woman on the table in a way he'd failed to be there for Teresa, to accompany her into death. He stayed out of pity and respect, the way other cops attended the funerals of other crime victims.

Because Helen Ellis's death was a crime. He was sure of that now.

But to prove it, he needed to find the weapon. A motive.

The murderer.

BAILEY thrust her hand to the back of her parents' mailbox, ignoring the barking of her neighbor's dog and the rumble of traffic behind her.

Although classifying the single car cruising down this

one-and-a-half lane rural road as "traffic" just proved she'd already been home too long.

The engine idled to a stop behind her. Bailey braced. All she needed to make her day complete was a verbal assault from a redneck in a truck.

"Come here often?" a man drawled.

Her heart raced. She knew that flat, deep voice. Clutching her parents' mail, she withdrew her arm and turned.

Lieutenant Steve Burke leaned across the bench seat of a black Ford pickup, his windows rolled down and his eyes amused.

She felt a jolt of . . . surely that was dislike?

"Not if I can help it," she said. "What are you doing here?"

"I came to tell you the body's been released. You can have your funeral."

She refused to feel grateful. "Shouldn't you tell Paul?"

Steve raised his eyebrows. "I did. He said you were making the arrangements."

His voice was neutral, no accusation at all, but she rushed to Paul's defense anyway. "He's very upset."

The detective unfolded from his seat, reminding her all over again how big he was—the kind of ex-jock who'd hung over her sister's locker in high school. He probably tried to use his size to intimidate people, Bailey thought scornfully as she watched him round the hood of his truck toward her.

She bet it worked, too.

"Upset enough to call a press conference?" he asked.

"What?"

"That's what he told my chief. Told me to wrap up the investigation, or he was talking to reporters."

Oh, dear. No wonder Steve's voice sounded flat. He was probably ready to murder somebody himself.

Not that anybody had been murdered, she told herself. It was purely a figure of speech.

Burke leaned against the door of his truck. "So tell me about this new book he's writing," he invited.

She eyed him warily. "Why?"

"Maybe I'm curious."

Maybe. And maybe he was looking for a way to defend his department by discrediting Paul.

She cleared her throat. "Well . . . It's about the Dawler murders. Are you familiar with them?"

"Mother was a prostitute. Grandma and probably sis, too. Kid gets drunk, decides he can't live with the shame anymore and, instead of offing himself, kills his entire family with a kitchen knife."

"That's an oversimplification of the story, but yes."

"Yeah, I heard your boss thinks the police case left things out."

"I think Paul wants to tell the whole story," Bailey said carefully.

"So he's going to sell a bunch of books by glorifying a killer and exploiting the deaths of two women and a fifteen-year-old girl."

"You don't understand the genre," she said. "Paul is very talented. This book is his way of doing justice to the memory of the victims."

"You do justice to the victims by putting their killer in jail. Not by making a living off their tragedy."

She crossed her arms. "Lawyers make a living off of tragedy. Police, too."

Acknowledgment lit his dark eyes. "Guess you could look at it that way. So, what's your role in all this?"

"I'm a former editorial assistant. I do research, correspondence, filing, publicity—whatever Paul needs me to do."

"Give me an example."

She drew a deep breath. "For example, right now I'm trying to find out how long it will be before we can get back into the house."

He raised his eyebrows at her change of subject. "Your boss gave his consent to search."

"Last night. But Regan—Helen's daughter—is flying into town tomorrow. She won't want to stay in a hotel."

"My team won't be out of the house until the day after."

"Thursday?" Bailey heard her voice rise and struggled to control it. "But . . . That's the day before the funeral!"

"It's the best I can do."

No apology, she noticed. As if his best was plenty good enough for her.

"You did get a signed death certificate, though, right?" she asked.

He inclined his head.

She didn't want to ask. She had to know. "Cause of death?"

"Drowning."

Relief weakened her knees. "That's all right, then."

He didn't say anything.

"Isn't it?" Bailey pressed. "If the medical examiner says Helen drowned—"

"*Cause* of death is drowning," he repeated. "Manner of death is still pending."

Bailey squeezed the letters in her hand until the envelopes crackled. "What does that mean?"

"It means the ME is waiting for the results of the blood alcohol test to determine if loss of consciousness contributed to Mrs. Ellis's fall."

That sounded reasonable.

Her chest hollowed. Too bad she didn't quite believe him.

Why would his team need another two days in the

house? What was he looking for? And how could she get him to tell her?

"Would you like to come in for a minute?" she blurted. "For"—*What? Coffee? Questioning?*—"something to drink?"

His eyes narrowed in surprise. Well, no wonder, she thought, her heart thudding. She'd surprised herself.

"You're inviting me in for a drink." A statement, not a question.

"Yes, well, I thought . . ." She wasn't thinking. Did she really want to introduce this man to her mother? "It's awfully hot."

He smiled at her, teeth white in his dark face, and the temperature climbed another ten degrees. "Yes, it is. But I'm afraid I can't."

No. Of course not. Good, she told herself, pretty sure that rush she felt was letdown and not relief.

It wasn't like he was actually rejecting her. She wouldn't care if he did. She was an aspiring writer, a veteran of New York's Dating Wars. She should be inured to rejection.

Anyway, it wasn't personal.

She stuck out her chin. "Right. You wouldn't want somebody to catch you getting chummy with a suspect."

"Actually, I have a prior engagement," he drawled.

Like a date? He was dating someone?

Maybe it was personal.

"Well, hello." Dorothy Wells's greeting flowed down the drive, sweet and sticky as molasses.

Trapped like a fly, Bailey turned to see her mother picking her way down the gravel driveway in size six strappy slides from Marshalls.

Dorothy smiled at Steve like a toddler spotting the cookie jar. "And who is this?"

He nodded at her politely. "Steve Burke, ma'am."

"Burke," Dorothy repeated. "Eugenia Burke's boy?"

Most men would have revealed some discomfort at being referred to as "boy." The police detective didn't even twitch. "Yes, ma'am."

Dorothy's smile widened. "And you're here to see Bailey?"

Bailey groaned silently. Of course. Steve Burke was practically designed to her mother's specifications: a white, Southern professional. Not a practicing Methodist—anyway, Bailey didn't recall seeing him at Sunday services—and at least ten years older than Bailey. But clearly Dorothy was prepared to compromise.

Bailey was not.

"He was just leaving," she said, fixing Steve with a "run away, run away" look.

"Oh." Not every fifty-six-year-old woman could pull off a pretty pout, but Dorothy had been practicing in her mirror since 1958, and even Bailey admitted the effect was charming. "Won't you at least come in for a minute? Bailey has so few friends in town anymore."

"I never had friends in this town, Mama," Bailey said, deliberately flip. Steve Burke already suspected her of lusting after her boss, not to mention murdering her boss's wife. Her lack of a social life wasn't likely to lower his opinion of her any. "Let the man go."

"Actually, I'd love a cold drink," Steve said, making Dorothy beam and Bailey's eyes narrow in suspicion. "If you all don't mind."

"What do you think you're doing?" she hissed as they strolled up the drive to the house. Dorothy minced ahead, her heels punching holes in the ground.

He looked down his strong, crooked nose at her. "Accepting your invitation."

"What about your 'prior engagement'?"

He actually glanced at his watch. "I have a few minutes. We can talk some more about what kind of work you do for Paul Ellis."

Was that why he'd changed his mind? Because he saw the opportunity to pump her?

"Not with my mother listening."

Steve raised his eyebrows. "She doesn't like your job?"

Not her job, not her life, not her wardrobe.

"Crime stories make my mother uncomfortable. She doesn't even read the newspaper."

"You should be glad." He opened the kitchen door, earning another approving smile from Dorothy.

Bailey paused on the stoop. "Why?"

"Because if your boss holds a press conference, your name's going to be in a lot of papers. Your mother won't like that."

He was right.

She scowled. "How would you know?"

Humor touched his hard mouth. "Because if she's any-thing like my mother, she believes a lady's name should only appear in the paper three times—when she's born, when she marries, and when she dies."

"Who's getting married?" Dorothy called from the kitchen.

"Nobody, Mom." Bailey stalked inside and turned to face the detective, crossing her arms over her meager chest. "Lieutenant Burke is here because somebody died."

FIVE

DOROTHY Wells's expectant face collapsed like a leaking balloon.

Not good, Steve thought, and did his best to defuse the situation.

"I'll bet your mother already guessed why I'm here." He smiled wryly at Dorothy. "Those middle of the night phone calls are tough on parents, aren't they? You think your children are grown, but when something like this happens, they need their mamas."

"Actually—" Bailey said.

"She didn't call." Bracelets jangling, Dorothy opened a cabinet, a petite, well-put-together woman with a mission and a grievance. "Her sister would have called. Not Bailey. I didn't even know something was wrong until I came down this morning to make Frank's coffee and found her sitting at the kitchen table."

"I didn't want to wake you," Bailey protested.

"And what time was that?" Steve asked.

"Six-thirty? Seven?"

Bailey had told him she got home at three. What had she done for three or four hours?

The memory of her white face and dilated pupils tugged at him. She might have been in shock. She could have been too numb or strung out or flat-out exhausted to make up a story that would satisfy her parents.

Or she could have been with her married lover.

That thought didn't sit well with Steve at all. He was tired, hot, and sweaty. Now he had to make time to talk to Lewis and the clerk at the desk to find out when Ellis had checked into his hotel. And with whom.

"Well, of course it was a shock." Dorothy snapped a glass down on the counter. "But I told her how it would be when she got involved with those people."

Bailey stirred from her post by the kitchen counter. Her crossed arms lifted her shirt in front, revealing a pale slice of belly above the drawstring of her black pants.

He forced his gaze up, into her eyes.

"I don't think Lieutenant Burke is interested in your opinion of my employers, Mom," Bailey said.

"But I am. Very interested."

Her gaze clashed with his. She probably thought he was a middle-aged pervert.

Maybe he was.

He cleared his throat. "You weren't friends with Helen Ellis?" he asked Dorothy.

"Helen was all right." Dorothy opened the refrigerator door, where plastic vegetable magnets squeezed in between family photos: a whole gallery of a towheaded boy and a curly-haired toddler in pink; several shots of a smiling blonde with various hairstyles and in different stages of pregnancy who must be Bailey's sister; and one candid of an earnest, much younger Bailey squinting from beneath her mortarboard at the camera.

Steve narrowed his eyes. *Only one?*

"Although I always thought she could have done more for Bailey," Dorothy confided, turning. "Taken her to the right places. Introduced her to the right people." Ice rattled into a glass. "The right *men*."

"I didn't come home to Stokesville so that Helen Ellis could invite me to Saturday night dinners at the club."

Dorothy poured his tea. "It just breaks my heart to see you waste your opportunities."

"I am *not* wasting my opportunities," Bailey said loudly. She took a deep breath. "I have a good education and a valuable research position with Paul Ellis." She made his name sound like it was splashed in capitals on a freaking book cover. "He won the National Booksellers' Optimus Award last year," she told Steve, like he should know or care what that was.

Dorothy sniffed. "Paul Ellis." The name sounded a lot different when she said it. She handed Steve a frosted glass.

"Appreciate it," he said. "You don't like him? Ellis?"

Bailey glared. "Don't you have to pick up your date?"

"After I finish my tea."

"You have a date?" Dorothy asked.

But he'd been a cop too long to let a pair of women turn an interrogation on him.

"You were saying about Paul Ellis . . . ?"

Dorothy pursed her lips. "Well, he's Not From Around Here, is he?"

"That's not a crime, Mom. It's not even a bad thing. Not everyone wants to live in Stokesville all their lives."

"There's nothing wrong with Stokesville," Dorothy said. "Isn't that right, Steve?"

Teresa had never been able to stand a visit of more than a few days. Hell, there was a time when Steve himself had . . .

He shut the thought down.

"Good place to raise a family," he said.

"Unless you have kids whose horizons stretch farther than the town limits," Bailey said.

Irritation flicked him. What the hell did she know about it? About him.

"Do you have a lot of experience with children, Miz Wells?" he asked in a flat, dangerous voice.

"I was one. How much experience do you have with life outside Stokesville?"

She didn't back down. He tried not to like her for that.

"Steve used to be with the Washington police department," Dorothy answered. "Didn't you, Steve?"

He nodded, watching Bailey.

She moistened her lips with her tongue. "State, or . . . ?"

"Metropolitan," he told her.

Washington, D.C. Murder Capital, USA. A combustible mix of privilege, politics, and social problems, of overlapping jurisdictions and warring gangs.

Bailey's eyes shifted and darkened as she reevaluated him. As a cop? Or as a man? he wondered, and despised himself for the question.

"How many years?" she asked.

"Twelve." Impossible to keep the pride from his voice.

"You must miss it. It's not like you get a lot of challenging cases in Stokesville."

He didn't let himself think about it. He sure as hell wasn't going to talk about it. He sent her a slow smile, designed to distract. "There's yours."

But she refused to be distracted. "That doesn't explain why you've come back."

"Why did you?" he countered.

"Because of my job."

He raised his eyebrows. "Because of Ellis, you mean."

"They're not involved," Dorothy broke in. "Not romantically involved. Bailey isn't seeing anybody now."

Except her boss, Steve thought. But maybe her mother didn't want to acknowledge that.

Bailey met his gaze, her dark eyes rueful. A shock of liking shivered through him. "Mom is letting you know, in her own subtle way, that I'm available."

Maybe Bailey didn't want to acknowledge it either.

"I have your number," he drawled. "Maybe I'll call."

"I don't think that would be such a good idea."

"Bailey!" her mother protested.

Upset by her daughter's lack of manners? Or her dismissal of a possible suitor?

"I'm busy," Bailey said. "I've got work."

Steve sipped his cold, too-sweet tea, observing her over the rim of his glass. "You can't get much writing done with the house shut up."

"I don't write." Her tone was too sharp. She softened it with a smile. "I run interference."

He raised an eyebrow.

"The accident made the local news at noon," she explained. "We've already received some reader response."

Ah, crap. Walt wouldn't want to hear that. Media attention was fine if you had a missing child or a fleeing suspect or even a traffic situation, but any speculation about Ellis's role in his wife's death could tip Steve's hand. And it couldn't help his case or his standing with his boss to have some nosy reporter stirring up Ellis's fan base.

"What kind of response?"

She looked surprised. "Condolences, mostly. E-mails."

"You brought a computer with you?" he asked, careful

to keep his voice neutral. Removing evidence from the scene. How had he missed that?

But Bailey shook her head. "No. Paul has a laptop, of course, but I prefer a desktop. I logged on to his account from here."

"Frank has a computer in his office," Dorothy put in.

"I screen Paul's mail and flag anything he needs to answer personally," Bailey explained.

"That's what you've been doing today?"

"A little. Paul's fans like to feel they're in the know, especially . . ."

"When it comes to crime?" Steve supplied dryly.

Bailey's slender shoulders straightened. "I was going to say, when it's a tragedy that affects him so personally. Most of today I've been handling Helen's final arrangements. You know."

He did know. God, he remembered. Hushed, impersonal meetings in quiet, chilly rooms with the funeral director, the florist, the organist, the priest, while his heart raged inside him like an angry child. He'd done it all without help.

He hadn't accepted help.

Or comfort, either.

Paul Ellis's Little Helper was watching with wide brown eyes, waiting for his reply.

He pulled himself together. "That's what I wanted to talk with you about. The arrangements. I'll need days and times for the viewing and the service. Was Helen a church member?"

Bailey nodded. "Saint Andrews Episcopal."

The church-going population in Stokesville divided between the Baptists, who didn't drink, the Episcopalians, who didn't sing, and the Methodists who fell somewhere in between. And the Catholics, too few to matter. It figured the upwardly mobile, imbibing Ellises attended Saint Andrews.

"Nice pew?" he guessed.

She smiled, surprising him. "Great vestments."

"Minimal commitment."

She shrugged. "Church was a social thing for Helen."

"What about for her husband?"

"He attends—attended—with her sometimes."

"And you?"

"Interested in my morals, Lieutenant?"

"Maybe I'm just making conversation," he suggested.

"Uh huh."

"We've always gone to First Methodist," Dorothy said. "Same as your people."

He didn't go there anymore. But his mother did. It was another connection he might use. Another complication he didn't want.

"What else do you need to know?" Bailey asked.

"The name of the Ellis's lawyer."

She was already backed against the kitchen cabinets with her arms across her chest. But her chin came up at that. "Does he need one?"

He'd been angling for a reaction. Hell, this whole visit was a fishing expedition. She was hooked, no doubt about it. That didn't mean he had to enjoy watching her squirm.

"I want to talk to Helen's executor," he explained. "Who's handling her estate?"

"Oh." Bailey's face cleared. "Pierce and Reynolds, here in town. Does that help?"

It could. Especially if he found out Helen Stokes Ellis had left a whopping pile to her husband.

His cell phone vibrated. He glanced down at the caller's number. *Gabrielle*.

Shit.

"Is something wrong?" Bailey asked.

Yeah. He checked his watch. He was late, and his daughter was going to be furious. Or worse, disappointed.

He was supposed to do better. He had to do better.

"Nope," he lied. "But I have to go."

Mother and daughter stared. He could trace their family resemblance in the narrow, oval shape of their faces, in their nearly identical fine-boned frames.

The reminder of what he had lost, of what he had left to lose, swept over him.

"Thanks for the tea," he said, and was gone.

"WELL." Dorothy huffed in disappointment. "He certainly left in a hurry."

Your fault, her look said. *Men never leave your sister.*

Bailey shrugged. "So we were lucky this time."

"You could have at least tried to stop him."

"Mom." Bailey regarded her petite, attractive mother with exasperated affection. Burke was investigating her. But in her mother's world, male attention was always a good thing. "The guy is six feet four and built like a linebacker. Not to mention he carries a gun. I couldn't even slow him down."

"A woman has ways," Dotty said.

"Some women, maybe."

"You know, Bailey, honey, you're not bad-looking. If you'd just make an effort—"

"I don't want to make an effort. I'm happy the way I am."

Happy enough.

"The right man could make you happier."

"Steve Burke is not the right man."

She'd already met the right man. At least, she'd thought she had. When Paul Ellis smiled at her on his way into his editor's office, when he sent flowers after she completed an exhaustive line edit, when he plucked her from her miserable corner at the Christmas cocktail party, Bailey had felt like Cinderella attracting the notice of the prince. Paul was more than charming. He was educated, urbane, sophisticated, successful . . .

And married, she learned later.

Had been married. He was widowed now.

Oh, God. Guilt scorched in her cheeks and burned in her stomach. She was absolutely going to hell.

"What's the matter with him?" Dorothy demanded.

Him? Bailey pulled her thoughts together. *Oh, Burke.* "He's too . . ."

"Too what?"

Too large. Too harsh. Too aggressively masculine, with his hard, cop's eyes and broad, muscled body.

Bailey had already battered her heart and bruised her ego fishing the pool of available men in New York. It was better—safer—to nurse a crush on her married boss than to risk her heart, her health, and her sanity on another disappointment. At least with Paul, she knew the limits of their relationship up front. At least Paul appreciated her.

"Well, for one thing, he lives here," Bailey said.

"So do you."

"Only temporarily. I could never get involved with a man who expected me to stay."

Dorothy sniffed. "You mean, like Paul Ellis does?"

Bailey's mouth dropped open. She snapped it shut. She didn't expect her mother to be perceptive. She didn't want her to be right. "I don't have time for this."

"Exactly," Dorothy said. "You're twenty-six years old. Almost twenty-seven. When your sister was your age, she was already pregnant with Bryce, Junior."

And pasting her perfect life into even more perfect

photo albums. Which was fine, if that was her sister's dream. It had never been Bailey's.

Not that she had anything against kids. But in her adolescent dreams, she'd always imagined herself creating new fictional worlds. Writing books, not editing scrapbooks.

"Can we please put off the biological clock discussion until dinner? I need to get back to work."

"And that attitude doesn't help you any. No man wants to compete with a woman's work schedule. Why, your father—"

Bailey's cell phone played the opening bars of "The Trouble With Love Is" from her pocket.

Reprieved. She snatched it out. "Hello?"

"Thank God you're there." Paul's voice flowed, warm and fervent, over the line. If she'd been less distracted by her mother, less annoyed by Lieutenant I-Have-A-Prior-Engagement, her heart would have leaped. "Bailey, I need you. I'm in trouble."

Anxiety clenched her chest. She forced herself to breathe deeply. To speak calmly. To think.

Steve had just left her mother's house. Had he even had time to drive to the Do Drop and make an arrest?

"Have you called a lawyer?" she asked.

"What are you talking about? I called Feinstein in New York, but he won't be in until tomorrow."

Feinstein was Paul's doctor.

"Are you all right?" Bailey asked.

"Of course I'm not all right," Paul said. "That's what I'm telling you. My Xanax is in the house, and I can't reach Feinstein for a new prescription. I need you to get it for me."

Relief washed over her in a warm tide. Relief and shame that she had ever doubted him. Only for a second, but the twinge lingered like the residual ache after a dentist appointment. It was Burke's fault, she decided, poking in where he wasn't wanted, prodding her with his questions and his bold, black eyes.

"Sorry," she said. "I'll call the pharmacy."

"You're not listening," Paul chided. "The prescription can't be refilled. I need you to get my pills from the house."

Can't be refilled? How much had he been taking?

But of course she couldn't ask him that. Not when he was under so much stress.

She turned to the counter, hunching her shoulders so she wouldn't have to see her mother's avid eyes and disapproving mouth. "Won't there be an officer on duty at the house?"

"You think I should ask him to go through my medicine cabinet and get my drugs for me?"

Bailey's flush deepened. Paul could be such an asshole. "I meant . . . What if he objects to my being there?"

"He can't. It's my house. You're my assistant. If he doesn't like it, I'll revoke my consent to search. I won't be inconvenienced because some stupid cop is hunting for evidence of an intruder when it's perfectly plain to the chief and everyone else that Helen drowned."

Bailey suspected Steve Burke wasn't stupid at all. *Twelve years with the Metropolitan police force.* But that wasn't what Paul needed to hear right now.

"I'll go right away," she promised.

"I never should have signed that damn consent."

Privately, she agreed with him. But he had been eager, even insistent, that he had nothing to hide.

"I'm sure they'll be done soon," she said soothingly. What had Steve said? "One more day. Maybe two."

"I didn't pack for two days. I only expected to be away overnight. I need things. Socks. Boxers. My laptop. I can't write the damn book on hotel stationery."

Bailey jammed her tiny mobile under her ear, stretching

her other hand for the paper and pencil her mother kept by the kitchen phone. *Underwear,* she wrote. *Laptop.*

"Of course not," she said, while a small, disloyal part of her wondered how Paul could even think about the book with his wife's funeral scheduled for Friday. "Anything else?"

"My black suit should go to the cleaner's. I'll need it for Friday."

Dry-cleaning, she wrote. So he *was* thinking about the funeral. But something about the request niggled at her like a persistent toothache.

Before she could figure it out, Paul spoke again. "Has Regan called about her flight?"

"Not yet."

"Find out when she's coming in. She'll need a ride from the airport."

Bailey made another note. "Did you book a room for her at the Do Drop?"

"I haven't had time," Paul said stiffly. "I can't think of everything."

He was upset, Bailey reminded herself. Overcome. She wrote *reservations* next to *taxi.* "How many rooms?"

By mid-July, most of Helen's social set would already have fled New York for the Cape and the Hamptons. But surely some of them would brave the heat and humidity of Stokesville, North Carolina, for her funeral?

"How should I know? Just take care of it."

"Can do." Bailey drew a circle around *reservations* and added a question mark. "What about Richard?"

Richard and Regan—attractive, headstrong, and disagreeable—were the children of Helen's first marriage to local developer Jackson Poole. They resented their mother's second husband bitterly. All Paul's charm and all Helen's assurances had failed to convince them he hadn't married her to get his hands on their inheritance. Bailey they simply despised as his stooge.

Paul sighed. "Who can say what Richard will do? But you'd better reserve a room, in case he shows up."

"I'm sorry," Bailey said gently. "Is there anything I can do?"

Paul hesitated. "I don't want to bother you."

Who else could he turn to? He was a brilliant, driven, difficult man. He was estranged from his own family. He had fans and admirers and precious few friends.

"It's not a bother," she assured him.

"Do you think while you're at the house you could pick up the mail?"

Bailey winced. She wasn't his therapist. She was his gofer. He didn't need her sympathy.

"Got it." *Mail,* she wrote, her pencil point digging into the paper.

"And don't forget my suit."

Bailey underlined *dry-cleaning* with two short, sharp jabs of her pencil. "I won't."

"That's my girl." The warm approval in his voice more than made up for her irritation at being called a "girl." "I don't know what I'd do without you."

"Oh." She flushed with pleasure. "Just doing my job, that's all."

"You're amazing. I'll see you around five. With my laptop, remember."

"Five o'clock," she promised.

The line went dead.

Bailey tightened her grip on the phone, as if she could hold on to . . . something.

"You're not meeting him, are you?" her mother asked.

"I work for him, Mom." Bailey kept her tone light. "He just needs me to run a few errands."

"Most girls your age are driving carpool. Or running errands for their husbands."

Bailey grinned at her. "But they don't get paid."

"And he pays you enough to make you drive all over town?"

Not really. But it wasn't about the money. Paul was her mentor. Her inspiration. Okay, so her time wasn't her own, and her manuscript was nowhere close to submission. Paul still understood her goals. He valued her intelligence. He made her feel smarter, more worldly, and infinitely more appreciated. *I don't know what I'd do without you . . . You're amazing.*

She would never make her mother understand.

"I make more than three-quarters of the women who live in Stokesville," Bailey said. "Anyway, Paul doesn't have his car."

And then it struck her.

Neither did she.

THE lobby stank of popcorn and soda-saturated carpet. Steve scanned the line in front of the concession stand. He must be the only male over thirty in the whole multiplex. He for damn sure was the only one carrying a gun.

Unless that ponytailed mama over there wrangling her toddler off the velvet rope was carrying concealed in her diaper bag . . .

A cluster of teens slouched and postured by the bank of video games, the girls in skinny spaghetti-strap tops and lip gloss, the boys in baggy shorts and overpriced sneakers. Steve watched one boy's hand drift down his date's back to rest on the belt of her low-rise jeans and narrowed his eyes.

"What's the matter?" Gabrielle asked from beside him.

He rearranged his face in a smile. "Nothing, sweetheart."

Not as long as she was still with him and not playing *Bloodlust 4* while some fourteen-year-old punk groped her behind.

"Are you really okay with the movie?"

All Steve knew about this afternoon's feature was that it had some vaguely recognizable teenage star and the word "princess" in the title. But it was rated G, and Gabrielle had elected it as an acceptable alternative to Orlando Bloom. He could probably nap through most of it.

"Wouldn't miss it for the world," he told his daughter.

"Liar," Gabrielle said. But she was smiling, and for at least a minute he felt like they were complete again, a unit, instead of something broken with a part horribly missing.

"What do you want?" he asked as they inched to the front of the line.

"Popcorn?"

With some vague thoughts about saturated fats and spoiling her dinner, he asked, "How about Raisinets?"

Raisinets was a fruit, right?

Gabrielle looked at him with big, sad eyes. "Okay."

Shit. Wrong answer.

"Large popcorn, medium Coke, and a bottle of water," Steve told the kid behind the counter.

"Extra butter?" asked the kid.

Steve looked at Gabrielle. She nodded, beaming.

"Yep. Thanks," he said.

"No problem," the kid said.

Steve forked a ten over the register, knowing he'd been manipulated by a nine-year-old and feeling pretty good about it. Maybe Gabrielle wouldn't mind so much not getting her way in the big things if she had some control of the small.

"Come on," she urged, clutching her red-and-white tub. "We'll miss the previews."

As he turned to follow her, his police pager went off.

PROBLEM *solved,* Bailey thought, as she maneuvered the rear end of her mother's dark blue Mercury Grand Marquis toward the road, feeling like a teenager borrowing the family sedan on a Saturday night. Back in high school, her mother had been too grateful when Bailey went out at all to ask awkward questions. Bailey figured the police officer on duty at Paul's house wouldn't be so complaisant. But she'd deal with that problem when she came to it.

The car lurched as a wheel ran off the drive. She strong-armed it back onto the gravel. So her driving skills were a little rusty. She hadn't needed a car in New York. Longing for her old life in the city seized her chest: the bright awnings and dingy lights, the smells pouring from restaurant kitchens and rising from subway tunnels, the choked traffic, the swimming sidewalks, the rush of life.

She gave herself a shake. If she were back in the big city, she'd have even less chance of talking her way past the cop.

But the officer on duty, pink-eared and regretful, held firm against both Northern aggression and Southern charm.

"I'm sorry, ma'am," he said after about five minutes. "I'll have to call Lieutenant Burke. He's in charge of the scene."

Bailey's heart bumped.

Somehow she didn't think Steve Burke would tolerate the contamination of his alleged crime scene. Besides, he had a "prior engagement."

Not that she cared about that.

"Oh, I'd feel terrible bothering him on his afternoon off. If you could just ask the chief about Mr. Ellis's medication . . ."

She held her breath while the young officer, Lewis, considered.

"I could do that," he allowed, finally. "If you'd wait in your car a minute . . ."

Bailey waited, palms sweating and heart racing, while Officer Lewis spoke into his cell phone. The street was quiet. No chugging lawnmowers, no barking dogs, no curtains twitching at the windows.

She wasn't doing anything wrong. She didn't even want to go into the house. She was simply doing her job.

Her skin felt clammy. Like Helen's skin. Bailey shivered, cold despite the heat that lay like a wet wool blanket over everything.

That's my girl . . . You're amazing.

The young officer approached the car and bent down to her window. "All right, ma'am. Chief said it would be okay to let you get Mr. Ellis's pills. But I'll have to accompany you into the house."

"That's fine. That's great." Maybe once they were inside she could persuade him to let her take Paul's suit as well.

Unpeeling herself from the damp upholstery, she sidled from the car. "This will only take a minute," she promised. "Five, tops."

But it was closer to twenty minutes later when they left the house, Bailey's vision half-obscured by the pile of absolutely essential items in her arms. With her purse on her shoulder and her keys in her teeth, she turned to lock the door behind them.

"What the hell do you think you're doing?"

Her heart leaped into her throat.

SIX

MACON Reynolds III stepped outside the 1930s clapboard house that sheltered the law offices of Pierce and Reynolds, glancing up at the sky. The sun was shining, he had a nine o'clock tee time tomorrow, and all was right with his world.

He strolled the cracked sidewalk in the direction of the two-block center of town. An unusual number of cars crowded the parking lot of the Do Drop—was that a Channel 5 news van?—but for the most part, the streets were quiet. Flags hung limply from front porches. Orange ditch lilies bloomed by the side of the road. Cannonballs rusted in a pile by the courthouse steps. God, he loved this town.

Oh, he'd been wild enough to leave once, he remembered, bored with high school and hot to conquer the world beyond its borders. But he'd felt adrift in the unfamiliar waters of the big state campus, despite its ready access to college bars and fresh pussy. He'd done what was expected of him, of course, finished his four years at Carolina and then struggled through law school. Grades didn't matter. His place in his father's firm was settled before he was out of diapers. So he'd passed the bar and come home to this backwater town, where he'd always be one of the biggest fish around.

Macon rounded the corner to the diner. After he'd made partner and then councilman, his old man had been after him to run for the state senate, but Macon suspected mayor would suit him better. The mayor had real power in this town, more than any rookie legislator in Raleigh, more than any party politico, more than the chief of police, even.

Macon smiled at his reflection in the diner's glass door: only thirty-six years old, trim and still handsome, with affable blue eyes and blond hair kept short by regular visits to Buddy's Barber Shop. *Mayor Reynolds.* It was just a matter of time.

"Hey, Macon."

"Howdy, Mr. Reynolds."

He nodded to the regulars in ball caps and Wrangler jeans chatting at the counter, accepting their greetings as his due as he slid into his booth by the cash register. The lunch buffet was closed, of course, but there was still time for a cup of coffee, plenty of time to see and be seen.

Charlene, wearing a hair net and a polyester dress that had been in style in his daddy's day, brought him his coffee without being asked. "Slice of pie, Macon? Or we got a nice banana pudding left from lunch."

He patted his flat stomach. "Just coffee today, honey. Can't spoil my appetite, or Marylou will have my hide."

Marylou wasn't likely to give a damn. His wife didn't cook. Hell, they barely spoke anymore. The two kids shuttled between piano lessons and soccer practice while Marylou put in her time with the Junior League, the PTA, the Ladies' Guild and the tennis pro. For all he knew, she was putting out for her tennis instructor, too, between lessons, on her back behind the clubhouse locker room. But she'd be waiting when Macon got home. Marylou understood the importance of keeping up appearances. That's why he'd married her.

Charlene dipped into her apron pocket for two creams. "Terrible thing about poor Helen Stokes."

Macon nodded seriously, like he cared. It wouldn't do to seem indifferent toward a client, and Helen, with her waxed snatch and catty tongue, had at least been entertaining. "She sure will be missed," he said, which was a lie, but in Stokesville you didn't speak ill of the dead. Particularly not when the dead were named Stokes.

Charlene set her coffeepot on the table. "I hear her own son isn't coming to her funeral."

Did the stricture against speaking ill of the dead apply to their children? Macon thought not. "That boy was always trouble."

Drugs, he'd heard. Thank God his children weren't inclined that way. There must be bad blood in the Stokes family somewhere.

"Did she . . . You know." Charlene leaned over the table, smelling of breath mints and fried okra. "Disinherit him?"

"Oh, no." Macon was genuinely shocked at the notion of leaving money outside the family. "Old Jackson made sure of that. His estate goes to the children. With conditions, of course."

"What about that husband of hers? The writer."

The Yankee.

Macon shrugged. "He's provided for."

And handsomely, too. As part of her prenup, Helen had taken out a four-million-dollar life insurance policy designed to keep Paul Ellis in comfort for the rest of his natural life . . . or until he remarried.

"Well, that's good." Charlene shifted her weight in her orthopedic shoes. "I just love his books."

Macon grunted, losing interest.

"I think it's so exciting he's setting the next one here." Charlene chattered on, oblivious. Macon raised his cup, hoping she'd take the hint and leave. "Wouldn't it be something if the police really did make a mistake in the Dawler trial."

Hot coffee scalded Macon's tongue. He swallowed. "What are you talking about?"

Charlene looked surprised. "That's what he does. In his books. He takes these real famous cases and he shows where the police went wrong."

"Paul Ellis is writing a book about the Dawler murders," Macon said carefully. Son of a *bitch*.

Charlene nodded.

"But Billy Ray confessed."

"Well, I know he did. But it's interesting, don't you think? My cousin Clayton—he's a deputy over in Guilford—told me Paul Ellis has been in three times to visit Billy Ray."

Panic skittered in Macon's chest like a mouse behind the baseboards. He willed himself to stay calm. It didn't mean anything. Charlene was a silly bitch and Billy Ray Dawler was a moron.

"Sure you won't have that pie?" Charlene asked.

"No, thank you, Charlene." He gave her his good-old-boy smile. "Got to save room for dinner."

Any appetite he'd had was gone.

STEVE'S head pounded as he watched Bailey back out the front door of Paul Ellis's house: her pale, narrow feet in black flip-flops, her pale, narrow back exposed by black drawstring pants riding low on her hips. His blood pressure rose.

"What the hell do you think you're doing?"

She didn't scream. Too bad. She flinched once like a startled cat, and something—a man's black dress shoe—tumbled and bounced on the porch.

Her shoulders squared. Turning, she smiled at him ruefully over an armload of clothes. "We have got to stop meeting like this."

Steve stared stonily back. "You mean, at crime scenes?"

Bailey's smile faded. "I meant you have a habit of sneaking up behind me."

"I don't sneak. But apparently you do."

Her chin lifted a notch. "Oh, right, because anytime I plan on committing nefarious acts under a cloak of secrecy I call Chief Clegg and request a police escort. What are you doing here?"

Steve didn't answer. He had no authority to stop her from going into the house. He knew it, and from her attitude she knew it, too.

Her gaze cut to Lewis, standing beside her on the porch. "You called him, didn't you?"

Lewis bent to pick up the shoe. When he straightened, not only his ears but his whole face was red.

"Officer Lewis felt I should know about any attempts to remove evidence from a crime scene," Steve said.

Bailey sighed. "You're angry."

"I am not angry." He bit the words out.

He was deeply, coldly furious. With Walt, for failing to keep him in the loop. With Ellis, for forcing him to tip his hand. With Bailey, for going behind his back to contaminate the scene and incriminate herself.

And with himself, for caring. The vise tightened around his head.

"Look, I'm sorry I interrupted your date," Bailey said.

He ignored her apology. His "date" was sitting in the front of his air-conditioned pickup nursing a large tub of popcorn and an even bigger attitude.

Compartmentalize. Depersonalize. Detach.

He had hoped to keep the investigation neutral. As long as he treated Ellis as a victim, there was still a chance the writer would cooperate. But no way could he let Bailey leave the crime scene with an armload of Ellis's clothes.

He was already too late to prevent the folds from rubbing together. But maybe whatever blood was on them had dried. Maybe there was no blood.

Steve's jaw clenched. Yeah, and maybe there was a Santa Claus.

He nodded toward the bundle in Bailey's arms. "What have you got there?"

"Medicine," she answered promptly. "Paul forgot to pack his prescription last night, and I stopped by to pick it up."

"Medicine." Not a question. A challenge.

"In my purse."

He ran his fingers lightly under the strap at her shoulder, observing the slight widening of her eyes. "This purse?"

She nodded, speechless.

"May I?" he murmured.

Without waiting for her reply, he slid the bag down, his fingers brushing the crook of her elbow, the inside of her wrist. He kept his touch impersonal as he maneuvered the strap under Paul's clothes and over her arm. But he was close enough to hear the faint catch of her breath. To notice the baby-fine texture of her skin. To *smell* her.

Shit. He took a step back.

"Do you mind?" His hand paused on the zipper.

She shrugged. "I've got nothing to hide."

He wished he could believe her.

He withdrew the brown prescription bottle with two fingers. "This it?"

She eyed him warily, as if she expected him to bust her for drug possession. But she said, "Yes."

"Where did you find it?"

"In Paul's medicine cabinet. Why?"

"Did Officer Lewis see you take it from the cabinet?"

She glanced uncertainly at Lewis, red and stoic beside them. "I guess so. He was standing right there."

"Lewis? You confirm you observed Ms. Wells remove this bottle from Ellis's medicine cabinet?"

"Yes, sir."

Now things got dicey.

"Is it okay if I take these for analysis?" Steve asked. He watched her draw a breath, the objection forming on her lips and in her eyes, and added, "Just one."

One pill and the bottle, for fingerprinting. That was all he needed. He waited, intent on getting this one small concession. If he could lull her into saying one yes . . .

"Why would you . . ." He watched her intelligent, expressive face as she puzzled it out.

"The toxicology screen," she said slowly. "You told me the ME was waiting to see if Helen's blood alcohol levels contributed to her fall."

Steve didn't say anything. He didn't need to.

"You think she was drugged," Bailey said.

He didn't want to spook her. He hadn't tipped his hand yet. "I'm keeping an open mind," he said. "She could have taken the pills herself. I have to eliminate as many possibilities as I can."

"I guess that would be all right," Bailey said. "Just one?"

"That's all. I'll just put the rest . . . Lewis? We need a kit." The officer scrambled for the evidence bag in his car.

"The lab folks will want the original container," Steve told Bailey.

"Why?"

"The label," he lied without hesitation. "It's got the strength and dosage on it."

"Won't they get that from an analysis anyway?"

He ignored her question. When Lewis returned, Steve transferred the bottle's contents into a baggie and dropped the remaining pill and the bottle itself into a paper evidence bag to preserve the prints.

"Well." Bailey's tone was dry as she tucked the baggie full of pills into her purse. "You've got what you came for. Can I go now?"

He glanced at her sharply. Had she understood the significance of the two bags?

"In a minute." No way around it, he decided regretfully. He couldn't let her leave with Ellis's clothes, even if stopping her revealed his suspicions . . . and aroused hers.

"What else have you got there?" he asked.

"A suit," she said with exaggerated patience. "For the funeral."

"Why isn't it on a hanger?"

"I'm taking it to the dry-cleaners."

"And whose idea was that?"

She stiffened as his implication sunk in. "Oh, no. You can't actually think—"

"Dad?"

DAD?

Bailey jerked her gaze from Steve's grim face to the child standing on the sidewalk behind him. A pretty girl, nine or ten, with smooth, honey-toned skin, butterfly earrings dancing at her ears, and big dark eyes.

Not his date.

His daughter.

Bailey's stomach was in knots. Her mind spun like a hamster in a wheel, pumping furiously, going nowhere, as she struggled to reconcile the hard-eyed, hard-assed detective questioning her with the existence of a child. His child.

He didn't wear a wedding ring. She'd looked. Not that she was interested in him in *that* way. But after a few months in New York, checking a man's ring finger became an instinct, a survival reflex, like learning to ignore panhandlers on the street or carrying your purse up under your arm.

"You're married?" she asked Steve.

"My mom is dead," the girl announced.

Oh. A little of Bailey's indignation leaked away.

"I'm sorry," she said with genuine sympathy. Anything less made her a monster. "That's tough."

The girl ducked her head between her shoulders. "Can we go now?" she asked Steve.

He rubbed the back of his neck. "I told you to stay in the truck."

Her lower lip stuck out. "It's hot."

"That's why the air-conditioning is on. Turn on the radio."

"The stations here suck. Can't I wait out here with you?"

The cool, tough detective looked hot and harassed. Bailey hid a grin. Karma was a bitch. "No, you can't."

"Are you going to arrest her?"

Bailey laughed.

Steve shot her a hard look, and she sobered up fast. Maybe he was.

"Not today," he said. "Get in the truck."

The girl turned her large, dark eyes on Bailey. "You're in trouble."

"Yeah, I got that." Bailey shifted the itchy load in her

arms, trying not to drop anything else. Trying not to think too hard about that *"not today."* "But I said I was sorry."

The child nodded. "That always helps. He'll get over it."

"Gabrielle," her father said in quiet warning.

"I have to go now," the child told Bailey politely. "It was nice meeting you."

"Nice to meet you, too," Bailey said, surprised to realize it was true. She watched the girl drag her feet to the curb before she said, "Cute kid."

Steve's lips tightened.

"Good manners," Bailey added, goading him.

"She takes after her mother."

The dead wife.

Which was a hell of a conversation stopper, but still a better topic than, say, what Bailey was doing sneaking out of the house with Paul's dry-cleaning. "How did she . . . That is, how long since her mother, ah . . ."

Died.

The word lay between them, unspoken. Unavoidable. Southern ladies considered euphemisms for death just plain tacky. Nice folks did not "pass away." "Lost" was acceptable, but the word had always implied a certain carelessness to Bailey. She was pretty sure Steve Burke hadn't lost anybody. His wife had been taken from him, and from the tension in his body, he was still pissed off about it.

His expression shuttered. "Two and a half years. Cancer."

That poor kid. She must have been, what, like six? Seven? And her father . . .

Steve used to be with the Washington police department, Bailey's mother had said.

That's why he'd left. That's why he was here. In Stokesville. *Good place to raise a family,* he'd said.

Oh, God. Bailey's assumptions splintered and shifted like a kaleidoscope.

"I am so sorry," she said, and she wasn't only expressing sympathy for his loss. She was apologizing for misjudging him.

"Thank you." His face was like stone.

O-kay. Obviously his impression of her hadn't changed one bit.

"Well." She fidgeted. "I'm sure you want to get back to your daughter. I'll just—"

"Why that suit?" he asked.

Sweat collected under her arms, in the small of her back, between her breasts. "Excuse me?"

"Did you pick out that suit yourself? Or did Ellis ask for it?"

"He asked for his black suit. He only has one."

"So he told you to take it to the cleaners."

She could see where this conversation was headed. She didn't like the direction. "He needs it for the funeral."

"Which is Friday. Why not wait? Take it to a one-hour cleaners on Thursday, when you're back in the house."

"This is Stokesville," she reminded him wryly. "There is no one-hour cleaners. Anyway, Paul asked me to take care of it. So I did."

"Do you do everything he asks you to?"

Pretty much.

She recoiled from the realization like a slap. Some things you didn't think about. She had enough on her plate without exploring the flaws and failings of her relationship with Paul.

"It wasn't that big a deal. I was over here anyway. To pick up his medicine."

"And that's the real reason?"

Her heart beat faster. "What other reason could there be?"

Steve shrugged. "He's a crime writer. Him sending you back to a closed crime scene, tracking fibers, leaving fingerprints, removing evidence . . . It looks bad, that's all."

For her, he meant.

She could barely breathe. It looked bad *for her*.

"I didn't . . . He's upset. I'm sure he never thought of that."

Steve met her gaze, his dark eyes almost pitying. "Maybe he didn't. But he should have, shouldn't he?"

SEVEN

CHIEF Walter Clegg stared out his office window at the tree-lined, flag-draped streets of his town, his hands clenched behind his back.

He couldn't argue with the results of the autopsy. Or with Burke's carefully prepared affidavit for a warrant to search the Ellis home. That didn't mean he had to like them.

At this moment, Walt wasn't feeling any too warmly toward Burke, either. Steve Burke was a good cop, dogged, honest, and imaginative. But the very qualities that had led Walt to hire him also made him a pain in the ass.

Walt fumbled for his handkerchief and mopped the sweat from his forehead. Once the media learned the contents of the warrant, they would know the police were looking for a murder weapon. And once that happened, interest in the case—and in Ellis and in his books—would explode.

Damn writer deserved what was coming to him, poking around where he didn't belong. But once the media was let loose on a story, they might sniff out even an old, cold trail. A trail Walt had believed buried twenty years ago.

Walt turned away from the window, folding his handkerchief back in his pocket. It couldn't be helped now. Steve Burke would do what he had to do.

And so would Walt.

REGAN rode the escalator down to baggage claim, her mind reeling and her stomach churning with grief and caffeine. She shouldn't have drunk a Red Bull for breakfast. She should have bought a bagel at the airport instead. She shouldn't have taken a plane at all. I-85 was a bitch around Charlotte, but if she'd tackled the six-hour drive from Atlanta to Stokesville she'd at least have her car. She'd have control. She wouldn't be stuck waiting for a ride at the fucking airport, the way she had every Christmas holiday from seventh grade on.

Slinging her purse over her shoulder, Regan stalked to the carousel. The other passengers got out of her way.

"Help you with your bag?" offered a middle-aged guy in a suit.

Regan narrowed her eyes and he backed off.

"Regan?" A woman's voice, almost unaccented, like one of those newscasters on TV. "Regan Poole?"

So she didn't have to wait after all. Regan grabbed her Louis Vuitton bag off the moving belt and turned.

The voice belonged to Paul's dweeby secretary, Bailey something, standing there wearing an uncertain smile and really awful clothes—a black T-shirt and totally boring khaki slacks. Honestly, you'd think living in New York would have taught her something about fashion.

Regan raised her eyebrows coolly, pretending not to recognize her. "Yes?"

Dweeb girl flushed. Her gaze was dark, direct, and insufferably kind. "Bailey Wells. We met in New York. I'm so sorry about your mother."

I just bet you are, Regan thought.

"Where's Paul?" she asked.

"He couldn't get away. Can I take your suitcase?"

Regan gripped the handle tighter. "I can manage. Where's the car?"

She was being a bitch. So what? She was entitled. Somebody should be as miserable as she was right now. Paul wasn't here, Richard wasn't coming, and her mother . . . God, her mother was dead.

Bailey made an obvious and convenient target. Helen used to make fun of her. And while Regan made a point of never seeing eye to eye with her mother, adopting Helen's dislikes now that she was dead seemed an excellent way to demonstrate her loyalty.

Bailey's smile faded. The pity in her eyes didn't. "I parked in the hourly lot. It's not far."

"I know how far it is."

Flying to and from boarding school for six crappy years, Regan had learned her way around fucking Raleigh-Durham airport.

Only the airport had changed. Everything changed. Regan glared when Bailey touched her arm, silently redirecting her steps, and waited in sullen silence as her stepfather's secretary fed a dollar into a new, automated parking kiosk.

"All set." Bailey reached again for Regan's suitcase, and this time Regan let her have it. It was hot, and she was sick of lugging the damn thing anyway. "Right this way."

The rattle of luggage wheels and the clack of Regan's heels echoed through the dim, cavernous garage.

Bailey fished in her purse. A keyless entry code bleeped from the line of cars along one wall.

Regan stopped dead, staring at the parked silver Lexus. "That's my mother's car."

"Paul thought you would be more comfortable in this than in *my* mother's car." Bailey opened the trunk and hefted Regan's suitcase inside. "And having driven my mom's car around for the past couple days, I can tell you he's totally right."

Her dry tone invited Regan to share the joke, but Regan didn't want to share anything. Certainly not with the dweeb. She had no right to drive Helen's car.

Regan flung herself in the front seat, flipped all the air-conditioning vents in her direction and dropped her head against the headrest.

Bailey eased the Lexus out of its slot, exiting the parking deck so slowly Regan wanted to scream. Sun slammed through the windshield. Outside, the landscaped curves and staked-out trees withered in the heat as the car picked up speed.

"So, how was your flight?" Bailey asked.

Like she cared.

Regan turned her face to the window. She didn't have to talk to Bailey. Bailey was nothing. Nobody. A glorified geek who'd gone to the public school with every other hick in town. She'd escaped on some kind of scholarship, but she couldn't be that smart, or she wouldn't be working for Paul.

For almost an hour, they drove in silence. The sun glittered on the concrete median and glared on the road. Regan's head pounded from an overload of caffeine and not enough sleep. She closed her eyes.

"We're here."

Regan started. Blinked.

Bailey cut the engine and turned to face her, cheerful and falsely confident as a substitute teacher in middle school. "I'll take your bag to your room. Can I get you something to eat?"

Regan dragged herself together. "No."

All she wanted was sleep.

And for her father to be alive, and for her mother to be lying out by the pool nodding off over a drink and a cigarette, and for this nightmare to be over, but none of those things were happening. She might as well nap.

Paul acted exactly as expected, lots of deep, tragic looks and fake paternal hugs. Regan leaned in from the shoulder to keep him off her boobs and stepped back.

"Dear girl," he kept saying.

The dweeb had the decency not to stick around while Paul acted all grateful and relieved Regan was here for her own mother's funeral. She heard the secretary tromping upstairs lugging the bag and then in the kitchen talking to some other women. The church ladies must have been in and out all day, delivering the covered dishes, plates of ham, Co-cola cake and cheese straws that accompanied death in Stokesville. Regan knew she should go out there and thank them, but just the thought of all that food made her want to hurl. Let Little Miss Efficiency deal with it.

"I'm going to lie down," she announced. "See you at dinner."

Paul gave her a small, sad smile. "Whatever you want, dear girl. We're just family tonight."

Family, my ass. He wasn't her family. She didn't have family anymore, except for Richard, and he wasn't here. She should have told her brother he didn't get any money unless he showed up.

Regan stopped at the top of the stairs. Now there was an idea. Maybe she could sell it to the lawyer.

She shoved open the door to her old room and dropped her purse on the bed. A splash of color on the dresser caught her eye: flowers, fresh garden flowers, in a tiny silver bud vase beside a pile of magazines. Tears sprang to her eyes. Ah, shit.

The last few times she'd visited her mother in New York, Helen had done the same thing, left flowers and fresh towels, a bottle of spring water and the latest magazines beside her bed. Her mother had never been big on the kissy-face stuff, so the gesture had really meant something—a sign of her mother's love, a tacit acknowledgment of Regan's new, grown-up status. She touched the flowers' petals. Thumbed through the magazines. All her favorites were there, *Cosmo, People, Us,* just like before.

Her head pounded. Exactly like before.

Which meant . . . Which meant . . .

Her chest tightened. The magazines hadn't been her mother's doing. Hadn't been her mother's idea. The magazines, the water, the flowers, everything, were from fucking efficient Bailey.

Heat swept Regan. She stormed out of her room and down the stairs, her rage and grief boiling inside her.

Bailey had left the kitchen and was talking quietly with Paul in the hall. Something about the way they stood—too close, heads bent together in easy intimacy—hit Regan in the gut.

"What is she still doing here?"

They looked up at her with nearly identical expressions of controlled patience. Like a couple. Like a unit. That was wrong.

Bailey hesitated, as if waiting for Paul to speak. When he didn't, she said gently, "I'm just helping with the funeral arrangements."

Like she'd "helped" with the flower arrangement in Regan's room?

"I can do that. She was my mother. You can buzz off."

"No, she can't." Paul sounded cool, almost amused. "She lives here, too, Regan."

Which made it worse. How much worse, Regan wasn't sure yet. She only knew she didn't want another woman in her mother's house, taking her mother's place.

Bailey hadn't lived with them in New York.

"That's bullshit," Regan said.

Paul drew himself up in displeasure. "I know you're upset, dear girl, but you can't talk that way in front of Bailey."

The dweeb frowned at him. "Actually, I think—"

"I'll fucking talk any way I want," Regan interrupted.

"Not in my house," Paul said.

"This isn't your house. It's mine," Regan said, pulsing with misery and triumph. Her gaze cut from her stepfather to his secretary. "And I don't want her here."

"THIS isn't your house." Gabrielle's chin stuck out. "It's Grandma's. And Grandma said I could paint the chair."

The chair in question, now a lurid reddish purple, glowed in the dim garage, its feet in tiny puddles of paint. Bright, graffiti-like whorls decorated the scattered newspaper. Discarded cans of spray paint—two of them—bled and rolled on the cement floor. A fine purple spray misted the handles of Eugenia's garden tools and the nearby lawn mower.

Steve shook his head. What was his mother thinking?

His daughter was easier to figure. Steve surveyed her from her paint-streaked hands to her miserable, defiant eyes, and realized it was payback time. She still hadn't forgiven him for skipping out on the movie the other day.

If Teresa were here . . . But she wasn't.

If he'd spent the morning at home . . . But he hadn't. He'd gone in early to prepare an affidavit for a search warrant of the Ellis house.

"I told you to wrap things up," Walt had complained.

"You told me to do my job," Steve had replied.

And damn the consequences.

So in two hours, when the magistrate returned from lunch, Steve had to go back to convince him he had probable cause to search for a weapon. He only hoped the judge would be less hostile than the chief.

Or Gabrielle.

So did he give his daughter the talking-to she deserved or the attention she so obviously needed?

"The chair, fine," he said evenly. "Not the garage."

Gabrielle's chin wobbled. "I tried outside. But the wind blew the newspaper, and it stuck to the paint."

"I can see that would be a problem," Steve acknowledged. "But now we've got another one."

Her gaze slid from his. He watched her shoulders slump as she took in the purple carnage. "I'm sorry," she muttered.

That always helps, she'd said to Bailey.

Well, she had him pegged.

He rubbed his jaw. "Need a hand with cleanup?"

She bit her lip. Nodded.

She was a good kid, Steve thought. A great kid. She deserved a father who spent more time with her. "Let's move this onto the driveway so it can dry."

"Do you like it?" Gabrielle asked as he slid the chair onto a piece of cardboard and dragged it outside.

"It's very . . ." The paint blazed in the sun. ". . . purple."

Gabrielle scowled. *Wrong answer.* "It's not purple. It's fuchsia."

"Fuchsia, huh? It's bright."

Teresa had loved bright colors.

"But do you like it?" his daughter asked.

He liked anything that made her happy. He shook out a trash bag. "Yep. You pick out the color yourself?"

"Uh huh. Grandma said I could. And she gave me the chair from the attic."

Steve hunted paint thinner on the cluttered shelves. "Where are you going to put it?"

"In my room. To make it more . . ." Kneeling, Gabrielle busied herself bundling newspaper.

Steve glanced at his daughter's bowed head. He knew when a subject was holding back on him. "To make it more . . . ?"

"Like home," she said.

Steve felt sucker punched. "Honey . . ."

"It's okay," she said, not looking up.

It wasn't. But for once Steve wasn't sure how to make it right.

"We won't always live with Grandma," he said. "As soon as we sell the townhouse, we're going to buy a nice house here. And you can paint your room any color you want."

"I don't want to sell our house in D.C.," Gabrielle said, her voice muffled.

His heart wrenched. "We talked about this, Gabby. It's better for us to live in Stokesville now. It's nice here, right?"

Unless you have kids whose horizons stretch farther than the town limits, Bailey had said.

"I know it's tough without Rosa. But there are people here who can take care of you," he continued doggedly.

"I don't need a nanny anymore. I can take care of myself."

"Not according to Child Services."

"Well, you take care of me."

Not well enough, he thought.

"Sometimes I have to work," he said. "And then it's good your Grandma is here."

"Grandma says she won't always be here."

His chest squeezed. Hadn't his daughter had enough

experience with death and dying without Eugenia sharing her fears of her own mortality? "Well . . ."

"She said she's going to Asheville on Friday with her book club group."

He breathed again. "But she'll be back Saturday night."

His daughter watched him from the corners of her eyes. "Grandma says what I really need is a mother."

"Your grandmother talks too much," Steve said grimly.

Gabrielle ignored this. "You could get married again."

Jesus.

"I don't think that will work," Steve said gently.

She sat back on her heels, giving him her full attention. "Why not?"

He didn't have the time or energy to invest in another relationship. He didn't have the heart. Or the guts.

"Well . . . I don't really know anybody."

Gabrielle cocked her head.

Steve felt uneasy. He'd seen that look before when Teresa wanted something. It used to presage a shopping trip. But Gabrielle couldn't go shopping for a mother.

He tried to clarify. "Before two people can get married they have to do a lot of other stuff first. Like go on dates."

"Oh." Gabrielle sighed. "Yeah, I guess you wouldn't be good at that."

"Right," Steve said, relieved. But curiosity wouldn't let him let it go. "Why not?"

Gabrielle grinned. "Because you'd make your date leave the movie."

He laughed.

"I think that's everything," Bailey told Paul, desperately upbeat. She popped the flash drive from his laptop's USB port. "I've backed up all your files and the documents folder. I can work from my parents' house."

As long as she could persuade her dad to stay out of his office and her mother to leave her alone.

Dorothy, who preferred even the TV to her own company, had never understood or approved of her younger daughter's desire for solitude.

What are you doing up there? she would call up the stairs when Bailey used to escape to her room after school. *You're not doing anything.*

Nothing but reading or writing or dreaming.

Nothing her mother considered worthwhile.

And leave your door open! she'd say, as if she could save her daughter from the perversion of privacy that way.

How can you expect to get anywhere if you spend all your time in your room?

Well, maybe Mom was right on that one.

Because here Bailey was, almost twenty-seven years old, unpublished, unmarried, slinking home to escape the scandal of an unconsummated love affair and an ongoing murder investigation, moving back under her parents' roof and driving her mother's car.

As a career development, it pretty much sucked. As personal achievements went, it was an all-time low.

Paul slouched against the corner of his desk, stretching out long, elegant legs in perfectly pressed khaki. "I want you to stay."

Bailey ignored the lick of longing and dropped the lipstick-sized flash drive into her purse. "My being here makes Regan uncomfortable."

He held her gaze, a smile touching the corner of his mouth. "And you're being gone makes *me* uncomfortable."

She resisted the lure of that long look. Being needed was

one thing. Being stupid was another. "I can't stay. Regan thinks—"

"Regan's opinions are hardly my biggest concern right now."

"What Regan thinks, other people will be saying."

Paul shrugged. "Small town, small minds."

"Big mouths," Bailey said. "People talk."

"So what? As soon as I finish this book, we'll be gone. Back to New York, where we belong."

That "we" should have thrilled her. Wasn't that what she wanted? Paul and New York. She didn't belong in Stokesville. She never had.

And yet . . . Her family lived here. Her father owned the hardware store. Her sister belonged to the Junior League. Her mother . . . How would her mother hold up her head in church if the whole congregation was whispering about her daughter's relationship with her famous boss?

Didn't Paul see that? Or didn't he care?

"It's going to be difficult to leave town if—" *You're arrested for murder.* She gulped. "—if the police decide to listen to gossip," she finished weakly.

"Let them. You of all people know I was faithful to Helen."

Bailey flushed guiltily. Yes, she did.

"I *loved* her," Paul said dramatically.

Bailey winced. But a small, cold kernel held aloof, observing, as if she were watching a mediocre actor in a very bad play. She didn't much like her own role, either.

"Unfortunately, the police are more interested in your dry-cleaning than your feelings," she said.

"The police are incompetent."

Bailey didn't think Steve Burke was incompetent at all. But she said, "All the more reason for you to be careful."

"I am being careful. I spoke to my lawyer. And I revoked that consent to search."

After she'd told him Steve Burke had confiscated his best black suit to test for blood stains.

"Are you sure that was a good idea?" Bailey asked.

"I'm under no obligation to cooperate with Barney Fife. Besides, as you pointed out, I could hardly host Helen's funeral from my hotel room."

He'd picked a heck of a time to start listening to her. "Yes, but now the police might think you have something to hide."

"I don't care what they think. They can't prove anything, and I don't have to let them in my house."

"Regan's house," Bailey corrected without thinking.

Paul glared.

She flushed.

"It's ridiculous." Lines of temper marred his lean, handsome face. "She'll want me out next."

"I'm sure she'll calm down," Bailey said soothingly. "Once I leave—"

"How am I supposed to get any work done?"

Had he always been this self-absorbed? Or was she simply more aware of it since the move back home? In New York, she had been dazzled by his notice and blinded by her own loneliness. Now, without even her little studio to provide escape, she saw too clearly how dependent she had become—financially, professionally, and emotionally.

The thought made her wince.

Paul depended on her, too, Bailey reminded herself. That's why he was so upset.

"If you need anything, all you have to do is call," she reassured him.

He studied her, his head angled to one side. "I suppose you could take the evidence boxes with you."

Bailey blinked, sure she hadn't heard him correctly. "What?"

"I'll be far too distracted to work. You might as well use your little time away to go through the evidence boxes."

After Billy Ray Dawler's conviction, the evidence from his trial had been packed away into heavy cardboard file boxes. The police didn't want to keep them; the department had a storage shortage. The district attorney's office didn't want to destroy them; the DA worried about the possibility of appeals. So for twenty years, the boxes sat forgotten in the DA's property room. The current DA had been only too happy when celebrated crime writer Paul Ellis expressed an interest in the old case and offered to take them off his hands. But as far as Bailey knew, Paul had never touched them.

"What do you mean, go through them?"

"I want you to inventory the contents."

Okay, that made sense. Paul was already reading the trial transcripts, hundreds and hundreds of pages. He had begun setting up interviews with Billy Ray and his jurors, his high school teachers, and the chief of police. Sooner or later, Paul would want to review the actual physical evidence.

But couldn't he wait to play detective until after the funeral?

"You want me to do that now?" Bailey asked.

Paul looked pained. "I suppose you think *I* should do it."

She felt hot and uncomfortable. Angry, and that made her even more uncomfortable. This was to be her punishment, she thought, for abandoning him. "I don't even know what you're looking for. Everything's disorganized."

"So organize it. That's what you do."

The implication was clear. That's what he paid her for.

Bailey drew another deep breath.

"Right. Can do."

Paul smiled, appeased. "I'll help you take the boxes out to the car." She must have looked surprised, because he added, "They're heavy."

She expected he'd forget his offer by the time she came back downstairs.

But her own packing didn't take that long. Her apartment furniture—the stuff she didn't sell, the rose wing chair with the velvet worn in spots, the 1920s steamer trunk she'd used as a coffee table—was still in storage. She planned to move her clothes in stages. Maybe by the time she emptied her closet, she'd have found a way to tell her mother she was moving home for good.

The thought made her shudder. Or maybe she'd find another place to live. Someplace close. Someplace cheap. In New York, she'd scrounged from paycheck to paycheck, and she hadn't been in Stokesville long enough yet to save the security deposit for an apartment.

Paul carried the final carton to her mother's car and closed the trunk with a final sounding slam. "I'll see you tonight."

She nodded. "Hobart Funeral Home, seven o'clock."

"Come by the house first. I don't want anything to go wrong tomorrow."

She understood his concern. The funeral of Helen Stokes Ellis was sure to be well-attended. Helen might not have been well-liked, but she was One Of Our Own. And every soul at the church would show up at the house afterward, eager to eat and drink and talk in hushed tones about the flowers, the music, and the circumstances surrounding her death. Someone had to be on hand to see the silver was polished, the donated dishes were listed and labeled, and the ice didn't run out. But . . .

"Is Regan going to want me handling the arrangements for her mother's funeral reception?"

"I don't give a damn what Regan wants. I need you, Bailey."

Her objections stuck in her throat. She swallowed, unable to resist his appeal. "I'll be there."

Paul's tired smile crinkled the corners of his eyes. "That's my girl."

Thawing, she returned his smile. But when he reached for her, she stepped back, uncomfortably conscious of the watching windows.

"So, I'll see you at six, then," she said.

Which gave her barely enough time to drop off her suitcase and change into a black skirt. No time for dinner, which was bad. No time for explanations, which was good.

No time to think. Maybe that was best of all.

She let herself in through the back door less than an hour later to find dirty dishes in the sink and a scooped out casserole drying on the counter. Bailey shook her head over the mess. For this she got her BA in creative writing? But she was glad to see Paul and Regan had eaten.

Rolling up the sleeves of her good white blouse, she scraped, wrapped, rinsed plates and wiped counters.

Most girls your age are driving carpool, her mother had said. *Or running errands for their husbands.*

Or doing dishes or putting their kids to bed . . . Was she kidding herself, pretending she was any different?

At least she got paid. Bailey loaded the last glass into the dishwasher. At least she was appreciated.

"What are you doing here?" Regan's hostile voice cut through the rush of running water.

Bailey turned off the tap and held on to her temper. The girl was grieving, she reminded herself. Distraught. "My job."

"Washing dishes?" Regan sauntered forward, her face heartbreakingly young, her chic black shift accented by her mama's pearls and her very own diamond studs. Big ones. Her gaze swept Bailey's plain white blouse and simple black skirt. "Well, at least you're dressed for it. You look like a waiter."

Distraught, my ass. The girl was a bitch.

"Thank you, Miz Scarlett," Bailey muttered.

Regan's eyes narrowed. "What?"

"Was there something you wanted?"

"Yes. Your key." Regan held out her hand. "You don't live here anymore."

The doorbell rang. Both women ignored it.

"But I work here," Bailey said.

The two notes chimed again.

Regan held her gaze and smirked. "Then I guess you can answer the door."

It would have been really satisfying to walk out at that moment. But not particularly adult. Not responsible. Not helpful. The girl had just lost her mother. Bailey couldn't know what that was like. She couldn't offer Regan sympathy, couldn't alleviate her grief or her rage. All she could do at this moment was answer the damn door.

Steeling her spine, she stalked past Regan into the hall and jerked open the door.

"Lieutenant Burke!"

He looked so big in the lengthening shadows of the porch, big and solid and calm and safe, a rock against the storms of emotion that had swept the house all day. For one foolish moment, she was almost glad to see him.

Of course he spoiled it. "Is Ellis home?"

"I . . . He . . ." She glanced past him to the curb, where his truck vied for position with a black-and-white squad car and a dark blue sedan. This was so obviously not a social call. Where was Paul? Why hadn't he answered the door? "He must be upstairs. The viewing is in half an hour."

"Who is it?" Regan asked from behind her.

"Lieutenant Burke, ma'am." His hand slid into his jacket like a man reaching for his gun. "We have a warrant to search these premises."

EIGHT

He should have expected this, Paul told himself as he gazed down at Burke, looming over the two women in the foyer. He did expect it. Clegg, the old hound dog, could be shaken off. But Burke had a bite like a pitbull. He wouldn't let go so easily.

Paul assumed a pained, polite expression and started down the stairs. "What seems to be the problem, Detective?"

He took some small satisfaction in not addressing the man by his rank. But Burke didn't react, didn't correct him, didn't respond at all. How disappointing.

Bailey's face turned up, her eyes dark and distressed. "He has a warrant. A search warrant."

Not an arrest warrant. Paul breathed again. "May I see it?"

"This is my house," Regan said. "I should see it."

Paul turned on her. "My dear girl, you have neither the experience nor the presence of mind to have any idea what you're looking at."

Regan flushed an ugly red.

Paul held out his hand. "The warrant, Detective?"

Burke surrendered it.

Paul scanned the forms quickly. *Personal home computer* . . . His temples pounded. That was bullshit. *Objects consistent with injury on victim's skull* . . . More bullshit.

The police had nothing. And they wouldn't find anything, either.

He handed the warrant back. "This is hardly a convenient time. We're expected at the funeral home in less than half an hour. I could accuse you of harassment."

"Your attorneys will have to advise you on that, sir," Burke said stolidly. "I figured it would be less distressing for the family if you all weren't on the premises while my people do their job."

Stupid, arrogant redneck. It would be an absolute pleasure to watch him waste his time.

"I won't leave while you're in the house," Paul said.

"You're not *staying*," Regan blurted.

Paul allowed a hint of pain to show in his face, a trace of impatience to creep into his voice. "I don't have any choice. Someone has to protect your home. Your inheritance."

"That's a crock of shit," Regan said. So crude, his stepdaughter. So like Helen. "I'm not going to Mom's wake alone."

"Bailey will go with you." He was rather proud of the suggestion, seeming to soothe, calculated to inflame.

Regan's mouth opened to blast him.

But before she could expose herself in front of the police, Bailey intervened. "I'm sure Regan would rather have your support," she said gently. Pointedly. Was she actually attempting to tell him what to do? "And of course all your friends will want to see you to pay their respects. If you want someone here to keep an eye on things, I can stay."

Paul hesitated. She might be right. Not that he cared

about the local yokels, but Helen's friends would certainly expect to see him at her viewing. Speculation about his absence wouldn't add weight to the police case, but perhaps it would be wise to keep public opinion on his side. Better if he appeared as the grieving widower while devoted Bailey kept tabs on the police.

"I don't know . . ." He raised a shaking hand to his face. "I want to do what's right."

"You go," Bailey said. "Let me stay. It's no big loss if I'm not there."

"You got that right," Regan said.

Burke's mouth thinned. *Good.* The man might be utterly lacking in intelligence and imagination, but even he couldn't miss that Regan was a bitch. And that Bailey, dear Bailey, would do absolutely anything for her employer.

Paul lowered his hand, taking care not to smile. *Yes, much better.*

STEVE waited until the door shut behind Ellis and the sulky-mouthed blonde before he switched his gaze to Bailey. She stood controlled and motionless under the chandelier, plain and tidy in stark black and white, her dark hair loose on her shoulders. How the hell did she stand them?

"Are they always like that?" he asked.

Humor flickered in her dark brown eyes, and he felt that stir of instinct again. Not his back-of-the-neck cop instinct, either, but below-the-belt, male-to-female instinct. *Shit.*

And then she primmed up her mouth and said, "You show up at people's homes with a search warrant, you can't expect to see them at their best."

He respected her loyalty, even if he thought it was misplaced. "All part of the job," he said.

"Your job sucks. And so does your timing."

"I'm just trying to make things easier for the family."

"You are not. And you made me miss the viewing."

He shrugged. "Your choice. I thought maybe you wanted out."

She didn't deny it. "I should still be there. In case anything goes wrong."

"Uh huh. You make yourself responsible for everything that goes wrong around here?"

Awareness brought her gaze up to his. "Not everything. Only the things Paul can't be bothered with."

Like bumping off his wife? Steve wondered.

But he didn't believe it. Or maybe he just didn't want to believe it.

"That must keep you busy," he drawled.

Her chin firmed. "All part of the job," she said, mimicking him. "Are you going to call the others in, or did you want a private tour?"

He hid a grin. He liked her attitude. He didn't want her to be guilty. But he wouldn't put up with her getting in his way.

"No tour," he said. "You sit."

"While you cut up the carpets and get fingerprint dust everywhere?" She shook her head. "I don't think so."

He forgot she had some idea how the police worked. It was something he'd never shared with Teresa. Or had to worry about, either.

"It's not an issue," he said shortly.

"Excuse me, but I have over a hundred people stopping by after the funeral tomorrow. So the condition of the house is most definitely an issue."

"It's not an issue," he repeated, "because this is a cursory search. We processed the pool area Monday. Unless we find something unexpected, we're not cutting carpets or throwing dust."

"What exactly are you expecting to find?"

He didn't answer.

She caught his eye and smiled crookedly. "Oh, well. You can't blame a girl for trying."

He didn't blame her. He admired her. But he couldn't let that stop him.

At his continued silence, her expression shuttered again, making him feel guilty. Which was stupid, he was just doing his job, and she was . . . Hell, maybe she wasn't guilty, either, but he couldn't take that chance.

"Where do you want me to wait?" she said.

He'd reviewed the layout of the house before coming over. Unfortunately, the only place he could stash her was the one area he'd already searched.

"Out back," he said.

Her dark eyes widened. "By the pool?"

Steve rubbed the back of his neck. He knew the scene was clean. But it couldn't be pleasant. She probably hadn't been back there since the night she pulled Helen out of the water.

Or pushed her in. He couldn't let himself forget that.

"Is that a problem?"

"No," Bailey said, her tone grim. "Like you said, this was my choice."

"Officer Conner will wait with you," he offered.

"Is she the only female officer in Stokesville?"

The only female officer who would come tonight. He'd asked for a full team, but Walt hadn't been willing to reduce police presence on the street or pay overtime for what he persisted in regarding as an unnecessary investigation.

"You got your warrant," the chief had said. "You'll have to grab whoever's available."

Steve had been relieved when rookie Wayne Lewis stepped up as responding officer, surprised when soft-spoken detective Sergeant Darian Jackson volunteered, and flat out grateful for Officer Margie Conner's offer of help. Maybe the chief's current displeasure had lessened his colleagues' resentment. Or maybe they regarded a little honest-to-God investigative work preferable to staying home with their spouses or pulling traffic duty at the funeral home tonight.

Steve opened the door and signaled them to come in. "Conner volunteered."

Bailey hugged her arms. "Right. I'm sure she's thrilled by the chance to baby-sit me again."

Without meaning to, Steve smiled.

Bailey smiled back. She had a long, wide-lipped mouth, surprising in her thin face. He didn't realize he was staring until her gaze dropped and she blushed. "So . . . before you put me out back, can I get you anything? Coffee?"

Coffee was good. Coffee was safe.

He remembered Bailey on Monday night, face pale, eyes stunned, bustling around the kitchen, pouring coffee into mugs, setting out milk and sugar for Conner, using simple, routine chores to maintain a measure of control, to hold the demons at bay.

Do the job.

Get through the day.

Go through the motions.

He recognized it. Hell, he lived it.

"Coffee would be good," he said. "Thanks."

AFTER two hours, the coffee was cold, and Bailey was sweating, her thighs sticking to her chair.

The ghosts of Monday night haunted the patio. The lounge chairs sprawled at awkward angles, the table pushed out of the way, bore silent witness to the paramedics' frantic activity. The tang of death and all trace of blood had been overlaid or eradicated by the smell of the pool chemicals and the very efficient pool filter. The lights shone, pure and eerie, beneath the sparkling surface. But every time Bailey glanced at the blue water, she expected to see Helen's body floating dark against the glowing depths.

Had Helen cried out? Had she struggled? Or had she slipped mercifully into unconsciousness and death?

Had she slipped at all?

Bailey shuddered and clasped her arms. "It's taking him long enough."

Him. Steve Burke. When did he become so significant he could be identified simply by a pronoun?

Officer Conner shrugged. "It's a big house."

"He said the search was cursory."

"But thorough. Lieutenant's a careful man."

"I hope so," Bailey muttered.

Despite Steve's assurances, she was concerned about the condition of the house. Even if his team took care, they were not responsible for restoring the premises to their pre-search condition, and it would be impossible to get the house cleaned before the funeral service tomorrow.

Worrying about disarranged drawers and furniture was bad, Bailey knew. But as a distraction, it beat worrying about what the police were looking for.

Or what they might find.

She slapped at a mosquito on her bare leg.

"When will the Ellises be back?" Conner asked.

Gratefully, Bailey focused on the little things she could control instead of the looming disaster she couldn't. "Paul and Regan? Viewing hours are over at nine-thirty."

Which didn't mean they would be home right away. Paul never left any gathering where he was the center of attention. And he would definitely attract attention tonight. Some of the mourners would be there to honor Helen's family, to respect her memory and offer their sympathies. The rest would come to satisfy their curiosity. There was no getting around the fact that after the corpse, Paul was the night's big draw.

Bailey scratched the bug bite blooming on her leg, drawing blood. "Will Burke be done by then?"

"Could be," Conner said. Maybe she was itchy, too, because she offered, "Having only three officers to search slows things down."

"That's not enough?"

"Lieutenant told us he wants the location of every piece of evidence verified by two officers. He's not taking chances the defense will throw anything out in court."

That was good. Wasn't it? Bailey's thoughts whined, as persistent and annoying as mosquitoes. Steve's precautions meant he wasn't planting evidence that would incriminate Paul.

But what did he expect to find? And what consequences could it have for Paul? For her?

A tall, dark shadow loomed beyond the French doors. Her pulse kicked up, her body recognizing Steve's presence before her mind had quite identified him.

The glass door opened, and he stepped out, soles silent on the patio tile. She thought again how quietly he moved for such a big man. The temperature on the patio crept up several degrees. Like, ten. The man practically exuded testosterone, his broad body in its rumpled suit seeming to absorb all oxygen, the indifferent light emphasizing the harsh planes and angles of his face.

He nodded to the two women. "Nice night," he drawled.

Bailey folded her arms. "If you like bugs."

The corners of his mouth deepened in a near-smile. "You can come inside now. We're done."

Bailey stood. "What did you find?"

In answer, he handed her two thin, pink sheets.

He'd given her a copy of the search warrant.

Her heart pounded. "For me?"

"I have to leave a copy with the home owner."

Bailey flushed. She knew that. Being so close to him was making her stupid. The man had the gravitational pull of a very large planet, Jupiter or something. And since he showed no signs of moving away, she stepped back, angling the paper to catch the light so her retreat didn't look like a rout.

He had written a list. A numbered list of maybe a dozen items, each with a description of where it was found and the names of the officers who found it. Heavy, flat items with straight, square edges. She flipped back to the first page. *Objects consistent with injury on victim's skull.*

Oh, God. Bile rose in her throat.

Swallowing, she read through the list carefully, the neat print swimming in her vision. Tool box. Bookends. Trivet. Metal tray. Cutting board . . . She stopped and went back.

"This is wrong," she said. "You can't take this."

He crowded her. "Take what?"

She pointed. "This tray. It's not ours—the Ellises, I mean. It wasn't even in the house Monday night. Mildred Wheeler brought it over yesterday, a nice ham-and-cheese plate."

"We didn't find any ham," Steve said. "Or cheese."

Bailey searched for a likely explanation. "I guess Paul must have eaten it for lunch." She frowned doubtfully. "Maybe while I was picking up Regan at the airport?"

Steve raised his eyebrows. "And then washed the tray and put it away in the cupboard under the microwave?"

Okay, not so likely.

"But I can prove it's Mildred's tray," she said.

"How?"

Bailey felt an uncharacteristic wave of gratitude for her mama. Whatever Dorothy's faults, no one could say she hadn't raised her daughters To Do the Right Thing. "When anybody drops off food, I write their name on the list for thank-you notes. And then I put a little piece of masking tape on the bottom of the dish so I can return it to the right person."

Steve's eyes narrowed. "Show me."

She led the way into the house. Wayne Lewis and a tall, black officer were talking in the kitchen, their heads together over a large cardboard box. At Bailey's entrance, they fell abruptly silent. Her gut clenched. Did they always react that way to Steve's presence? Or were they silent because of her? Were they talking about her?

"The list," Steve prompted behind her.

Bailey pulled herself together. "On the refrigerator." She pulled down the list of funeral foods taped to the fridge. "Your mother brought a lemon cake."

His eyebrows rose. "You met my mother?"

"I answered the door," Bailey said, doing her best not to sound defensive. "She seemed very . . ."

"Nosy?"

Bailey flushed, remembering Eugenia Burke's bright eyes and warm smile. "Nice," she said firmly. She tapped her finger on the list. "See? There's her name."

Steve studied the list over her shoulder. Crossing to the table, he removed the pewter tray from the carton and flipped it over.

"Well?" Bailey demanded, her heart thumping.

He turned the tray so they all could see the piece of blue masking tape stuck on the bottom.

And then he put it back in the box.

"Hey," she protested. "What are you doing? That's Mildred's."

"The sticker is in your handwriting."

"Of course it is. I wrote it."

"So how do I know you didn't slap a piece of tape on this tray just to get it out of the house?"

"That's incredibly devious."

Steve shrugged. "You have to learn to think like a criminal."

"But I'm not a criminal," she said. Too loudly. She caught the two male officers exchanging glances and made an effort to lower her voice. "I don't know whether to be flattered you think I'm that resourceful or terrified you believe I'd actually do something that bent."

He looked amused. "If you're innocent, you don't have anything to worry about."

If you're innocent. If.

Condescending son of a bitch.

"What about Mildred's tray?" Bailey asked.

"What about it?"

"I need to return it to her."

Steve rubbed the back of his neck. "I'll take the tray to Miz . . . Wheeler, is it? If she identifies it as hers, I'll return it for you."

He'd made a concession of sorts. She should let it go. She had nothing to gain by antagonizing him and maybe everything to lose. *If you're innocent . . .*

Her teeth snapped together. "What else are you taking?"

He nodded at the form in her hand. "It's all listed there. You're pretty much looking at it. One box and the computers."

"Both computers?"

He watched her closely. "Is that a problem?"

Normally, it would have been a disaster. Paul took his laptop everywhere. But hardware could be replaced. And she'd just backed up his files, all his files, on her flash drive so she could work from home. Thank God.

"We'll cope," she said.

Paul would complain, of course, about the inconvenience. But it would be several days, surely, before he got back to work? He didn't interview Billy Ray again until next week. Plenty of time for her to shop for a new computer and reinstall his files. But . . . A doubt bumbled at the back of her mind like a moth against the patio lights.

"Was there something else?" Steve asked.

She blinked. *Was there? Something?* But it eluded her, blundering into the shadows. Should she tell him about the flash drive? "I don't think so."

"Sure?"

She was pretty sure his search warrant didn't include the contents of her purse. And she wasn't about to offer it up and risk losing all Paul's work. Not to mention her job.

She stuck out her chin. "Yes."

Steve scowled as if he didn't believe her. Reaching into his pocket, he took out a business card and scribbled on it. "Here's my cell number. You think of something, you can call me anytime."

The sharp white edges dug into her palm. Accepting his card felt vaguely disloyal, a connection she had not sought and did not want.

Of course she wouldn't call.

But she tucked the card away carefully in her purse, along with her tissues and Tic Tacs, mace, condoms, and a tampon, small precautions against the unforeseen.

She was as bad as her mother, Bailey thought as she drove home. Dorothy Wells had QVC on speed dial. As if Dale Earnhardt commemorative plates and coin sets from the Franklin Mint could protect her from death and the collapse of the global economy.

But fifteen minutes later when Bailey let herself in the front door, she found her mother surrounded by a wave of tissue paper and the contents of the hall curio cabinet.

"There you are!" Dorothy tucked a swaddled shape into a cardboard carton. "You're late."

"Not really." Bailey eased through the door to avoid colliding with a black plastic garbage bag. Outside, their neighbor's dog announced to all the world that she was home. "It's not even midnight."

Her old curfew. Twelve o'clock. The magic hour when, according to her mother, carriages turned into pumpkins, parties became unsanctioned occasions of sin, boys transformed to sex-crazed fiends, and good girls lost their clothes and their morals.

If you're innocent, you don't have anything to worry about.

Still fully dressed, Bailey slunk toward the steps.

"How was the viewing?" Dorothy asked in a distracted tone.

"Oh." Bailey pushed her hair behind her ears. She didn't really want to explain to her mother she'd missed visiting hours at the funeral home because Steve Call-Me-Anytime Burke was searching her employer's home for a murder weapon. "It went all right, I guess. What are you still doing up?"

"My *chi* is blocked," her mother said. "I'm making room for new opportunities to come into my life."

"Your *chi*," Bailey repeated. The last project she had edited before she quit her job had been a feng shui guide for Paragon. Was her mother attempting self-help through better *bagua?*

Dorothy waved at the half-emptied shelves. "There's too much clutter in this house. I need to free the flow of positive energy."

Bailey blinked. Her mother thrived on clutter. Doll collections and tea sets, candles and candy dishes, the relics of clearance shelves and QVC . . . Why change? Why now?

Why not?

"Positive energy is good." Bailey edged towards the stairs. It was late. She had work to do. Just because her mother had decided to turn over a new leaf didn't mean she had to give up her sleep or disrupt her own life.

Dorothy grabbed a vase and rolled it vigorously in tissue paper.

Bailey paused with one foot on the steps. "Aren't you coming to bed?"

The paper crackled. "In a while."

"Is Dad, um . . ."

Dorothy nodded toward the living room. "He's up."

There, but not there. Only the red glow of his cigarette and the muted sound of ESPN in the darkness beyond the hall indicated his presence in their house. In their lives.

Bailey sighed. "Do you need any help?"

Dorothy's distraction dissolved in smiles. "That would be wonderful. If you could just hand me that bowl. . . . Oh, and can you put that box over there?"

"Sure."

And forty minutes later, as Bailey taped the last carton to go into the attic, she had to admit the entry appeared lighter, cleaner, and more elegant.

"Looking good, Mom."

"That wall opposite the door was blocking my ability to move forward in my life," her mother asserted.

"Yeah, I know how that goes."

Dorothy surveyed the space, her head to one side. "I was thinking a mirror would help."

Bailey's satisfaction suffered a jolt. "What?"

"A new mirror. To redirect my energy. And a fountain to activate my *chi*. I saw some really darling ones at Marshall's today that would be perfect."

"A fountain," Bailey repeated. Her mother hadn't really changed. She'd just . . . redirected her energy.

"You could go with me tomorrow," Dorothy suggested. "To pick one out."

Right. Or she could take a sharp stick and jab herself in the eye. She hadn't gone shopping with her mother since she'd rebelled against matching outfits at the age of ten.

But Dorothy looked so happy. So hopeful.

Bailey swallowed. "That would be great. But I, um . . . the funeral's tomorrow, Mom."

"Oh, that reminds me." Dorothy scrambled past the pile of cartons to the closet. "I bought you a purse."

Maybe lack of sleep was making her stupid. "A what? Why?"

"A new purse," Dorothy said, rummaging in a shopping bag. "Your old one looks so worn. You want to look nice tomorrow."

"Thanks, Mom. That's—"

Hideous, Bailey thought, staring at her mother's latest bargain, a huge shapeless bag with an adjustable strap, gleaming with gold hardware and bristling with zippers.

"—great," she finished weakly.

"And it's black," Dorothy declared. "I know you like everything to be black."

It was certainly black. Bailey slung the purse over her shoulder.

Dorothy smiled.

Obeying impulse, Bailey put her arms around her mother, feeling the purse slide and bump between them, feeling Dorothy's start of surprise.

Her mother's shoulders were thin and bony, the skin of her upper arms soft and loose. But she smelled the way she always had, like Dove soap and White Shoulders perfume.

Bailey breathed in and held on, fighting unexpected, inexplicable tears.

"It's really great," she repeated. "Thanks."

She trudged up the stairs to her blue-flowered bedroom, the dusty yearbooks lining one shelf and the faded posters of Melissa Etheridge and Lisa Loeb decorating the walls. Paul's evidence cartons were stacked beside the white painted desk where Bailey used to do her homework.

She refused even to look at the three-ring notebook on top, the manuscript Paul said wasn't ready to show anyone else. That she hadn't touched in almost four months.

Too much clutter, she thought, blocking my *chi*.

Or maybe it was the ghosts of the departed Dawlers— Shirley, Tammy, and Tanya—held to this place by this forlorn collection of their possessions, the grisly mementos of murder.

Was the murder weapon in there?

She hadn't checked.

She didn't want to know.

But she was powerfully tempted to look, like a rubbernecker slowing to stare at an accident on the highway. She eased the lid off the top box to find . . . paper, a long row of manila folders and photocopied pages grouped by grubby rubber bands. She exhaled in relief and disappointment.

One item stuck out. Literally. A spiral-bound notebook was crammed along the box's side, its silver coils rising above the sea of paper like some exotic ocean creature.

Bailey tugged it free and turned it to the light. Bold black letters marched across the purple cover: TANYA DAWLER. MY DIARY. KEEP OUT.

Bailey felt a tickle at the back of her neck, a prickle in her fingers. Billy Ray's fifteen-year-old sister. *His victim*.

Curious, she carried the book to the bed with her. Propping her pillows against the headboard, she curled her legs under her and began to read the childish, rounded handwriting.

Detention again. I'm always in trouble even when I haven't done anything. Which I didn't. This time, anyway!

Bailey smiled.

But it's like the teachers expect it. Dawler trash.

The words were underlined. *Dawler trash.* Even after twenty years, she could see the mark where the pen dug into the paper.

You can see them thinking it. Like they know my brother and they know my mom so they think they know me. The male teachers mostly stare at my tits.

Bailey's smile faded. She didn't believe Steve's charge that Paul exploited his subjects. But until now, Tanya Dawler hadn't been quite real to her—a research subject, a sad chapter of the Billy Ray story. With every word and exclamation point, Tanya took on depth. Substance. Personality.

Did Bailey really want to start identifying with a teenage murder victim?

But the loopy purple handwriting drew her on and drew her in.

So, anyway, in detention you have to do homework, even if you don't have any, which is totally unfair!!! Mr. D. keeps coming by my desk to say, "What are you doing, young lady?" and squeezing my shoulder in that fakey fake way. What a perv.

So I'm writing in this notebook, Tanya continued in her defiant scrawl. *That'll show him.*

Bailey turned the page.

NINE

THE Stokesville Police Department wasn't *CSI: New York* or *Miami* or anywhere else glamorous with television cameras and inventive scriptwriters and swarms of evidence technicians. Hell, it wasn't even the Metropolitan Police Department, which at least had its own crime lab.

Steve hefted the carton containing his selection of potential murder weapons into the trunk of Wayne Lewis's Crown Victoria, dropped and locked the lid, and initialed the shipping manifest.

"Is that everything?" Wayne asked.

"Not quite."

"I didn't see the tray. In the box, I mean."

"That's because I returned it to its owner."

"Ellis?"

"Nope." Steve folded the manifest and put it in his pocket. "Mildred Wheeler."

Wayne digested this as they retraced their steps. "So the girl's story checks out."

Steve opened the back door of the station house. "So far."

"Did you, like, dust it for fingerprints anyway?"

"I dusted."

"And?" Lewis asked eagerly.

Steve rubbed the back of his neck. He appreciated the rookie's enthusiasm. He appreciated him volunteering to make the drive to the state crime lab in Raleigh even more, especially since the chief resented the time his officers were putting in on this case. But . . .

"Turned up prints on damn near everything from damn near everybody, including the cleaning lady and the deceased."

Wayne frowned. "What about blood?"

"Nothing visible."

"You spray with Luminol?"

Steve shook his head. "I'm not going to jeopardize the evidentiary value by doing my own testing."

"So you think there's something there."

"Not really." Steve nodded a greeting to Sergeant Darian Jackson, writing reports at his desk.

"Why not?"

"There are multiple prints on everything," Steve explained patiently. "If Helen Ellis's attacker wiped her blood from the object he struck her with, he would have wiped away the prints, too."

"But the lab might still find something," Wayne insisted.

"Maybe."

Maybe not. He'd had one chance, one shot, to find the murder weapon, and he'd blown it. If he didn't come up with something soon, Walt would have his ass and his job. Unless the chief was so relieved at being able to drop this case he only demoted Steve to crossing guard.

Steve forced a smile. "We'd need SBI to do the DNA testing anyway."

Which the State Bureau of Investigation would get to in their own sweet time. DNA results took weeks or months, not hours. But juries were more and more reluctant to convict without high-tech forensic evidence. Steve blamed it on television.

Wayne nudged a box with his foot. "What about the computer?"

Steve managed to back up his own files. He even paid his bills on-line. That didn't qualify him for the Geek Squad. "I don't have the expertise to conduct a search of electronic data. It's too easy to destroy or tamper with the evidence. The computer should go to an evidence preservation lab."

Darian spoke up from his cluttered desk. "You really think it'll help your case to find out Paul Ellis bookmarked a bunch of porn sites?"

"Porn sites, no. Unless he's making assignations in private chat rooms. If he's having an affair—"

"He doesn't need to go on-line to have an affair. Not with that little Wells girl living right upstairs."

Tension gripped the back of Steve's neck.

Wayne's ears turned red.

In his gut, Steve didn't believe Bailey was guilty. Of an affair or anything else.

But his gut wanted to have sex with her. He couldn't trust his gut any more than he could trust her.

"I'm looking into it," he said. "You find anyone yet who saw her on her walk?"

"Martha Grimes was out watering her roses that night," Wayne volunteered. "She saw Bailey cross the street."

Steve had been gone too long to know Martha Grimes. "Which street? What time?"

Wayne fumbled for his notebook, flipping through the pages. "Church Street. Right around the corner from the Ellis place. About nine o'clock."

"Kind of late to be watering flowers," Steve observed.

"Less evaporation. Saves water," Wayne said.

"Plus, Martha was probably out sneaking a cigarette," Darian said. "Her husband's been after her to quit."

Steve nodded. "So, Bailey would have gotten back . . ."

"A little after nine."

That matched her story. Plenty of time for her to return to her room and do some reading before she came downstairs to fix herself some ice cream and discover Helen's body.

Or to hit her employer's wife over the head, dump her body into the pool and sneak upstairs.

He looked at Darian, who had volunteered to do followups with the neighbors. "Anybody remember seeing anything after that?"

"You mean, like a murder?" Darian shook his head. "Nope. Fellow across the street let his dog out about eleven. Thinks he saw lights on in the front bedroom window and in the study. That's about it. You get anything else from that lawyer?"

Two days ago, Steve had gone to Helen's executor to question him about the Ellises' financial affairs. The lawyer, Macon Reynolds, informed him Helen Stokes Ellis had taken out a four-million-dollar life insurance policy as part of her prenup—enough to convince Steve her husband had a motive for murder, more than enough to convince the judge Steve had probable cause for a warrant.

"Just that the insurance company won't pay out as long as the manner of death is 'pending.'"

"He told you that?" Wayne asked. "Isn't that, like, breach of confidentiality or something?"

"Not if he doesn't represent Paul Ellis. Helen was his client."

"But she's dead."

"He still has to act in her best interest." Steve smiled

thinly. "I just convinced him her interest was best served by cooperating with the police."

Which hadn't been hard. Reynolds claimed to remember Steve from high school, so Steve had played the hometown connection. Despite her years away, Helen had been One Of Our Own. Ellis was a Yankee interloper who didn't deserve his dead wife's fortune.

Steve picked up the carton that housed the flat-screen monitor and cables, all tagged and labeled, hoping Wayne would take the hint and grab the computer box.

"So we dump all this with the state crime lab and wait for them to tell us why Ellis suddenly needed money?" Wayne asked.

"We don't have to wait. Most criminal investigation isn't rocket science. We have bank statements. Bills. Correspondence. Let's start there."

Wayne's eyes lit as he saw his opportunity to be involved in something more exciting than lost dogs and public disturbances. "I can help. When I get back."

"Aren't you forgetting something?" Steve asked.

The younger man's face fell as he remembered. "Funeral at eleven."

Darian looked at Steve. "You got traffic duty, too?"

Steve bared his teeth in a smile. "Not yet."

REGAN heaved behind a headstone. Another stream of coffee and bile arced to the grass, spattering her black $275 Kate Spade pumps.

Fuck, fuck, fuck.

Tears leaked from her eyes. She sagged against the back of the marble headstone where she had taken refuge, fighting the buzz in her head. The hum of mourners leaving her mother's grave site blended with the whisper of leaves and the rising whine of the cicadas. Despite the sun beating down on her unprotected head, she felt flushed and cold. She should be out there now, a brave little smile on her face, accepting the condolences of people she barely knew and couldn't care less about, inviting them back to the house. Her house.

She doubled over, her stomach rebelling in fury against an overload of uncertainty and grief, of tranquilizers and caffeine. *Fuck them all.*

Something white fluttered at the corner of her vision like a ghost. Regan's heart crowded her throat along with what was left of her stomach contents. But it was only Bailey coming to check up on her.

"Tissue?"

Regan snatched it, pressing it to her mouth. "Go away," she ordered.

But maybe dweeb girl had some spine, after all, because she didn't leave. Not right away. She rummaged in her monster purse—like Mary Poppins's, only uglier, big and black with gold zipper teeth—and came up with a mini-bottle of water and a packet of Tic Tacs.

"Here." She unscrewed the bottle of water. "Rinse, don't swallow."

Leaning weakly against the tombstone, Regan reached for the water. She rinsed and spat on the thick green grass. Rinsed and—ignoring Bailey's instructions—swallowed. Her stomach lurched, but the water felt so good against the parched tissues of her mouth, against her hot, tight throat.

"Are you all right?" her stepfather's assistant asked gravely.

"What do you care?"

Bailey shrugged. "I just . . . Your mother . . ."

"I'm fine." Regan closed her eyes. "You've done your little ministering angel bit. Now get the fuck away from me."

When she opened her eyes, Bailey was gone. Regan's chest squeezed. *Good.* She knew that caring act was a bunch of crap. She took another swig of water.

"Regan, honey, how you holding up?" That smooth baritone flowed like molasses, rich and slow.

She lowered the bottle. A guy stood on the other side of the grave. Blond hair, pocket square, expensive suit, polished shoes. She recognized him. Reynolds something. Her mother's lawyer.

"How do you think?"

He smiled. "I think you look like a lady who could use a drink. And I don't mean water."

Regan considered. For an oldie, he was kind of a hottie. And he was on her side. He was the one who told that greedy bastard Paul he wouldn't get a penny of her father's money.

"What did you have in mind?" she asked.

He looked her up and down, and the cold inside her ebbed. "Well, now, that's up to you. I imagine there's sherry back at the house."

She pulled a face. Sherry and a bunch of chattering old farts who would expect her to listen to their stories about her parents.

"Or we could go someplace quiet for a vodka and tonic," he continued smoothly.

"Make mine an appletini," she said. "And you've got yourself a deal."

"How about a date?" he said, still smiling.

He wore a ring. Asshole. Married asshole. Unlike dweeb girl, Regan didn't waste her time on married men.

But she deserved a little comfort, didn't she? Or at least a drink. Her mother was dead. Her brother wasn't here. And the hot male appreciation in the older man's eyes warmed the edges of the cold void inside her.

Don't do it, her instincts whispered, but that little warning voice sounded annoyingly like Bailey.

Regan pushed away from the headstone. "Sure, why not?" she said.

SOUTHERNERS appreciated a good funeral.

His wife's death thirty-one months ago had blunted Steve's enjoyment of such events, but the folks around him, drifting away from the grave and toward their cars and the buffet line, seemed to be having a good old time. Maybe it was the weather, incongruously bright, decorously hot, cooperatively dry.

Teresa had died two days after Christmas, her spirit fading with the waning year. She was buried in Saint John's churchyard in the short, bleak interval before New Year's. Her parents flew up from Brazil for the funeral. Steve remembered holding Gabrielle's small, damp hand, listening to Rosa's soft sobs as the organist played "Ave Maria" to a nearly empty church.

People had packed the sunlit pews this morning at Helen Ellis's funeral. The older ladies of the congregation counted the turnout, their lips moving silently. The service was beautiful and decorous: the flowers, the candles, the sedate, brief hymns, the even more sedate and briefer sermon. But Steve felt like he was watching a play. The tasteful, traditional ceremony in the packed church seemed more empty of real feeling than Teresa's quiet, sparsely attended mass.

Who had loved Helen Ellis? Who mourned her?

Jamming his hands in his pockets, he strode towards his truck.

"Lieutenant Burke?" Bailey's voice was slightly breathless, as if she'd hurried to catch him.

Steve felt the blip of sexual attraction, like the warning whoop from a squad car. Something about being pursued by an attractive woman, even if she was a person of interest in an ongoing investigation. . . . He turned.

She smiled apologetically, pushing her dark hair back from her face. "Sorry to bother you. But have you seen Regan? Regan Poole?"

"Why?"

She blushed, or maybe that was the sun on her face. "I thought . . . I saw you watching everyone, and I hoped you might have noticed where she'd gone."

Steve shook his head. "Not why did you ask me. Why are you looking for her?"

"Oh." This time she definitely blushed. "She's supposed to ride back to the house with Paul. The limo's waiting."

Steve took his hands from his pockets. "She already left with the lawyer."

Her brows drew together. "Macon Reynolds?"

"Yep."

"You know him?"

She'd given him the name of Helen's lawyer. Did she remember? "We've met," he said. "Turns out he was a year behind me in school."

"Right. This is Stokesville. Everybody knows everybody. So did you two have a little reunion party?"

"Not really. We didn't exactly run with the same crowd in high school."

"Which crowd was that?"

"Macon Reynolds," he said carefully, "was one of those kids who drove their own cars and raided their parents' liquor cabinets after school."

A smile touched her lips. "And you didn't drink and drive."

Steve shrugged. "Not during football season. And the

rest of the time . . ." He stopped. He wasn't here to tell her the story of his childhood.

"The rest of the time," she prompted.

This was Stokesville, he reasoned. Everybody knew everybody. What he didn't tell her, she could learn from somebody else.

"I worked for my dad in the lumber yard."

"Is he here?"

Steve looked out over the sunlit hill, his hands in his pockets. "He's dead."

"I know. Mama told me," she added. "I meant, is he buried here?"

Memories of his father's funeral crowded him like ghosts: his daughter's warm weight, his mother's drawn face, Teresa, slim and elegant in her good black coat . . .

"On the other side. In the low-rent district."

"I'm sorry," Bailey said. "It must be hard."

"It was five years ago," he said flatly.

"I don't imagine you ever get over the loss of a parent." *Grandma says I really need a mother. Maybe you could get married again.*

"We manage," he said.

Bailey bit her lip. "I wish Regan hadn't gone with Mr. Reynolds."

Steve pulled himself together. "You don't like him?"

"I hardly know him. But Regan was supposed to ride with Paul. He's waiting for her."

Steve didn't see what the big deal was. Unless Bailey couldn't bear to disappoint her boss.

"So you go," he suggested roughly.

"I'd rather not."

"Why not?"

"I'm not family. It wouldn't look right."

True enough. According to Eugenia, folks in town were

already speculating about Bailey's role in the Ellis household, their talk fueled by Regan's obvious hostility.

But he said, "You worry too much what people think."

"That's not true. I gave up caring what other people think in high school."

He recalled the photo on her mother's fridge, the skinny girl squinting at the camera with hope and defiance. She'd had enough confidence then to dream her own dreams. Enough courage to tackle New York. "So what happened?"

"Nothing happened. I have certain responsibilities now."

He met her gaze. "To Ellis."

"Well . . . yes."

Disappointment pinched him. What the hell had he expected? *Nothing.* He knew where her loyalties and priorities lay.

And his.

"Better run along, then," he said. "Tell him his stepdaughter took off with the lawyer."

"I will."

But she stayed rooted on the sunlit slope, pink-cheeked and warm and alive, while the dead stretched around them in all directions. A breeze teased a strand of hair across her face.

Steve fisted his hands in his pockets. "What are you waiting for?"

At his impatient tone, her chin came up. "How about a ride?"

"A ride," he repeated without expression.

"I told you. I don't want to take the limo with Paul."

"How did you get here?"

Her gaze dropped. "In the limo with Paul. But Regan was with us." She looked up at him through her lashes, and something stirred in his belly. "You could offer me a lift."

He wasn't here to flirt with her. "Knock it off. You're not the type."

"Excuse me?"

"The 'I have always depended on the kindness of strangers' act," he said. "It's not you."

"Well, I wouldn't have said you were the type to quote Tennessee Williams, either, so we're even."

She waited, as if she expected a response. But he didn't have one to give her. Didn't have anything to offer any woman.

Her smile faded. "Right. Never mind."

She turned away.

Good, he thought. *Let her go.* He didn't mix his personal and professional lives. He didn't need her blundering in where she didn't belong, blurring his careful boundaries.

On the other hand, she was a piece of the puzzle, part of the picture he was assembling of Helen Ellis's life and death. And she'd been holding out on him last night. He was sure of it.

He watched her wobble down the hill, head high, heels sinking in the soft, bright grass, and felt as if the sun had ducked behind a cloud, leaving everything dim and cold.

"I'll pick you up at the front gate," he called after her.

She didn't stop her march down the green slope. "Forget it. I don't accept rides from strangers anyway."

"So get to know me," he replied.

She turned then, folding her arms to glare up at him. "What good will that do?"

No good at all.

Reason whispered he didn't have to give her a lift to talk to her. He knew where she lived. He could set her down for a come-to-Jesus meeting at her mother's kitchen table. Hell, he could drag her attractive ass down to the station and interview her in the presence of Margie Conner.

"It's just a ride," he said. Who was he trying to convince? Her? Or himself?

Bailey hesitated. "I'll have to tell Paul."

Right. Couldn't forget old Paul.

"You do that," he said, and stalked off to get his truck before either of them could change their minds.

IT was just a ride, Bailey reminded herself as she hurried toward the cemetery entrance. Headstones glittered in the sun. Tall groupings of cypress cast short, sharp shadows against the grass. Bailey's face flushed. She was sweating. Glowing, her mother would have said, but Bailey had no illusions.

Beyond the heavy iron gate, Steve's truck stuck out from the line of parked vehicles, as oversized and aggressively masculine as its owner.

Her steps slowed. Her heart beat faster.

He swung from the cab, big and dark in his loose-fitting suit, and opened her door.

"I can do that," she protested automatically.

He slanted a look down at her. "Yeah, but why should you?"

She sidled past him. His white dress shirt practically steamed with heat. Her nipples, clearly unconnected to her brain and receiving signals from somewhere else, stood at attention. "Why should you?"

"Because it's polite?" he suggested.

She climbed into the passenger seat, tugging on her skirt. She should have worn pantyhose. "Men use gestures of courtesy to establish status. If you open my door, I'm proceeding at your discretion. It sets you in a superior position to me."

"Try telling that to my mother."

"Excuse me?"

He looked up from her bare legs, a gleam in his eyes. "When I was a kid, my mother tanned my hide if I didn't hold the door for her. If you want to call over her knee a superior position . . ."

Bailey relaxed enough to smile. After the heat outside, the air-conditioned cab felt like heaven. Sinking into the deep leather seat, she gave herself up to the luxury of being driven.

Steve slid into the seat beside her, his shoulders filling the cabin, his right knee jutting into space. Her space. She pressed her thighs together and shifted them toward the door. They drove a while in silence—not uncomfortable, but with a crackle to it like the static from the police radio in the dash. His square, strong hands rested easily on the wheel.

She cleared her throat. "Nice truck."

He shot her a look. "I didn't take you for a pickup girl."

"A double entendre. Should I be impressed?"

His mouth quirked. "Just making an observation."

"Contrary to what you may have heard in truck commercials and country songs, not all women go for men who drive trucks."

"You never dated a guy because of his ride?"

She shook her head. "You have me mixed up with my sister."

"I never dated your sister."

He was probably the only football player at Jefferson High who hadn't. So what?

"Why not?" she asked.

His grin spread. "Not interested."

"Everybody was interested in Leann," Bailey said with equal parts pride and resentment. *Oh, you're* sisters, the teacher would say on the first day, looking up from her gradebook, obviously struggling to connect the beautiful fairy child from years ago with the squat brown dwarf before her. *I hope you'll do as well in school as Leann.*

And she had. Academically, at least, Bailey had always done better than her sister. Better than poor Tanya Dawler, whose journal, continued in fits and starts over weeks of detention, was full of misspellings and complaints.

Bailey was a spelling whiz. But she skipped ahead in her reading, she argued with her teachers, she scribbled stories in class. She never made it look easy, the way Leann had. She never made people like her.

"Leann was the most popular girl in school."

Steve frowned. "Blond, right? Cheerleading squad?"

"And homecoming court," Bailey said, making an effort to be generous.

"She was a freshman."

"Only for one year."

"My senior year. She was too young."

Leann was almost nine years older than Bailey.

"Or you were too old," Bailey said tartly.

Steve grunted. "You would know. Your boss is what, fifty-two?"

"Forty-seven. And what does that have to do with anything?"

"I'm just saying. He's too old for you."

She clutched her fat, zippered purse in her lap. "I didn't know there was an age limit for employers."

"Is that all he is?"

She glared. "Is that a personal question, or should I call a lawyer?"

"You could just answer," he suggested mildly.

"I thought we'd been over this."

"You told me you worked for him. Your mother told me you weren't romantically involved. Which is what you would have told her whether you were or not."

Bailey felt a hot pricking in her chest like a smattering of cinders.

She'd known she was a suspect. She'd accepted that he had a responsibility to investigate her.

But he had no right to lay her open for his judgment, to dissect her feelings, feelings she had never once, in two years, acted upon.

"Not," she said.

"You can tell me if you were." His voice was deep. Confiding. "No shame in not coming right out with it."

She recognized the burning in her chest as anger. She took a breath, to steady herself and her voice.

"No shame," she repeated.

"Nope."

"In lying."

He shrugged. "A lot of people are reluctant to talk to the police."

The anger flared, brief and bright. She damped it. "What about adultery? Any shame in that?"

He hesitated. She had the impression he was choosing his words carefully. "You're not married. You've been all alone in the big city for a couple of years. Must have been pretty overwhelming at times. It's not hard to see how you might imagine yourself attracted to an older man."

The anger collapsed and fed on itself like a building in flames. She could hardly breathe. This was horrible. Horrible, because it was true. Or close enough, anyway.

"You have no idea what it was like," she said, her chest burning, her throat tight.

"Why don't you tell me?"

No way.

She stared through the windshield without seeing anything. She'd never told anyone how she felt—how pressured, how discouraged—as her work piled up and her social life dwindled. Months and opportunities slipped away while she divided her evenings between the uncorrected manuscripts she carted home on the subway and the unsuitable men she tried to avoid bringing home at all. Men who seemed cute enough or nice enough or intelligent enough until—surprise!—they revealed a penchant for cocaine or spanking or women's underwear.

She had thought working for Paul would be better. She had hoped her schedule as his assistant wouldn't drain her time and creative energy the way the stacks of unread, unproofed manuscripts had done. She had imagined indulging a crush on her married boss was less damaging than endless, joyless dates with hopeless men.

Wrong, wrong, wrong.

Three strikes, and you're out.

She took a deep breath. "Okay, maybe I was attracted, a little. But I never did anything about it."

Even in her own ears, that sounded lame.

"Why not?"

Because she had morals. Standards. Didn't she? But with all her self-deceptions and self-justifications scraped bare, she wasn't prepared to argue the point.

"He's married. Was married," she corrected. "And he's my boss."

"So? It wouldn't be the first time an employer took advantage of an employee."

"Paul wouldn't do that."

Steve raised his eyebrows without looking away from the road. "Seems to me he does it all the time."

Bailey winced. She wanted to protest she didn't know what he was talking about. But she did. Steve already thought she was a doormat and a slut. No point in convincing him she was an idiot and a liar, too.

"That's different," she mumbled. "Anyway, Paul was devoted to Helen."

"Helen's dead."

She hugged her arms. "I didn't kill her."

"I'm not saying you did."

"But you're thinking it."

The truck turned a corner. Almost there. Her hands tightened on her purse. The buckle dug into her palm.

"I'm keeping an open mind," he said.

She stuck out her chin so it wouldn't tremble. "Yeah? Is that why you're questioning me about my relationship with Paul?"

"Maybe I'm trying to warn you."

Her heart thumped. "Warn me about what?"

"Keeping bad company."

"That sounds like something my mother would say," she said, forcing herself to speak lightly.

He shrugged. "I thought it sounded better."

"Better than what?"

He looked at her with flat, dark eyes. Cop's eyes. Her breath clogged in her throat. "Accessory after the fact."

TEN

"WHO invited Officer Grumpy?"

Regan's loud voice attracted glances, scandalized and indulgent, from the funeral crowd surrounding the buffet table. Paul wondered how many of Stokesville's senior citizens were there for the free food and how many had come for the gossip.

Bailey stood beside him, tray in hand, doing her best to keep the food flowing.

And Regan, it seemed, was doing her best to add to the gossip.

"He's staring at me," she continued petulantly.

His stepdaughter liked to imagine everything revolved around her. Just like Helen.

It was true Burke kept looking in this direction.

It was even possible he was attracted by Regan's big breasts, blond hair, and overstated makeup. *Slut Barbie*.

But Paul suspected the detective's true target was Bailey.

Or Paul himself.

Paul brooded and drank. They'd arrived together—Bailey and Burke. She had told him, of course, she'd found another ride. She hadn't told him with whom.

What else hadn't she told him?

And what had she and Burke talked about on the fifteen-minute drive home?

"It is an open house," Bailey said, balancing her overloaded tray. "Anyone who showed up at the funeral could come."

"Beautiful service," Macon contributed heartily, helping himself to a deviled egg.

Regan tossed her head. "I'm so glad you liked it."

Bailey, of course, said nothing about her own part in the arrangements. She never claimed credit for her work. Paul found that very useful.

He allowed himself a small, sad smile. "I think Helen would have been pleased."

"Nice turnout, too," Macon said.

Regan swallowed the contents of her wineglass. "I think they all came to see if Paul would be arrested."

Vicious little bitch. Paul felt the rage surge inside him, the blood drain from his face.

Macon laughed uncomfortably.

"Does anyone want coffee?" Bailey asked.

It would take more than coffee to shut up his stepdaughter. More than Bailey's pitiful attempts at distraction to counteract Regan's poison, allay Burke's suspicion and get public opinion to Paul's side.

"It's the police's fault," Paul said. "But I suppose I can't expect them to be impartial. They're just looking for ways to discredit me."

Regan rolled her eyes. "Oh, please."

"It's true," Paul insisted. "This fuss over Helen's accident is all some absurd payback because I wouldn't drop my investigation of the Dawler case."

Macon put up his eyebrows. "Seems to me there's not much to investigate. That boy confessed."

"Which is all the police based their case on," Paul said.

"Are you saying he didn't do it?"

"Let's just say the case was far more complicated than Chief Clegg wants people to believe. Or bothered to find out at the time."

Macon's face creased. "Now, I don't know. Family like that . . . Bound to be trouble. Billy Ray didn't have an easy time of it. Whore for a mother. Tramp for a sister. Folks around here figured he just finally had enough."

"She wasn't a tramp," Bailey said.

"Excuse me?"

"Tanya Dawler. She was only fifteen."

"Old enough to get into trouble," Macon said.

"Literally," Paul said. "She was three months pregnant when she died."

"Did you know her?" Bailey asked Macon.

He smiled down at her. "I was in school with her brother. Same as everybody else. But I hadn't heard she got herself knocked up."

"It was in the autopsy report," Paul said.

"Nobody gets pregnant all by herself," Bailey said. "Somebody had to be the father."

Macon shrugged. "Sure. But in that family, it could have been anyone. Including her own brother."

"*Eww*. Didn't the cops do, like, a paternity test or something?" Regan asked.

Her question caught Paul by surprise. He hadn't expected his stepdaughter to be paying attention. Or to ask an almost intelligent question.

"This was nineteen years ago," Bailey explained. "DNA testing was just being introduced."

"So I guess we'll never know," Macon said.

Paul allowed himself a smile. "Investigative journalism isn't like an episode of *CSI*. It isn't all about the science. It's about people. And people talk."

Regan emptied her wineglass. "Well, this girl—Tanya, is that her name?—can't tell you anything. She's dead."

"Her brother isn't," Paul said.

Macon's face relapsed into that smooth, grave expression most people assume at funerals. Quite appropriate, under the circumstances. "You didn't hear?"

"Hear what?" Bailey asked.

"It's all over the sheriff's department. Billy Ray was murdered in prison."

Paul froze, genuinely shocked. His heart seized. Billy Ray couldn't be dead. Paul needed him.

Macon was wrong, that was all. He must be wrong.

"You're mistaken," he said stiffly, his heart galloping again. "Someone would have called me."

He'd certainly spent enough in charm and in bribes over the past few weeks to warrant a goddamn phone call.

"No mistake. My firm represented him, you know. Well, my father's firm. We got the call this morning."

"But I spoke with him last week. He was fine."

Better than fine. The inarticulate Billy Ray was finally beginning to trust him. It happened with every book, when writer and subject forged a symbiotic bond. The killer relied on Paul to give him a voice. And Paul depended on Billy Ray to give him a story.

Everything was finally falling into place. One more interview, one more twist, and he would have the sensational revelation that would take his book beyond the common criminal-done-wrong story and launch it onto the best-seller lists.

To get it, he had dangled the promise of understanding in front of Billy Ray like the prospect of salvation, skillfully playing on his subject's need for approval. Twenty years ago, that need had driven Billy Ray first to murder and then to confession. Now it would drive him to tell Paul the whole story. The true story.

All he needed was one more interview.

"Well, he's not fine now. Killed in the shower." Macon lowered his voice. "Sheriff said it was likely some sexual thing." He drew the word out. *Sex-you-all.* "I don't know the details and I don't want to know. You spoke with him, you said?"

Paul drew a shaking hand over his face. "Frequently."

What a waste. What a loss. Not a loss to society, of course, or even to him personally. Billy Ray had been an undereducated, overreligious boob. But . . . what would happen to his story now?

"Does this mean you have to give the money back?" Regan needled Paul. "If you can't, like, finish the book?"

Oh, God, the money. He couldn't possibly pay it back. Not until Helen's insurance paid out. How was he going to salvage this?

"I'll finish," he said. He had no choice but to finish. Somehow.

He watched the doubt dawning in Bailey's eyes and swore silently. He needed her loyalty. What had she and Burke talked about on the ride here? Goddamn it, did he have to worry about everything at once?

"What all did that boy tell you?" Macon asked. "Exactly."

"I can't tell you. Exactly," Paul said. "It will all be in the book."

Macon hesitated. "You know, I wouldn't put too much

faith in everything Billy Ray said. He never was quite right."

"The police put enough faith in his confession," Paul said. "I'm just going to set the record straight."

"Who cares?" Regan asked, slurring her words slightly. "He's dead, isn't he? Everybody's dead."

Macon patted her arm. "Let me get you another glass of wine."

Across the room, Burke's dark gaze fixed on their little group.

Let him watch, Paul thought. Let him wonder. The police got everything wrong anyway. They had in the Dawler case. Clegg's fault, that time, for rushing to bring charges in the notorious deaths of the town prostitutes.

Paul sipped his drink thoughtfully. Of course, Clegg might have had his reasons for wanting the case wrapped up so quickly. Pressure from the mayor, maybe, or the media, or other, personal reasons of his own . . .

It was worth thinking about. Paul was not above blackmail.

But with any luck, the police chief would be just as eager to resolve Helen's case, and Paul would be out of the woods. His wife's death was tragic, an unfortunate necessity. And if that damn detective, Burke, pushed the matter, well . . .

Paul would make sure someone else took the blame.

BAILEY couldn't wait to go home.

Okay, not home, exactly. The feng shui hall and blue-flowered bedroom in her parents' house no longer felt like home, and her studio apartment in East Village had been sublet to a massage therapist from Ohio named Ken.

But away from here.

The house was silent now. The guests were gone. Regan

was somewhere. Upstairs, Bailey hoped. Dorothy had shown up with a covered casserole made with Campbell's cream of celery soup. She stayed the requisite half-hour, finally leaving Bailey with a hissed reminder to reapply her lipstick.

As if she should be trolling for hookups at Helen's funeral reception.

Her mother had also given Bailey a hug and the keys to her car. Bailey appreciated both, even though accepting the keys reminded her sharply that at twenty-six she had nothing to call her own but a few pieces of furniture in storage and a three-ring notebook with the rough draft of her first novel inside.

She sprinkled powdered detergent into the dishwasher door and slammed it shut to run another load. She wanted better.

She wanted to matter. Somehow. Somewhere.

Not here.

It was hardly a choice. More a realization, whispering at the back of her mind, coalescing, heavy and cold, in her belly.

She shook a dish towel over the sink. She wouldn't find what she wanted here.

She'd thought she had. Or that she could. She did intellectually stimulating, well-paid work for a man who professed to admire her mind and support her goals.

And told her—again and again—her work wasn't ready to show to anyone but him.

Bailey twisted the towel in her hands.

Steve's dark drawl joined the whisper at the back of her mind. *It wouldn't be the first time an employer took advantage of an employee. . . . Seems to me he does it all the time.*

No, she didn't belong here. Not anymore.

She draped the dish towel over the bar of the oven to dry. But how could she leave so soon after Helen's death?

The heaviness settled in her stomach. How could she stay?

She set the coffeemaker to brew in the morning and propped the note for the cleaning lady in its usual place by the phone. Flipping off the kitchen lights, she made her way through the darkened first floor to the front door.

"Bailey."

Just her name, spoken out of the darkness, stopped her at the base of the stairs. She turned her head.

Paul slumped in one of the big leather chairs flanking the fireplace, cradling a brandy glass in his hands.

Bailey cleared her suddenly dry throat. "I was just leaving."

He didn't say anything. The light from the hall cast shadows on his haggard face and hollowed eyes.

She should go. She was going.

But habit and compassion made her say, "Can I get you anything first?"

"You left," he accused.

Bailey blinked. She hadn't gone anywhere yet. "It's late."

"Before," he said, a hint of impatience in his tone. "You didn't ride home with me from the funeral."

Bailey was relieved, both because he sounded more like himself and because he was making sense now. Sort of. "I told you I got another ride."

"And this offer, this ride, from—someone—was more important to you than the fact that I needed your support."

Bailey's heart plummeted to join her stomach. Obviously, he'd been drinking. And she'd had enough dates that began or ended in bars to know you couldn't reason with a drunk.

She tried anyway. "I didn't think it would look right, my being alone with you like that."

"And avoiding me looked so much better." Paul shook

his head. "You drove off from my wife's funeral with the detective trying to frame me for her death."

"It wasn't like that." Her voice sounded shaky. Defensive. Could he hear it?

"What did he want?" Paul asked.

Bailey's heart pounded.

Maybe I wanted to warn you.

"To talk, I guess," she said.

"What did you tell him?"

Did she really want to blurt out her confession of misplaced devotion and thwarted hope? *No shame in not coming right out with it.*

No. Bad enough Steve knew about her stupid crush. Telling Paul would only make the situation worse. Not to mention unbearably awkward. She couldn't stand his pity. And she wouldn't know what to do with anything else.

She hedged. "Nothing much. We talked a little about my work."

"About me." Paul rose impatiently. "What did you tell him about me?"

Bailey took a deep breath. "I said you were devoted to your wife."

"Dear Bailey." Paul touched her cheek. "Always so loyal."

She jerked her head back. Was he mocking her?

"Look, it's been a long day," she said. "I should—"

"It has been. A very long, very difficult day." Paul's hand dropped, skimming her arm, brushing her hand.

Bailey started.

"A difficult week." He braceleted her wrist. "A difficult year." He tightened his grip.

Bailey backed into an end table. "Uh . . ."

"It will get better," Paul promised. "Soon. When we're back in New York."

She could not believe this. Did not want to believe this could be happening now, when he was free and she was—literally, finally!—on her way out the door.

"I don't know how I would have made it through without you," he whispered. His breath was warm and laced with brandy.

"Always happy to help," she said, insanely perky.

Oh, God, she wanted to go.

He smiled. "That's what I'm counting on," he said, and lowered his head to hers.

His mouth was hot and wet. Invasive.

Shock kept her still for one second. Two. She couldn't breathe, couldn't move, while her mind raced in panic.

He was grieving. Drunk. He didn't know what he was doing.

She didn't know what to do.

She felt the bulge of his erection as he pressed against her, and revulsion rose in her, sharp as nausea. She flattened her palms against his chest to push him away.

"This is cozy." Regan's voice rattled into the overheated atmosphere like hailstones in July. "Are we celebrating something?"

Bailey stumbled back, almost knocking over the table. Regan stood at the base of the stairs, her blond hair blazing in the light of the chandelier, her face contorted.

"No, I . . . it's not what you're thinking."

"Gee, really?"

"I was just telling Paul how sorry I was."

"Sorry?" Regan's voice cracked. "You're not sorry. You're pathetic. He doesn't get anything, you know. Not if he killed her. And not if he remarries, either. So you're wasting your time."

Unreality gripped Bailey. "I'm not . . . It wasn't . . . Paul, tell her!"

But he looked at her as if he'd never seen her before.

"He didn't get anything in a divorce, either," Regan said. "But I guess he told you that."

"No, he didn't. We never . . ." This was a nightmare. "Paul?"

He roused himself to speak slowly. "Helen's death was an accident."

Under the panic, under the disbelief, anger grew. "Of course it was."

"She was in the pool when you found her."

"Yes!"

Oh, God, he didn't think . . . he didn't suspect . . .

He did. He and Regan thought she had killed Helen because she wanted Paul and Paul wanted Helen's money.

She was screwed.

"I don't believe you," Regan said. "And the police won't, either. Not when I tell them what I saw tonight."

She could deny it, Bailey thought. Steve might believe her.

Your mother told me you weren't romantically involved. Which is what you would have told her whether you were or not.

She shivered. Or he might not.

I'm keeping an open mind, he'd said.

But that was before Regan went running to him with the news that on the night of Helen's funeral she'd caught her stepfather kissing his personal assistant.

Bailey was the first one to find Helen dead. It wasn't that big a stretch to imagine she was the last person to see Helen alive. That she was the one who killed her.

"Regan." Even as she spoke, Bailey felt the hopelessness of her appeal. Except for the hectic color in her cheeks, the girl's face could have been carved in stone. "You're upset. We're all tired. Maybe we should talk in the morning."

She looked at Paul, willing him to get involved, but he wouldn't meet her gaze. His face was strained and pale.

He could still say something to support her. To protect her. All he had to do was tell the truth.

Why didn't he say something?

"I don't have anything to say to you," Regan said. "I want you the fuck out of my house."

Bailey struggled not to fall apart. "Okay," she said with as much dignity as she could muster.

Which wasn't much. Her knees wobbled as she crossed the marble floor to the front door. She tugged it open, her hands shaking.

She was never coming back.

SHE had to go back.

Bailey hugged her knees and stared at the blue-flowered wallpaper and faced facts. She couldn't duck her responsibilities. She still had Paul's backup files and the evidence boxes. She had to give them back.

She could go in the morning, early, when she wouldn't have to face her mother and her questions, when there was a good chance Regan would be asleep. She would stack the cartons in his office and leave her letter of resignation on his desk.

Under the circumstances, she didn't think he would require two weeks' notice. And if he did . . . well, he wasn't going to get it, that was all.

No more half-measures. No more going with the flow and hoping for the best and imagining things would somehow work out if she didn't ask for too much, if she made other people happy, if she made them like her.

She was quitting. Tomorrow. And then she would get on with her life.

Assuming she wasn't arrested.

Okay, she couldn't think about that right now. Later she would figure out what to do about what Regan saw and what she would say and whether to talk to Steve or immediately hire a lawyer. Right now she just wanted every vestige of Paul Ellis out of her life.

Scrambling off her bed, she gathered an armload of loose papers, printouts of articles and clippings of reviews, promotion schedules and sales reports, notes and maps and lists. She hesitated over the notebook on her bedside table, the one with the purple cover. Her fingers traced the bold black words: TANYA DAWLER. MY DIARY. KEEP OUT.

She flipped it open.

The guys who have sex with you at a party on Saturday night won't even talk to you at school on Monday morning. But they'll talk about you. In the locker room, in the hall. You can act like you don't care. I mean, they're assholes, right? But it hurts! It hurts.

Bet they wouldn't like it if I talked about them. Or their daddies.

Poor Tanya, with her dramatic exclamation points and defiant humor and desperate longing to be loved. The girl didn't deserve to have her words, her feelings, thrust back into a dark box. Paul would never give Tanya her due. But she was part of another life, the life Bailey was getting rid off.

She swept the lid off one of the evidence boxes, prepared to shove everything inside.

And froze.

This carton wasn't crammed with paper. This held labeled plastic bags and paper bundles, crime scene evidence.

She could deal with that. No problem. The problem was lying on top, a heavy, flat, familiar object, a granite plaque on a wooden stand—last year's National Booksellers' Optimus Award, presented to Paul Ellis for *Breathing Space*.

Bailey felt queasy. What was that doing here?

When—why—would Paul have added it to boxes she was taking away to inventory?

But she knew. She knew. Hadn't she read the search warrant? Toolbox. Bookends. Trivet. Metal tray . . . *Objects consistent with injury on victim's skull.*

She pressed her hand to her mouth. *Oh, God.*

She was so screwed.

No, she wasn't, she told herself, swallowing panic. She couldn't dump this on her parents. Paul had let her down, betrayed her, in every possible way. But there had to be something she could do. Someone she could turn to.

Steve, she thought, and lost her breath because she was so scared. And because he was the right person, the only person, she could call.

She held the picture of him in her mind, tough and solid and safe, those little lines of impatience between his dark brows.

Maybe he wouldn't believe her, but he would listen. He was open-minded, and he knew what to do.

Anyway, there was no one else. Not in this town. Not in this life.

She jammed the lid back on the box and scrambled for her cell phone.

ELEVEN

STEVE sat alone in near darkness.

His mother was in Linville. His daughter was in bed. The house settled around him, warm and constricting as a child's blanket.

Steve sprawled in his father's old chair, making notes. This used to be his favorite time, the quiet hours of the night, when a man could work uninterrupted or think slow, deep thoughts about his life or make slow, deep love to his wife.

His wife was dead.

He didn't like the company of his thoughts anymore, or the direction of his life.

At least he could work.

Once—six months or a week ago—that would have satisfied him. It didn't now. His fault, for letting personal feelings into an investigation.

This afternoon in his truck, he should have coaxed Bailey into confiding in him. Or scared her into confessing.

Except he didn't want her confession. He scowled at the lined yellow pad on his knee. Maybe the chief was right and he should withdraw from the case. Maybe he *had* been gone too long to be effective.

Or maybe he'd been back too long and lost his edge.

Compartmentalize. Depersonalize. Detach.

He reviewed his notes. The blood screen had arrived today, verifying Helen Stokes Ellis had died with a blood alcohol level of .10. She hadn't been drugged. So she hadn't helped herself to her husband's pills, and no one had slipped a Xanax in her nightcap, either.

Another dead end, damn it.

The only thing Walt Clegg hated more than a big case in his town was an unsolved big case. The chief had backed Steve's request to the DA to authorize a rush job on the items seized from the Ellises' home. But the special request hadn't done them a damn bit of good. None of the items removed in the search appeared to have been used in the attack on Helen. And now that he had the results—the negative results—Walt Clegg was more convinced than ever that Steve was blowing smoke up his ass. Unless he came up with something fast, he wouldn't even make it to his six-month review.

I'll give it another whack, friendly lab guy had promised, with a chuckle at his own little joke. But he didn't hold out much hope.

Neither did Steve. He'd gone to trial without a murder weapon before . . . in D.C. But folks around here would want concrete evidence to convict. Especially since Ellis's defense was sure to call an entire lineup of high-paid, high-profile expert witnesses to refute the prosecution's case.

To convince a jury, to persuade the DA—hell, even to get the chief on board and off his neck—Steve needed means. Motive. Preferably something besides Ellis screwing or wanting to screw his personal assistant.

Steve's hand tightened on his pen. The three most common motives for murder were sex, property, and insults. Steve doubted Ellis hit his wife over the head with an unidentified object and dumped her in the pool because she criticized his writing.

Which brought him back to Bailey. To Bailey and sex.

Okay, maybe I was attracted, a little, she had admitted. *But I never did anything about it.*

He could canvass her neighbors, see if anybody could ID Ellis as a visitor to her apartment. Right. Like Walt would spring for airfare to New York.

So either Steve believed her, or not.

He wanted to believe her.

Four million should be motive enough for anybody. Even a cursory examination of the Ellises' financial records revealed the couple had been living beyond their means in New York City. The rent on their Central Park apartment had been paid, but other debts—his car, her plastic surgeon's fees, their credit cards—had been allowed to pile up.

So how did Paul Ellis afford the services of a full-time personal assistant? What was Bailey getting from Ellis she couldn't get from her job with Paragon Press? Room? Board? Payment in kind?

The pen snapped.

Disgusted, he threw the pieces across the room. Thinking with his dick again. It was this damn case.

It was Bailey, a voice inside him whispered, but he ignored it. He'd had lots of practice ignoring things that didn't fit his plans—a dangerous approach for a detective, but it got him through the nights.

He walked across the room to get another pen.

Paul Ellis may have come to Stokesville to research, but

the move had also allowed the couple to retrench. Faced with several hundred thousand dollars in debt, Steve reflected, Ellis could have decided his wife was worth more dead than alive.

Selfish bastard. As if you could put a price on someone's life, a premium on the time you had together.

A memory of Teresa shuddered through him, her eyes begging for his understanding. *I'm not poisoning what's left of my life with treatments, Steven.* He'd reasoned and raged and fought with her about it. And poisoned the time they had left with his frustration and his fear.

There was no way to get it back. Each month, each week, each precious hour could never be replaced.

He thought of Bailey, pink-cheeked, scowling, and how he couldn't get involved with her, and wondered when the hell he'd made a habit of living with regret.

His cell phone vibrated. He reached for it. He wasn't on call tonight.

He checked the number. No one he knew.

"Burke," he said.

"Um. This is Bailey Wells."

He felt a shot of adrenaline that straightened his spine and cleared his head. "Are you all right?"

"I . . . yes."

Hard to tell from those two clipped syllables. He remembered the way she had held herself together after Helen's death. Something was up, or she wouldn't have called him. She certainly would never have called after eleven o'clock at night. He got up again to pace.

"What can I do for you?" he said easily.

Silence.

"Bailey?" Not so easy now.

"I need to see you."

Absolutely.

Not.

His instinctive male response was to rush to the rescue, club swinging.

But it wasn't so simple. He wasn't a caveman. He was a single dad working cop, and Bailey was a person of interest in an ongoing investigation. Even if he wanted to, which he didn't, he couldn't leave his sleeping daughter to meet with her.

"Can it wait until morning?"

He heard her sharp intake of breath and felt a twinge of . . . professional duty or personal concern? It really didn't matter.

"Bailey? Don't hang up on me now."

"I won't. I need to talk to you. Tonight."

"Okay." Who the hell was on duty tonight? There had to be somebody she could talk to. Marge Conner, maybe. "Can you get to the station?"

"Yes, I . . . I have my mother's car."

"Good. You get yourself to the station, and I'll have someone meet you there."

"No." Her voice was firmer. Louder. Scared. "It has to be you. I have to talk with you personally."

He couldn't invite her here. One of the first things you learned in training was to keep the job separate from your private life. Cops who crossed that line made trouble for themselves and their departments.

Her breath caught again. "Please."

Compartmentalize, he told himself. Depersonalize. Detach.

And heard himself say, "Let me give you directions."

"I know how to get to there."

"Not to the station." His voice was grim. "Five eighty five Sawmill Road."

"Five eighty five. Thank you." Her relief flowed over the line. "You won't regret it."

Her voice made him feel good. Foolishly good.

"Not a problem," he said, and hoped she was right. For both their sakes.

THE important thing was not to panic.

The intruder moved quietly through the darkened first floor of the big house, drawn like a moth to the light still burning in Ellis's study. It was unfortunate Paul persisted in poking into matters that were really none of his business. But he had the means and the opportunity now to make things right.

Didn't Daddy say folks mostly got what they deserved? Helen's death—and Burke's suspicion—provided the perfect justification for what he was about to do.

Really, Paul had brought this on himself.

He patted the bulge in his jacket pocket the way another man might touch a rabbit's foot. For luck.

Not that he believed in leaving anything to chance. That's why he had to do this. To protect himself. To protect his family and his way of life. A man had a right to do that. That's all he'd ever done.

Of course he'd regretted the waste all those years ago.

He'd been appalled by the mess and the fuss.

He would have managed the business much better himself.

And he had, hadn't he? The last death had been simple—a debt called in, a favor promised, no different from the deals he made every day at the courthouse or over a cup of coffee at the diner.

Things weren't quite so simple this time.

The knowledge sharpened his senses and thickened his

blood. His heart pounded. His palms were actually sweating. He could remember when sex felt like this, edgy and risky and raw.

A long time ago.

He blotted the sweat from his upper lip with his handkerchief, smoothed his hair and stepped through the study door.

BAILEY bowed her head, willing her hands to release their death grip on her mother's steering wheel.

She'd made the right decision. She had enough strikes against her without adding withholding evidence and obstructing justice to the list. She needed to tell Steve her story before Regan spewed her version of that awful kiss to the police, before Paul . . .

Bailey's stomach pitched to her shoes. She couldn't think about Paul yet.

She peered through the windshield. Steve lived in a white, two-story house in a block of other white, two-story houses with detached garages, mature shrubs, and neat lawns. The setting was familiar and nonthreatening. Much better than the police station. Really.

Her heart beat high and hard in her chest.

Uncurling her fingers from the steering wheel, Bailey dragged herself from the car. She hauled the evidence box from the back seat and stood staring at the yellow porch light.

She braced her shoulders and tottered up the walk. Before she reached the steps, the front door opened. Her stomach rocketed from her shoes to her throat.

Steve loomed, cut in light and shadow, framed against the dim interior of the house.

He gestured to the box. "Can I help you with that?"

She swallowed. "I hope so."

His eyebrows climbed, but he didn't say anything, just came down the steps and swung the box into his arms. Muscled arms. In the hours since the funeral, he'd changed from his suit into jeans and a plain dark T-shirt that clung to his broad chest and shoulders.

Bailey averted her gaze, unsettled by this sight of him, by the late hour and his casual clothes. He was a police detective. It was easier to think of him as a police detective when he wore the suit.

He opened the door for her with one hand and nodded towards the back of the house. "Kitchen's that way."

She walked past him, past the grandfather clock at the foot of the stairs, along a narrow hallway that smelled reassuringly of lemon furniture polish. Floral prints and faded family portraits of solemn-faced toddlers and smiling brides hung on the walls.

"Nice place." And not at all what she expected. She thought he'd be more the black leather and beer cans type. Unless this was stuff his wife had picked out.

His eyes were hooded. Unreadable. "This is my mother's house."

So they both lived at home. Dr. Phil would have a field day with that. Norman Bates from *Psycho* meets the crippled chick from *The Glass Menagerie*. Except Steve was way too virile to play old Norman, and Bailey was the one suspected of murder. . . . She winced.

"She's out of town this weekend," Steve continued easily. "Back tomorrow night. She goes with her book club to the Highland games in Linville every year."

Bailey collected herself enough to ask, "She's interested in log throwing?"

"The correct term is caber toss. But I think she just likes men in kilts," he said.

Bailey smiled wanly. He was trying to put her at ease,

she knew, filling the awkward silence, hiding his curiosity and impatience. As if it were perfectly okay for her to invade his home and his privacy at a quarter to twelve on a Friday night. No problem, he'd said.

If only he knew.

She had to tell him.

"Something to drink?" He set the carton on the table in the breakfast nook, looking surprisingly at home against the oak cabinets and white ruffled curtains. Well, why not? He probably grew up here.

"Oh, no. No, thank you," she added politely.

A smile touched the corners of his hard mouth. "You want to sit down?"

Sitting would be good. Her knees were about to give out anyway.

They faced each other across the table, the carton between them.

Steve's gaze flicked to it and then fixed on her face. "What can I do for you?"

She opened her mouth, and nothing came out. Panic dried her mouth and constricted her throat. Maybe she should have accepted that drink after all.

Steve sat motionless. Patient. Polite. Waiting.

She worked enough moisture into her mouth to swallow. Could she do this? Once she confessed her suspicions, once she laid out her case, there was no turning back. Everything would change.

Everything had changed already.

She took a breath. Released it. And said, "I found the murder weapon."

EXCITEMENT hummed through Steve's system like a low-level electrical charge.

Easy, he told himself. Maybe she found the murder weapon. That would certainly explain her urgency in seeking him out tonight. But maybe she was mistaken. Maybe she was lying.

He didn't want to believe she was lying.

Something shifted tonight when she showed up at his door lugging that box, her eyes full of desperate hope. Or maybe it happened this afternoon, when she climbed into his truck and he got that long look at her legs.

Whatever it was, whenever it happened, the line had been blurred. Whether he liked it or not, whether he admitted it or not, he couldn't regard her only as a suspect anymore.

So here she was, in his mother's kitchen, invading his territory, disturbing his peace, shaking his assumptions.

And about time, too, Eugenia would say.

Steve eased back in his chair, observing the strain in Bailey's face and the resolute set of her shoulders. He hadn't sat in a kitchen with a woman late at night since the early years of his marriage when he worked the swing shift. Not that he and Teresa talked about his cases. Teresa, loving, laughing Teresa, had never been comfortable when he walked through the door with the job still clinging to him like cigarette smoke, the tang of danger, the taint of family disputes, the stink of deals gone bad. He learned to shower before he joined her in bed, and he never brought the job home.

He didn't have that choice with Bailey. And if what she said was true . . . it would change everything. She could save this investigation and his ass. Or bury him in the hole he'd dug with Clegg.

He cleared his throat. "Want to tell me about it?"

"Why don't I show you instead?"

He glanced at the box between them. "In there?"

She nodded.

Standing, he lifted the lid of the box. No point worrying about fingerprints. He'd already lugged the thing into the house. And . . . yes. All right. There it was. A heavy, blunt object with sharp, squared edges.

The hum grew from a buzz to a whine.

"Looks like a tombstone," he said.

Bailey stood, too, her hair brushing his shoulder, and he felt a jolt that wasn't electricity or suspicion. "I think it's meant to."

He read the name—Paul Ellis—and below it, etched into the granite where "Beloved Husband" should be, were the words *National Booksellers' Optimus Award,* the book title, *Breathing Space,* and last year's date.

"Where did you get this?"

"I found it in the box about half an hour ago."

"See it before?"

She nodded again, and her hair slipped forward over her shoulder, slippery as silk and distracting as hell. "Paul used to keep it on his desk as a sort of paperweight."

Steve took a step away from the table. Away from her and her hair. "When did you notice it was missing?"

"I didn't. I mean, you don't take much notice of stuff you see every day, do you? Unless you're Sherlock Holmes or something."

Her attempt at humor didn't fool him. He knew her well enough now to recognize the tiny signs of stress and to appreciate the effort she made to hold herself together.

"Did you pick it up? Touch it?"

"Recently?" she asked.

"Ever."

"Possibly. Probably." She pushed her hair back from her face. "That means my fingerprints will be on it, won't they?"

Oh, yeah.

"Unless somebody wiped it," he said grimly.

"Would that be better or worse?" Her throat moved as she swallowed. "For me, I mean."

Things looked bad for her either way. But she was smart enough to have figured that out, and he didn't have the heart or the knowledge yet to tell her how bad.

So instead he said, "Why don't you tell me what you were doing with the box."

"It's an evidence box."

"I can see that."

She cleared her throat. "Paul used his connections with the district attorney's office to get them to release the evidence collected for the Dawler trial from their property room."

He lifted an eyebrow.

She plunged on. "When Regan . . . When I moved back to my parents' house, Paul suggested I take the boxes with me. To inventory."

"Why would he do that?"

"I assumed because he didn't want to do it himself. It's a time-consuming job," she explained.

"And you had the time," Steve said flatly.

"Well, no. Not really. But I thought I might get to it. After the funeral."

"Okay."

Echoes of their earlier conversation played in his head. *It wouldn't be the first time an employer took advantage of an employee.*

Paul wouldn't do that.

Seems to me he does it all the time.

"So you took the boxes," Steve prompted.

"Yes. Well, no. Paul offered to carry them to the car for me while I packed."

His intuition hummed like a tuning fork, raising the hair on the back of his neck. "And this was when?"

"Thursday around five." Bailey met his gaze, her dark brown eyes determined and unhappy. "Before the search."

Well, shit.

"Anybody see Ellis move the boxes?" he asked without much hope.

"I don't know. I don't think so. Regan might have."

He made a mental note to ask. "Did you open them? Inspect the contents?"

Bailey pleated her fingers together in her lap. "Not then. I opened one that night, but I didn't find anything."

"What were you looking for?"

Her head snapped back as if he'd slapped her. "Nothing. Something to do. Something to read. If you must know, I found Tanya Dawler's diary. Which doesn't have anything to do with why I had to talk with you."

"Why me? Why now?"

She hesitated. Preparing to lie? he wondered. The possibility bothered him more than it should have. People lied to him all the time.

"You know how in books or movies when the girl gets a threatening letter or hears a scary noise in the basement, and instead of contacting the authorities, she decides to handle whatever it is herself?"

Where was she going with this?

"You mean the girl who winds up dead?"

"Exactly." She met his eyes with devastating frankness. "I don't want to be the dumb dead girl."

Their gaze held.

She wasn't dumb. She was sharp and competent, loyal to a fault . . . and in a shitload of trouble. It took guts for her to come here tonight. His respect for her grew. As did his concern.

. . "Not dumb at all." He leaned back in his chair in a wasted attempt to restore some distance between them. "So what's my role in this movie of yours?"

"I don't know," she admitted. "But I could really use a hero about now."

His lungs expanded. Was it possible . . . could she possibly . . .

No and *no*.

Do the job. Go through the motions.

Maybe it wasn't very heroic, but if he was going to save her, he had to do it by the book.

He got out his notebook. "Tell me again what you were doing with the box."

He took her back over and through her story until he was satisfied she'd told him everything she remembered. But he still didn't know how she felt or what she thought, all the things any competent defense attorney would toss out as speculation that were suddenly, vitally important for reasons Steve didn't want to think about.

"What made you think this could be the object used in the attack on Mrs. Ellis?"

Bailey considered his question, her head to one side. "You gave me a copy of the search warrant, remember? This is exactly the kind of thing you were looking for. Plus, it was so obviously out of place in this box."

"Any idea how it got there?"

"I can't be sure. I didn't see."

"But you have some idea."

She nodded silently.

Still protecting that asshole.

"Can you tell me? For your statement," he said.

"Right. All right. I think Paul put the award in the carton and carried it out to my car so that you wouldn't find it if you searched the house."

She almost had it.

"Or so I'd find it in your possession," Steve said.

Her eyes widened. He felt like crap. Like she was six years old and he'd just told her there was no Santa Claus. Or twenty-six and he'd told her the guy she'd had a crush on for the past two years had totally set her up for the murder of his wife.

"Did you two have a disagreement?" Steve asked gently. "Words, maybe?"

Her hands twisted in her lap. "No. Tonight he said . . . He wants me to go back to New York with him."

Son of a bitch.

"Is that what you want?" Steve asked. Very cool. Detached. Professional.

"Not anymore."

He fought a fierce flare of satisfaction. "Why not?"

"It doesn't matter." She gave him a small smile that struggled to match his, cool and professional. "Personal reasons."

It pissed him off. "How personal?"

She blushed. "It's not what you're thinking. More professional personal, if you know what I mean."

He didn't have a clue. Any more than she had any idea what he was thinking. Which was a good thing, because some of his thoughts weren't professional at all.

"Maybe you could explain it to me," he suggested.

She sighed. "I went to work for Paul Ellis because I wanted to write my own book. That was two years ago."

She was writing a book? he thought, amazed. Impressed. But what came out of his mouth was, "You haven't finished a book in two years?"

"Oh, it's finished." She looked down like it was no big deal. Like finishing a book was nothing. "But it's not ready to submit."

"How do you know?"

"Paul told me."

Anger bubbled through him. She was so smart. How could she be so dumb where this one guy was concerned? "You think a guy who killed his wife and stuck you with the murder weapon is the best person to turn to for career advice?"

Bailey winced.

Steve winced, too. This was not the detached, just-the-facts-ma'am discussion they should be having.

She rallied. "It's not like I knew two years ago that things were going to work out this way. Anyway, one doesn't have anything to do with the other."

Fuck detached.

"Sure it does. The guy's a user. He's proved he'll put his interest before yours. Maybe he doesn't want to lose you as a personal assistant. Or maybe he doesn't want the competition."

She shook her head. "That's a nice theory. And an even nicer compliment. But there's no way Paul could consider me competition. Even if I were any good, I don't write true crime."

He let himself be diverted. "What do you write?"

"YA. Young adult fiction," she explained, as if he might not know what that was.

"*The Princess Diaries,*" he said. "*The Outsiders.*"

Bailey's smile lit her eyes. Her face. "Your daughter?"

He nodded. "I'm no expert, but I bet I know more about what girls that age like than Ellis does. I bet you do, too."

Her mouth opened. He could practically see the wheels spinning inside her pretty head as she absorbed his words.

"Paul knows a lot about the industry," she said.

"Does he know you don't want to go back to New York with him?"

Her gaze dropped. "Not yet."

"When were you planning to tell him?"

"Tomorrow."

Steve made a disbelieving noise.

"It's true," she insisted, her big brown eyes fixed on his face. "That's why I was packing up the boxes. To give everything back to him."

"You were going to quit," Steve said with heavy skepticism.

"Yes."

"The day after his wife's funeral."

The chin came up. "Yes."

He didn't buy it. She was too conscientious, too self-effacing, too fucking loyal to leave her boss in the lurch like that.

"Why?"

Bailey moistened her lips. "There was a little, uh, awkwardness before I left tonight."

Awkwardness? What the hell did that mean?

"What kind of awkwardness?"

"Well . . . Paul was drinking."

Terrible images flooded Steve's brain. Had her boss hurt her? Hit her? What? "Are you telling me what happened or making excuses for him?"

Again.

She flushed. "I'm trying to tell you what happened. Paul was drinking, and before I left, he . . . kissed me."

TWELVE

THE intruder paused in the doorway, his heart pumping.

Ellis raised his head and stared blankly. "What are you doing here?"

Did he suspect? But there was no awareness in his face. No awkwardness. No fear.

Was it possible, after all, that he wasn't a threat?

"I was hoping we could talk."

"Now." Ellis didn't sound alarmed. Maybe curious, and a little drunk. *Perfect.* He sprawled in one of the room's big leather chairs, his legs stretched out on the Oriental carpet. The desk might have been even better, but the chair was positioned a good three feet from the bookcase behind him.

Plenty of room.

"I wanted to catch you without an audience around."

"If you mean my darling stepdaughter, she's upstairs." Ellis set an empty brandy glass on the table beside him. "You know she wants me out of the house."

"I heard." Hands in his pockets, he walked behind Ellis's

chair, pretending to study the books on the shelves. "These your books?"

"Some of them."

He scanned the spines. *Breathing Space. Murder-in-Law. A Time to Die*. Ellis was a clever guy. Just not clever enough.

"Shame about Billy Ray," he offered.

Paul rested his head against the back of the chair. "Shit happens. It won't affect me."

He looked down at Paul's full, graying hair, a little taken aback by his dismissive attitude.

"It will affect your book. Unless you plan to write about the Dawler murders without talking to the murderer."

"But I did talk to Billy Ray. Several times, in fact. And I have other sources."

"What other sources?"

"You want names, you'll have to get in line to buy the book. Just like everyone else." The bastard had the balls to sound amused.

Rage rose like bile in his throat, but he controlled his voice carefully. "If you've discovered new evidence, then it's a matter for the courts. Or the police."

Paul sniffed. "I'm not an officer of the court. I don't have to do your dirty work."

"You're bluffing," his visitor decided. "You don't know anything."

Paul smiled. "I know there was a witness."

He froze, his hand curled in his pocket. "To the killings?"

"Not quite. But according to Billy Ray, someone else was in the house that night."

His heart threatened to choke him. He dragged in air. "Did he tell you who?"

"He told me . . . enough to figure it out. Sooner or later."

Really, Ellis left him no choice.

He brought this on himself.

"Sooner, I think," his visitor said.

Hooking his arm around Paul's neck, he jammed the gun to his temple. Quick. Hard.

Paul's body arched. His eyes went wide.

He turned his head, the way he would from a camera flash, a popped balloon. And squeezed the trigger.

The blast shook him. Hot. Loud. Noisier than he'd reckoned. He had considered using a silencer, but Ellis was the type who would choose to go out with a . . . well, with a bang. Anyway, Regan was dazed with drugs and alcohol and grief. The noise wouldn't rouse her.

Slowly, he straightened, quelling the lurch in his stomach, and looked. Not bad. A round black hole to the side of the head, welling blood. A .22 was only one step from a BB gun. The bullet tumbled inside the skull without sufficient force to exit.

But it certainly did the job.

He eased his hold on Ellis. The body slumped, the head dropping forward. Very natural. If not for the blood and the spatter on his clothes, he could have been drunk or asleep.

Carefully, he took out his handkerchief and wiped the gun. He wrapped Ellis's flaccid hand around the butt of the revolver and, pressing the unresponsive index finger to the trigger, held the barrel to the small neat hole in Ellis's head. Done.

He released the hand and the gun together, surprised to notice his own hands shaking. Ellis's arm fell to his lap.

He stepped back to survey the scene. One gun. One glass. No sign of struggle. He didn't worry about footprints in the carpet. People had been in and out of every room of the house all day.

Ellis slouched almost as he'd found him, a suicide, overcome by grief or guilt.

Let the police decide. He tucked his handkerchief back in his pocket. Either theory suited him fine.

STEVE'S Inscrutable Cop Face set like stone.

Bailey's stomach sank.

"It didn't mean anything," she said, pushing away the memory of Paul's wet, invasive kiss. Of his erection prodding her belly. "But Regan saw, which makes the situation a little . . ."

Compromising?

Damaging?

Disastrous.

"Awkward," she repeated lamely.

"It meant something," Steve said in his flat, neutral voice. "To make you quit."

Bailey straightened her spine. "It means Paul was drunk, and I was stupid."

Steve shook his head. "Not stupid. Set up."

Great. He thought she was so undesirable even a drunken wife-murderer wouldn't want to kiss her.

But there was no way Paul had faked his hard-on.

"I don't think he was acting," she said.

Steve went very still. His eyes narrowed. "You don't think so?"

And no way she was telling him why.

"Anyway," she said hastily, "Paul couldn't count on Regan coming downstairs at that moment."

Steve shrugged. "Doesn't matter. He sets the stage. He makes his move. Or another move. He has no reason to believe you'll reject him. Sooner or later, stepdaughter's going to get the idea."

He has no reason to believe you'll reject him.

Oh, God. Her face, her stomach, her whole body burned.

"But why would Paul want Regan to think we're . . ." Bailey choked on the words. She swallowed and forced herself to continue. "It just makes him look more guilty."

"Of cheating on his wife."

"Of killing her. An affair is a motive for murder."

Steve shrugged. "Depends how he plays it. He can argue that while Helen was alive he had it all. A wealthy wife. A willing, adoring assistant. All he has to do is convince the police you were pressing for more and he told you no. Then, when the weapon is found in your possession . . ." He leaned forward. "Are you all right?"

She couldn't breathe, she was about to throw up, but other than that she was hunky-dory.

"Fine," Bailey assured him. It was sweet of him to be concerned. She struggled to form a coherent thought, to frame a coherent sentence. "I still think it's risky for Paul to pretend to have an affair with me."

"As long as he could sell his wife's death as an accident, sure. But once we start treating it as a possible homicide, he has to divert suspicion. Who else benefits from Helen's death?"

"Her children. Richard—"

"Was sleeping it off in a drunk tank in Chicago," Steve interrupted.

"Then . . . Regan?"

"Didn't leave the bank until five-thirty that night and went to her gym after dinner. Even assuming she could get into the house without somebody noticing, she couldn't make the drive from Atlanta in time."

Bailey gaped at him. He'd just shared actual information with her about the case. He was investigating other leads.

She felt—not safe—but suddenly less alone. Hot tears burned her throat and rushed to her eyes. *Oh, God*. Like she wasn't embarrassed enough already. She crossed her arms over her chest and stared at Eugenia Burke's white-painted ceiling, willing the tears not to fall.

When she looked down again, Steve was watching her, his eyes unexpectedly kind. "I told you I was keeping an open mind."

"Yes, you did." She cleared her throat. "Thank you. What happens now?"

"Tomorrow I'll contact the DA. He can authorize emergency testing at the state lab in Raleigh."

"You can't do it yourself?"

"I could spray it with Luminol, check for traces of blood. But that would jeopardize the value of the evidence when we go to trial."

When, not *if.* It was suddenly hard to breathe.

"How long will testing take?"

"If the chief pushes the request through, I could have results in a day."

Her stomach churned. "And then what?"

"You'll have to come in. Sign a formal statement." His gaze was sympathetic, his tone neutral.

That didn't sound too bad. She'd done that before. She nodded.

"And we'll need to take your prints," he continued, still in that kind, neutral tone. "For the purposes of elimination."

"Are you going to read me my rights, too?"

He frowned. "You're not being detained. Technically—"

Disappointment and fear made her sharp. "I'm not asking you a technical question. I'm asking you as a . . ." What? Friend? He wasn't her friend. "I'm asking you," she repeated. "Do I need a lawyer?"

He didn't answer right away. Her stomach pitched and rolled.

"You can get one if you want," he said finally. "I need to talk to the chief and the DA before I move forward on this."

"And Regan," she said. "And Paul. You have to talk to them, too."

His jaw set. "I will. Believe me."

"Regan saw Paul kiss me." It was a relief, Bailey discovered, to get all the bad stuff out, all her sins and fears. Like popping a blister. Or going to confession. "Even if you don't think I'm guilty, even if the DA doesn't think I'm guilty, Regan believes I killed her mother. Or conspired with Paul to kill her mother, which is just as bad."

"You were the one who came forward."

He leaned forward across the table, big and solid and competent with his deep drawl and seductive sympathy, his muscled arms and macho readiness to take her problems on to his broad shoulders.

Everything she'd never wanted.

"Why did you come here tonight, Bailey?" he asked quietly.

She couldn't admit, even to herself, what she wanted from him. But she gave him as much of the truth as she dared. "I didn't have anywhere else to go."

Something—could it have been disappointment?—flickered in his eyes. "So you decided to cooperate with the police. Smart."

"Only if you believe me."

He raised his eyebrows. "Why wouldn't I believe you?"

She swallowed hard. "I might just be trying to get a lesser sentence."

"You might," he agreed. "If I had any kind of case without the murder weapon."

"Or Paul and I could have had a falling out."

"You did," he said without inflection.

"Oh, God." She covered her face with her hands. "See? Even you think I could be guilty."

"I think," Steve said slowly, and stopped.

Had she offended him? She lowered her hands.

But he wasn't even looking at her. His attention fixed over her shoulder. Turning, Bailey peered into the shadows of the hall.

"Gabrielle? What are you doing out of bed?" Steve asked.

The nine-year-old rose from behind the hall table, four feet two of injured dignity in pink-and-gray striped pajamas. "I didn't want to interrupt your date."

Steve raised his eyebrows. "So you decided to eavesdrop instead? Apologize to our guest and go upstairs."

"I'm not a date," Bailey said. Not unless the kid was talking court date.

Gabrielle slipped forward into the kitchen light, her heart-shaped face creased in concentration. "I remember you."

"Hi," Bailey said. "I remember you, too."

"Are you still in trouble?"

Oh, yes. And she was getting in deeper by the minute.

"Not as much as you'll be in if you don't get up to bed," her father said. "How long were you down here?"

Bailey flushed. What exactly had she heard?

"I heard you talking about work."

"And?" Steve asked sternly.

Gabrielle grinned. "Bor-ing."

Steve narrowed his eyes with mock severity. "Did I ask for your critique of my dating technique?"

This wasn't a date, Bailey wanted to protest.

"Hey, I'm just trying to help," Gabrielle said. "You are out of practice."

"To. Bed," Steve said, enunciating each syllable.

The girl rubbed one bare foot on top of the other, looking

at him through her lashes. "Isn't somebody going to tuck me in?"

Steve's hard face softened. Amazing to watch the big, tough detective totally manipulated by a nine-year-old girl. "Right. Up we go."

The Look turned on Bailey. Once again she had the sense of being sized up for . . . something. "Can she do it?"

Bailey was flattered but wary.

Steve simply looked wary.

Of course. Whatever kind of show he was putting on for his daughter, he wouldn't want—what had he called her?—a person of interest in an ongoing investigation tucking his precious only child into bed. No matter how open-minded he was.

"I'm a lousy tucker-inner," she said, to get them both off the hook. "But thanks for asking."

"Maybe you could both do it," Gabrielle suggested, still shifting from foot to foot. Her toenails were painted sparkly blue to match the blue stones in her ears.

"Fine," Steve said before Bailey could think of another excuse. "But no more getting up."

"Yes, Daddy," Gabrielle said, all demure obedience now that she had her way. She flashed Bailey another grin. Bailey smiled back cautiously.

They all trooped upstairs.

Gabrielle's room, like the rest of the house, was conventionally feminine, with ruffled curtains at the windows and botanical prints on the walls. Bailey's gaze traveled over the polished mahogany furniture to a fuchsia chair, glaringly out of place against the seafoam carpet.

"Nice paint job," she said.

Gabrielle beamed. "Thanks." She jumped on her mattress, making the items on her nightstand bounce. "That's my mom."

Bailey studied the framed photograph beside the bed. Gabrielle's mother was exotically lovely, with her daughter's heart-shaped face and dramatic coloring.

Bailey felt plain and tongue-tied. "She's very pretty."

"Dad put her picture there so I can see her when I say my prayers. But it's not the same as really talking to her."

"Lights out," Steve said.

Gabrielle sniffed and scrambled between the floral print sheets.

"You could write her a letter," Bailey suggested before she thought better of it.

Gabrielle gave her a patient look. "No, I can't. She's dead."

"Um." Bailey didn't dare turn around to see Steve. She could just imagine what kind of look he was giving her. "Right. But that doesn't mean you can't put down how you feel to her in words."

"If she's dead, doesn't she already know how I feel?"

Bailey was so out of her depth here. Totally over her head. But she had plunged in, so she floundered on. "Yes, but the letter's not only for her. It's for you to feel closer to her."

Gabrielle flopped against her pillows. "But you couldn't mail it."

Clearly, she had inherited her father's logical mind.

"You wouldn't have to mail it," Bailey said, acutely conscious of Steve listening. "You could burn it. Or bury it." Did that sound too depressingly funereal? "Or . . . or tie it to a balloon and let it go. The important thing is getting your feelings down in words."

"The balloon thing could be cool," Gabrielle conceded. "Are you spending the night?"

"Gaah," Bailey said, which was bad, but better than asking if her daddy had sleepovers often.

"No," Steve said from behind her. "We're just going to talk awhile, and then Bailey has to go home."

Which apparently satisfied Gabrielle. She snuggled into her pillow. "Okay. Thank you for tucking me in," she added politely.

"Thank you for inviting me. It was . . . fun," Bailey said, because she wasn't going to be outdone by a nine-year-old in the manners department, and it was also weirdly true.

Steve leaned past her to kiss his daughter on her forehead. The sight of that tough, stubbled face so close to the delicate, smooth one created an emptiness low in her stomach, a fullness around her heart.

"Goodnight, sweetheart. Sleep tight," Steve said.

Gabrielle grinned and pursed her lips to kiss his cheek. " 'Night."

Bailey followed him down the darkened stairs, still with that odd, aching fullness in her chest.

"Thank you," Steve said.

She found her breath and her voice. "I didn't do anything. She's very . . ."

Pretty? No, she'd said that about the mother.

Precocious? That sounded presumptuous.

"Friendly," Bailey settled on.

"She would be." Steve's smile gleamed in the shadows of the hall. "She wants me to get married again."

Bailey stopped at the bottom of the stairs, one foot in the air. "Excuse me?"

"Gabrielle's convinced herself—or maybe my mother convinced her—that if I had a wife, we could all move back to D.C."

O-kay.

Bailey released her grip on the banister. "Do you want to move back to D.C.?"

He rubbed his hand over his face. "This isn't about what I want. It's about what's best for Gabby."

Not her problem, Bailey reminded herself. None of her business. But what actually came out of her mouth was, "Did you ask her?"

"She's nine years old," Steve said. "What does she know?"

"She seems to know what she wants," Bailey offered cautiously.

"But not what she needs."

"And you do."

"It's my job to know." He sounded tired. "I'm her father."

She admired his determination to take care of his daughter. She really did.

"My father—" she said, and stopped.

He frowned. "What?"

Was it her imagination, or did he sound the teensiest bit defensive?

Sympathy weighted her chest. She didn't have a lot of experience with in-control, protective Manly Men. But she could imagine for a type like that, a man like Steve, nothing could be harder than to be faced with a disease he could not control and a daughter he could not protect. His uncertainty touched her even more than his concern.

Would he be amused if he guessed how she felt? Or appalled?

"Nothing," she said, and went into the kitchen and sat, determined to restore an appropriate distance between them. "Like you said, I don't have any experience being a parent."

"But you were a kid once, you said."

She looked up, startled he remembered.

He held her gaze a long moment, his hard, dark eyes assessing. "Hungry?"

She struggled to find her place in the conversation. "Excuse me?"

"You sat down at the table. You want something to eat?"

Just the suggestion made saliva pool in her mouth. "I'm fine, thank you. I've been surrounded by food all day."

"And you didn't touch any of it. Too busy waiting on other people. I could make you a sandwich."

He'd been watching her? Closely enough to notice what she ate? The thought was warming. Flattering.

Terrifying.

"You can't make sandwiches at . . ." She looked at her watch. "Oh, my God, it's two-thirty in the morning."

"Eggs, then." His mouth quirked in one of those crooked, heart-bumping smiles. "We'll call it breakfast."

They didn't know each other well enough for him to make her breakfast. For heavens' sake, she'd had sex with men who hadn't made her breakfast.

Heat started in the pit of her stomach and rose in her face. Not that she was having sex with Steve. Or even thinking about it.

"I don't want to put you to any trouble. Any more trouble," she corrected.

"No trouble." He opened the refrigerator to remove eggs and butter. "We can talk while you eat."

She didn't want to talk anymore. She was all talked out, empty and light-headed from stress and lack of sleep.

He dropped butter into a skillet, and the aroma rose with a sizzle that seriously weakened her resolution. He looked very . . . not domesticated, she decided, watching his muscled forearms and strong, square hands as he beat eggs and added them to the pan. But he was housebroken. He looked comfortable. Competent.

Sexy.

The toaster pinged. Steve glanced over his shoulder as he reached into the refrigerator. "Milk or juice?"

"Uh . . . milk, please."

It was like playing house.

At least until he started questioning her again.

"What were you saying about your father?"

She blinked. That was the last topic she expected him to introduce. But lots better than, say, what she was going to do now that she had no job, no prospects, and no permanent address. And he was feeding her. He could question her about whatever he wanted.

"I don't think my father ever had any idea what was best for me." She shook her head, afraid that hadn't come out right. "I don't mean he didn't want what was best for me. He worked hard. He made sure I had food, shelter, clothes." She smiled. "A curfew."

"All the basics," Steve observed, buttering her toast.

"Mom wanted me to go to Meredith College, like Leann. We had these horrible fights when I got the Bryn Mawr scholarship, but in the end she let me go. I used to wonder if maybe Dad took my side, but I don't know. We never talked about it. We never talked about much of anything."

Steve set a plate in front of her, scrambled eggs with cheese and toast. "Guys don't."

Oh, wow, that smelled so good. She closed her eyes and breathed in.

When she opened them again, Steve was watching her, an arrested expression on his face.

Hastily, she picked up her fork. "You never talked to your father about your plans? Your life?"

"Nope."

"So the two of you weren't . . . close?"

Poor guy. No wonder he was having trouble connecting with his daughter.

He looked amused. "Sure we were. We did the usual father-son stuff."

Bailey swallowed and asked, "What kind of stuff?"

He shrugged. "Fishing. Catch. Cleaning out the garage. He came to all my football games." He looked away, a muscle working in his jaw. She remembered how he had looked standing alone in the graveyard, all tough, broad shoulders and lonely eyes.

"Are those the things you do with Gabrielle?" she asked softly.

"She's a little small for football," Steve said dryly. "We cleaned the garage the other day."

He was on the defensive again.

"I'm sure that was a treat for both of you." Diplomatically, Bailey turned her attention to her plate. "These are good eggs."

"Look, even if we did more together, it wouldn't be enough." The words burst out of him, rough with frustration. "I can't talk to her the way Teresa could."

"You don't have to talk," Bailey said, her heart hurting for him. "You just have to be there. To listen."

"We did grief counseling together," he said. "For a year. It didn't fix anything."

He was such a guy, she thought, bemused. Did he honestly think of his wife's death as something that could be "fixed"?

"You can't solve every problem," Bailey said, poking at her eggs. "Sometimes the best you can do is share it."

"By talking about it."

"Yes. Why not?"

"Because there's no point talking about something you can't fix."

"Except to make you feel less alone." She set down her fork. "Do you ever talk to Gabrielle about her mother's death?"

"I told you, we went to grief counseling. She didn't talk there, either."

"Kids don't talk on the clock. Or on a schedule. They find their own times. So if you don't make the time, they'll never talk."

Steve raised his eyebrows. "Speaking from experience again?"

She leaned forward, her eggs forgotten. "I never played football. I didn't have the slightest interest in football, even though my father watched it every Sunday afternoon and Monday night of my life. I never expected him to sit in the back of the yearbook room cheering my great layout of the senior pages. But I wish just once he'd said to me, 'Hey, honey, State's playing Florida this afternoon. Sit down and watch the game with me.' "

"And that would have been enough."

"Probably not," she admitted. "But it would have been . . ." She struggled for words. "A start."

His eyes were warm. "So, you're suggesting we make a fresh start."

Her heart thumped. Stupid. He was talking about his relationship with his daughter. Wasn't he?

Her mouth went dry. She didn't answer.

With slow, sure movements, he nudged back her chair and drew her to her feet. His hands on her shoulders were warm and firm. Her heart hammered wildly.

She could say something. She should say something. Her mind went blank.

He stood close enough for her to feel the heat emanating from his body, close enough to see the stubble of his beard give way to the smoothness of his throat. He didn't touch her except for his hands and his gaze like a caress on her face. Her mouth. He was looking at her mouth.

Her lips parted.

He kissed her. Gently. Firmly. Briefly.

And raised his head.

Bailey waited. That was it? She opened her eyes, relief and disappointment curling in her stomach.

It was over before she had a chance to react. She didn't know what to do with herself. With her hands. With him.

His gaze met hers, serious and steady, and she knew.

She wanted him to kiss her again.

Flexing her fingers in the soft fabric of his T-shirt, she pulled him closer and kissed him. Like that. Like this. Again, harder, taking him in tastes, in bites. *She wanted him.*

His arms came up to steady her as she inhaled him, attacked him, pushing her tongue past his teeth, plastering her body against his broad, hard body. And he kissed her back, pulling her even closer to support her weight, absorbing her clumsy assault with easy strength.

He felt so good. So safe. She pressed against him. Rubbed against him. If she could have crawled inside him, she would have.

He angled his head and used his tongue. Zings and tingles raced up her spine and shorted out her busy brain. He glutted her senses. He filled her mind. As long as she was kissing him, she didn't have to think about tomorrow.

And then his hands came up and gripped her hands. He straightened his arms, forcing her away from his solid, aroused body.

"Enough," he said.

THIRTEEN

BAILEY stared at him, her eyes unfocused and her lips swollen from the force of their kiss.

Steve inhaled sharply. She looked like his personal sex dream come true. Beautiful. Vulnerable. Available.

She looked like a big mistake.

He had kissed her as a sign of truce, a gesture of comfort. And because he really wanted to kiss her. But what he'd intended as an exploratory fresh start exploded when she detonated in his arms. Her response had completely blown him away. She blew him away. He was still reeling from the aftershocks. His blood pounded in his head. His erection pressed against the zipper of his jeans.

"Enough," he said roughly.

Her mouth, her sweet, slick, kiss-swollen mouth, dropped open. "Are you kidding me?"

He wanted to laugh. He wanted to jerk her into his arms and finish what they'd started. He shook his head instead, not trusting himself to speak. If he spoke, he might do something else impulsive and stupid, like beg her to trust him or invite him to his room to have sex or ask her to have his babies.

"Why?" she demanded.

"I don't mix sex with the job," he said. *Pompous ass.*

"You could have fooled me."

He wasn't fooling either one of them.

"That wasn't sex," he said.

Not only sex. He had feelings for her. He hadn't figured out yet what those feelings were, or what he was going to do about them, but they definitely elevated that amazing, full-body-contact, no-holds-barred kiss above simple sex.

Bailey stopped tugging against his grip and glared at him, the kiss-dazed, cloudy look fading from her eyes. "What are you, one of those Bill Clinton, it-has-to-be-penetration guys?"

His control frayed. His breathing was ragged. "No, I'm one of those I-shouldn't-fuck-a-woman-when-she's-vulnerable-and-came-to-me-for-protection guys."

Hot color swept her face. "Oh."

Shit. This time when she tugged at her hands, he let her go.

She looked at the ceiling, at her shoes, anywhere but at his face. "Sorry."

She was taking responsibility again for something that wasn't her fault. He'd kissed her. He started this. And it was killing him not to finish.

"My mistake," he said.

She grimaced. "Yeah. Thanks. That makes me feel lots better."

Damn it, he didn't mean it like that. "Bailey . . ." He reached for her.

Her chin came up. "Don't."

He stopped cold. "No. I won't. I just . . ."

Fucked up. Big time.

"Didn't want to take advantage," he said.

Not after the way Ellis had used her and betrayed her. She'd been taken advantage of enough.

"Thanks," she said again. "I'm sure I'll appreciate your restraint in the morning."

Frustration balled in his gut. "At least one of us will."

This time she managed a smile. *Thank you, Jesus.*

"Well." She hugged her arms, still not quite meeting his gaze. "It's late. I should go."

He didn't want her to leave. Not now. Not like this.

Not ever. He pushed the thought away. He had obligations, to his daughter and to his job. He couldn't pursue a relationship until he figured out how it fit into the rest of his life.

"Are you too tired to drive?" he asked.

"I'm fine. You have to stay with your daughter."

He did. At least Bailey recognized Gabrielle was his top priority. That didn't mean he couldn't make sure she got home okay.

"I could call you a cab," he offered.

"In Stokesville? At three-thirty in the morning?" She shook her head, making her dark hair swing against her cheek. "I'll be fine."

"I'll call you."

She smiled wryly. "Yeah, that's what all the boys say."

"I will. When I get back from Raleigh. I don't want you to go into the station alone."

"All right."

"And don't go to Ellis's house," he said.

Her head snapped up. Well, what did he expect? He'd kissed her, rejected her, and now he was ordering her around like he had some kind of right. Gabby was right. He *was* out of practice.

"Won't Paul suspect something if I don't show up at work?"

Steve hid his relief at her mild tone. "It's Saturday. Do you usually work weekends?"

Her silence answered for her. Of course she did.

"Jesus," he said.

"Only for a couple hours in the morning. I'm baby-sitting for Leann in the afternoon."

"Well, tomorrow morning stay home," Steve ordered. "Maybe he'll figure you're still upset over . . ."

Too late, he saw the pit he'd dug for himself.

". . . upset over a kiss?" Bailey finished for him. *Now* she met his gaze. "That would be pretty stupid, wouldn't it?"

"Understandable," Steve corrected. "He betrayed your trust."

"He did." She took a step toward him. He took a step back. "You didn't."

Raising on tiptoe, she kissed him, her soft, warm lips pressing his clenched jaw, her soft, warm breasts brushing his chest.

His hands curled into fists at his sides. He was in charge here, he reminded himself. He was in control.

But he couldn't breathe.

"Well." She lowered slowly, her gaze searching his face, watching, waiting for a response. A response he wasn't prepared to give.

She sighed. "I'll talk to you in the morning, then."

He let her out of the house, opened her car door and watched her drive away, leaving him staked out between his code as a cop and his need as a man. Aching, unsatisfied . . . and alive again.

He stood on the porch and watched her red taillights disappear in the dark.

REGAN steadied herself against the kitchen counter, still dressed in her cami and boxers, fumbling for the coffeemaker's "on" button. She should have slept in this morning. But her body clock was set for work. At six forty-five, her system jangled awake, and never mind the vodka and valium cocktail she'd downed the night before.

In consequence, she felt like five miles of bad road. Her eyeballs were gritty, her tongue coated with gunk. A headache jackhammered her skull. Even her muscles felt sore, like she'd been bounced over speed bumps or smashed into a concrete retaining wall.

She needed caffeine. At least when dweeb girl was around, she switched on the fucking coffeemaker.

Resentment flared, inescapable as loss and deep as sorrow. Regan hugged it to her. Anger was easier to cope with than grief.

She didn't regret for one second throwing her stepfather's little love interest out of the house. As soon as she was fortified with some coffee—and maybe a shower—she was getting rid of Paul, too.

She slopped the one-percent milk into her mug, ignoring the spill on the counter. Clutching her coffee, she padded toward the stairs.

And saw a black shoe, sticking out from one of the big leather chairs.

He was up already. Paul.

Or maybe he had never been to bed.

She hoped so. She hoped his night was as lousy as hers. Worse.

She stood in the study door, nursing her coffee and her grievance. "Hey."

He didn't answer.

"Paul?"

He had better be asleep. He'd better not think he could ignore her.

Balancing on one bare foot, she nudged his shoe with the other. *"Hey."*

And noticed the gun. In his lap, his hand half curled around the butt.

Her heart stuttered. She took another step forward. "Oh, hey, Paul . . ."

He slumped in the chair, his chin on his chest and a neat, dark hole in the side of his head. A dark line of blood ran down his cheek. More blood flecked his shirt.

Her breath deserted her. *Oh, God. Oh, God.*

How could he do this to her?

"JIM'S okayed the request," Walt told Steve over the phone. "You think maybe you have the actual murder weapon this time?"

The chief's displeasure vibrated clearly through the line. Steve couldn't blame him. Walt's last call to the DA to rush through lab tests hadn't yielded results. And with the council screaming about damage to the town's image and the Channel Five news van parked at the curb, Walt needed results. They all did.

"No reason for Ellis to plant it on Bailey otherwise," Steve said. "He got it out of the house before the search, and if anybody found it, it would be in her possession."

"In an evidence box, you said?"

"That's right. From the Dawler trial."

"So now her boss is dead, she can write the book for him."

Steve felt savage. "She's writing a book. It doesn't have anything to do with the Dawler case, though."

"But she has the evidence."

"What's your point?"

"No point. Except she could benefit from Ellis's death."

"I don't see Bailey Wells murdering her employer on the off chance she might get a book deal."

"Guess not," Walt said. "Well, you'll have to take this—what did you call it? Opti Award—to the lab yourself. I can't spare an officer to drive down to Raleigh every time you turn up a new piece of evidence."

"Not a problem," Steve said, which wasn't strictly true.

If he couldn't find an obliging neighbor to keep an eye on Gabrielle, he would need to take his daughter with him. But he wasn't about to plead another special circumstance to Walt.

"I'll be back by ten to take Bailey Wells's statement."

"You think you're the only one who can conduct an investigation around here?"

Not the only one. Just the best. Bailey had come to him. She trusted him. He'd be damned before he let her down.

He set his coffee mug on the hall table. "I'm the one who took her original statement," he said.

Continuity was more important in solving cases than the most sophisticated lab results. That was one of the pluses of small-town police work.

"As long as that's the only reason," Walt said.

Steve stiffened. "What other reason could there be?"

"You tell me. Tom Sherman saw Dorothy Wells's car parked in front of your place last night."

Steve's gut tightened. And that was one of the minuses. "I told you Bailey brought me the evidence."

"Yeah, but why you?"

He'd asked Bailey the same question when she'd sat

across his mother's kitchen table, her spine straight and her eyes bruised. *Why did you come here tonight?*

And been disappointed by the raw honesty of her answer. *I didn't have anywhere else to go.*

It wasn't nearly enough to satisfy Steve.

But it would do for Walt.

"Because I'm in charge of the investigation," he said. "I'll see you at ten."

Walt snorted. "Suit yourself. Just don't expect any overtime."

Steve cradled the receiver very carefully and stood in the hallway taking deep breaths. He needed this job. He wanted this job. He just hated working for Clegg.

"Where are you going?" Gabrielle asked.

Steve looked up and saw the reason he had to put up with Walt Clegg until the chief's retirement peering through the spindles on the stairs.

"I've got to drive to the lab in Raleigh," he said. "Want to come?"

Gabrielle looked skeptical. "To the lab?"

"I've got to drop something off at the lab," Steve said. Bailey's voice played in his head. *I wish just once he'd said to me, "Hey, honey, State's playing Florida this afternoon. Sit down and watch the game with me."* "I thought we'd stop by Krispy Kreme, grab some donuts for breakfast."

"We can buy donuts here."

"Not hot off the line. When I was in high school, we used to drive up there on Friday nights after football games, four or six of us piled into a truck, cruising to see if that 'hot' sign was flashing in front of the bakery."

"You drove to Raleigh for donuts?"

"Hot glazed donuts." Steve smiled at the memory, and then at his daughter. "You want some?"

"I guess."

"Go get your shoes on."

She ran for her room.

Bailey was right, Steve thought. It wasn't enough.

But it was a start.

"ARE you sure he killed himself?" Macon asked over the phone.

Regan stood in her mother's kitchen, her bare feet curling from the cold tile, listening to a lawnmower from several yards away.

She shuddered. "Of course I'm sure."

What did he think, she'd shot Paul herself?

And if he thought that, what would the police think?

"What should I do?" she asked.

"Call 911."

"You're my mother's lawyer." *You had sex with me last night, you bastard.* "And the best you can come up with is, 'Call 911'?"

"What do you want from me, Regan?" Macon said, his voice pinched. Patient.

She wanted him to be here. Her father was dead, her mother was gone, her brother was too messed up to make it through the fucking funeral, and she was alone in the house with a dead body. Somebody should be here for her, damn it.

"I want you to come over."

"This isn't a good time for me," he said. "You really should let the police handle this."

"But they'll want to talk to me."

"Oh, I'm sure they will."

"What should I do? What should I say?"

"Don't touch anything," he said.

That was such lame advice. Such impersonal, insulting, lame-ass advice.

Regan gripped the receiver tight. "That's not what you said last night."

There was a long, satisfying pause.

"I don't think we should bring up last night," Macon said. *Not quite so impersonal now, you son of a bitch.*

"No? Then you better get your ass over here," Regan said. "Because I'm not talking to the police without a lawyer present, and I'm calling the police now."

"THESE are good donuts," Gabrielle said, licking icing off her fingers.

"The best." Steve passed the white-and-green bakery box across to the passenger seat.

Gabrielle selected another hot glazed. "Grandma says donuts aren't a good breakfast."

"Your grandmother likes oatmeal," Steve said, and Gabrielle grinned. "Now, your grandfather liked donuts. Remember I told you how we used to drive down here in high school?"

Gabrielle nodded.

"Well, sometimes we didn't make it home until really late. After midnight. But as I long as I left Grandpa a box of donuts on the kitchen table, he didn't ground me for breaking my curfew."

His daughter's eyes widened. "Really?"

"Of course, I was older than you. Much, much older." He didn't want her getting any ideas.

She took another bite. "Does Bailey like donuts?"

Uh oh. His daughter had ideas, all right. Not about breaking curfew, but other, equally dangerous ideas.

Steve sipped his coffee, buying time. "Probably. Why?"

Her shoulder lifted in a shrug. He recognized the gesture as his own. "Maybe next time she could come with us."

"Why?" he repeated.

"I like her." Gabrielle's gaze slid to meet his. "Don't you like her?"

He did. He liked Bailey's intelligence and quiet efficiency, her loyalty and self-deprecating humor. He caught himself thinking about her at odd moments, the clean lines and angles of her body, the way she tucked her hair behind her ears, her wide smile lighting her thin face.

He thought about her a lot.

His preoccupation could have been a problem. It was certainly a distraction. But he was a grown man, with a grown man's needs and an adult's awareness. He could explore this new attraction, enjoy it even, without imagining it had to lead to a permanent relationship. He wasn't a lonely, impressionable nine-year-old girl. He had his feelings and the situation under control.

It was important to keep control.

To protect Gabrielle.

"That wouldn't be a good idea," he said.

Gabrielle twisted in her seat. "Why not?"

He eyed her uneasily. Bailey said he should make time to listen to his daughter. But what was he supposed to do when she kept asking questions?

Keep it simple, he decided. Keep it truthful. Most interview subjects incriminated themselves when they elaborated on the truth.

"Because I'm not looking to get involved with anybody right now."

"Why not?"

"Because we're doing fine on our own." *Better, anyway.* He had to believe that. Inspired, he added, "I want to spend my time with you."

"Right," said Gabrielle.

The flatness in her tone shocked him. "Gabby . . ."

She pulled the bakery box toward her and opened it. "It's okay," she said to the donuts. "I just miss Mommy. I miss being a family."

He was shaken to the heart. "Sweetheart . . ."

He didn't know what to say. He watched a tear squeeze between her eyelashes and streak her cheek and didn't know what to do. He couldn't take away her pain. He couldn't give her back her mother.

Moving the box to the back, he reached across the gear shift and gathered his daughter to him, all stiff shoulders and bony knees and streaming eyes.

You can't solve every problem. Sometimes the best you can do is share it.

His own eyes stung. Pressure built in his chest and burned his throat.

"I miss her, too," he whispered against his baby's silky hair, and he held her while she cried.

This is what she'd been missing. What they'd both been missing. For once, he didn't offer promises or solutions. Only comfort.

And maybe comfort was all Gabrielle needed, because her eyes dried quickly. Her grip on his T-shirt eased.

Gratitude filled him, for this chance and for the woman who had urged it on him. For Bailey, who claimed not to know anything about parenting.

Who didn't want to spend her life in Stokesville.

He frowned.

Gabrielle sniffled and rubbed her face against his shirt. "Is that why you don't want to invite Bailey to come with us?"

The truth, Steve reminded himself.

"It's trickier than that, sweetheart." He found a clean paper napkin for her to blow her nose. "She might not want to come."

"But you could ask."

"I could," he acknowledged cautiously.

She might even say yes.

It had been a long time for him, but he could still gauge a woman's interest. Her desire.

He and Bailey Wells had engaged in complicated mental foreplay for almost a week. Last night the tension building between them had erupted in a kiss, dark, thrilling, raw.

Not a situation he was comfortable with. Not a memory he could entertain with his daughter sitting beside him.

Gabrielle.

He needed to think about her. About the risk of letting her get too attached to another woman who would leave her. Leave them both.

His cell phone vibrated. Senses prickling, he stared at the unfamiliar number.

"'S okay," Gabrielle told him, swiping her eyes with the heel of her hand. "I'm okay."

Only partly reassured, he flipped the phone open. "Burke."

"Oh, Lieutenant Burke, thank goodness I reached you." The voice was female and familiar.

His gut tightened. "Who is this?"

"Dotty. Dotty Wells. Bailey's mother? I found your card on her bed."

The tightness constricted into slippery knots. "Where is she? Is she all right?"

"She's at the police station."

Worry and fury leaped in him like fire. He'd told her to wait for him, damn it. His voice cool, he repeated, "What happened? Is she all right?"

"Paul Ellis is dead. Shot. The police are questioning Bailey."

FOURTEEN

He could help her. Would help her. But only after he learned the truth, and only if he kept his cool.

The chief waved him to a chair. Steve ignored it, jamming his hands into his pockets, pacing a line to the file cabinet and back.

Not so cool, after all. But if he couldn't move, he'd explode.

"Who found the body?"

Walt Clegg drew in his chin at Steve's tone, but he answered readily enough. "The stepdaughter. Regan."

"When?"

"Call came in around seven-thirty."

Right after his own conversation with the chief this morning. *You think you're the only one who can conduct an investigation around here?*

"You should have called me," Steve said, keeping his voice even with effort.

"Why? You were on your way to Raleigh." Walt rubbed

the bridge of his nose. "Though I guess I could have saved you the trip."

Anger edged under the worry, a thin, sharp blade. "You're not taking me off the investigation."

Walt rocked back in his chair. The old springs squeaked. "What investigation? Ellis killed his wife and then shot himself. End of story."

Relief caught him like a wave. *Ellis shot himself.* Meaning Bailey didn't.

So why bring her in for questioning?

"You're sure," Steve said, not quite making it a question.

Walt shrugged. "Night of his wife's funeral. No sign of forced entry. No sign of struggle. The way I see it, he's drinking alone in his study, pulls out his revolver and puts a .22 in his head."

"Note?"

"We haven't found one yet."

Okay. His mind weighed, measured, considered options. Suicides sometimes hid notes in places significant only to them. An investigator had to know where to look.

"Who caught the call?"

"Tom Sherman."

Sherman, a ruddy-faced veteran with a diehard nicotine habit, was one of the detectives who had made his resentment of Steve plain. Steve wouldn't help department morale by questioning his handling of the crime scene.

Too bad. "He swab for powder residue?"

"Of course he did. And took the gun for prints." Walt leaned forward over his desk. "But I'm not chasing after zebras when I hear hoofbeats and can see the horse's ass in front of me."

Nothing wrong with that scenario, Steve told himself. Remorse might have driven Ellis to suicide. Maybe the writer couldn't face his guilt anymore. Or maybe, with the investigation closing in, he couldn't face prison.

His motive didn't matter as long as Bailey wasn't involved.

All Steve had to do was keep his mouth shut.

"Where did he get the gun?" he asked.

"What?"

"You said Ellis pulled out his revolver. I searched that house two days ago. There was no gun."

"So, you missed it."

Steve ignored the slur. "Who's it registered to?"

Walt frowned. "It's not registered."

"Then I didn't miss anything," Steve said flatly.

Walt's face turned red. "Except the murder weapon. Or are you wrong about that, too?"

Irritation licked him. He tried to keep any trace of it—or of apology—from his tone. "That award wasn't in the house when I searched. Ellis moved it."

"If you can believe the girl's story."

"I believe her," Steve said quietly. "And Regan Poole can testify she saw Paul Ellis carry a carton identical to the one holding the murder weapon out to Bailey's car. Now tell me why Sherman brought her in."

Walt's gaze dropped. "Goes to the victim's state of mind. She was with him yesterday."

"Hell, Walt, half of Stokesville was in and out of that house yesterday."

"Half of Stokesville wasn't lip-locked with Paul Ellis a couple hours before he put a bullet in his head."

Fuck, Steve thought.

"Is that what she told you?"

"That's what Regan Poole told me. She saw them together."

"Define 'together,' " Steve suggested through his teeth.

The chief waved his hand. "Together. Kissing."

"So he took advantage of her."

"I don't care if he was fucking her six ways to Sunday. But we have to look at her, you know?"

His neck prickled. "Look at her for what?"

"You're the hotshot detective. You need me to draw you a diagram?"

He needed the truth. It might be all he had to protect her.

"What's the time of death?" Steve asked.

"We're waiting on the ME's report."

"But you have some idea."

Walt sighed. "Victim was cold and stiff—fixed lividity, full rigor—at seven-thirty this morning. Say, six to eight hours."

Steve did the math. "So, even at the outside, Ellis was killed sometime between eleven last night and two this morning."

Walt shrugged. "Looks like it."

"Then Bailey wasn't involved."

"I'm not saying she was. But the stepdaughter—"

"Saw Bailey leave the house around eleven."

"She could have come back."

"No. I told you. She was with me."

"Until two in the morning?"

He could save her. He could provide her with an alibi. All he had to do was confess to his chief he had been up half the night with one of the main players in a high-profile case.

"Until after three."

"Well, now." Walt's eyes were as bright as the buttons on his uniform. "Isn't that convenient."

"It's not what you're thinking." *Not exactly.* "She came to me to provide a lead in an ongoing investigation."

"Or provide herself with an alibi."

His fury startled him. It was one thing for Clegg to yank his chain. But he had no call to pick on Bailey.

"She doesn't need an alibi. Not if you're convinced Ellis's death was suicide."

"I am. She isn't. Look, Steve . . ." It was first names now, Steve noted cynically, man-to-man and everybody friendly. "I'm satisfied Ellis killed himself. We'll wait on the autopsy results, of course, but I'm sure the DA will see things my way. Murder solved, case closed, everybody's happy. It's unfortunate, but it's in Miz Wells's best interest to just accept what happened and let all this excitement die down. Because otherwise, with this fuss in the papers, I'll be forced to investigate, and all kinds of things are going to come out that are best left private."

Steve wanted to punch something, a filing cabinet, the wall. He wanted to grab his boss by his pressed uniform shirt, haul him across his desk, and shake him until his service medals rattled. He fisted his hands in his pockets. "Are you threatening her?"

Walt looked genuinely offended. "Hell, no, I'm trying to *help* her. And if you care for the girl, you'll make her see she can help herself by dropping all this talk about how Ellis couldn't have committed suicide."

THE bare white walls, the vinyl upholstered chairs, the cold, hard table . . . Bailey felt like she was in a gynecologist's exam room. If she'd actually been flat on her back with her feet up in stirrups, she wouldn't feel any more uncomfortable.

Any more exposed.

Or alone.

The detective had left. Shivering, she hugged her arms,

her black pants and tank top no more protection against the air-conditioned interview room than a paper gown would have been.

When her mother had called up the stairs to say the police were there to see her, her mind had flown to Steve. Her heart had actually skipped a beat. She hadn't been prepared for Detective Sherman's sidelong looks and yellow teeth. She hadn't dressed for a ride in a squad car to the police station.

She hadn't expected the news about Paul.

He was dead. Shot.

The knowledge surrounded her without quite sinking in, like ice coating a statue. It walled her from the full force and implications of the detective's questions. Her brain felt frozen, her fingers numb.

Before Sherman left her to write up her statement, she had answered all his questions honestly and completely.

She had left the Ellis household around eleven o'clock.

Yes, there had been an altercation with Ms. Poole and Mr. Ellis before she left.

No, she and Mr. Ellis were not having an affair.

Yes, he had been drinking.

Yes, he had a prescription for the tranquilizer Xanax.

Of course he seemed depressed.

At that point, she had realized from the direction of the detective's questions that he believed Paul had killed himself. Her mind rejected the very idea. Her heart shrank from the possibility.

The man she had once imagined she could love—vain, self-absorbed, confident—could not have taken his own life. Paul would always believe he would eventually triumph over lesser mortals, that he could bend circumstances and people to serve his will.

Bailey had been shocked and horrified by the possibility

Paul had murdered his wife. But she could accept him as a murderer more readily than a suicide victim.

She said so, and the interview went downhill from there.

"Let's just go through the evening one more time," Detective Sherman had said, frowning.

Bailey's heart thumped. Her hands were icy.

"Do I need a lawyer?" she asked.

"You're free to go anytime," Sherman said. "But if you wouldn't mind answering just a few more questions . . ."

So she had stayed and answered them. She wasn't under arrest. She hadn't done anything wrong. Steve would tell them.

Pleating her fingers together, she glanced at her watch. Where was Steve? It was after ten o'clock. Maybe if she called him . . .

No.

He was probably on his way back from Raleigh right now. Just because he had kissed her once—*twice*. Her mind supplied details with vivid alacrity . . . Anyway, just because he had kissed her and cooked for her was no reason to consider him her personal protector. He had made it painfully clear last night he preferred to keep their relationship on a professional footing.

I don't mix sex with the job.

Good rule. Given the mess she'd made with Paul, she should have adopted something like it.

She was so cold.

The door cracked in the flat white wall. She braced.

"Bailey?"

Steve.

The door opened and he was there, strong and solid and safe, his big body crowding the tiny room. Her rush of relief embarrassed her. Her throat closed.

His gaze sharpened on her face. "You okay?"

She swallowed. Nodded.

He frowned and reached for his hip pocket. "Here."

A handkerchief.

It blurred as she stared at it. She hadn't realized her eyes were wet.

"Take it," he commanded.

Turning her back, she blotted her eyes and blew her nose. She didn't hear him come up behind her until his hands closed on her shoulders and turned her around. She felt a terrible urge to put her fate in his big, competent hands, to rest her head against his solid chest, and fought to get a grip.

She cleared her throat. "Thanks."

"Not a problem." Steve smiled, but his eyes remained serious, fixed on hers. "It's my day to have women cry on me."

"I'm not crying."

Lines appeared between his brows. "Maybe you should."

She wanted to. She could feel a torrent of mingled emotions rushing and bubbling inside her, like a mountain stream under winter ice.

She clutched his damp, crumpled handkerchief. "They said . . . Detective Sherman implied Paul shot himself."

He released her shoulders. "Looks that way."

The ice encasing her cracked. "He wouldn't."

"I know it's hard to accept," Steve said in a soothing voice, like a traffic cop delivering bad news to the relatives of an accident victim. "It's a natural part of grieving. When somebody we care about dies—"

"Bullshit," Bailey said.

His mouth compressed.

"I'm not grieving," she continued. "And I'm not in denial. I'm telling you Paul Ellis thought too highly of himself to end his own life."

Steve's professional mask flickered. He looked . . . not convinced. But at least he looked interested. He didn't dismiss her as Sherman had dismissed her.

"Under most circumstances, I'd have to agree with you," he said. "But Ellis was facing a specific, real threat. If he went to prison—"

"He wasn't thinking about prison. He was talking about New York. He wanted to go back there."

With me. The thought splintered through her, another warning crack in the ice. *He wanted to go back with me.*

Steve frowned. "Is that what's worrying you? You can't blame yourself for—"

"I'm not blaming myself!" she shouted.

Oops. Too loud. He wouldn't take her seriously if she sounded hysterical.

Wayne Lewis stuck his head through the door, his earnest young face concerned. "Everything all right in here?"

"Fine," Steve said without turning his head. "Close the door."

It clicked quietly shut.

"You can't blame yourself," Steve repeated, still in that calm cop's tone, "because Ellis never knew you weren't returning to New York. Or that you planned to quit. Unless you told him."

Bailey rubbed her bare arms. She felt cold again. "Are you trying to make me feel better? Or asking me if I talked to Paul after I left you last night?"

"Did you?"

She wasn't offended. She wouldn't let herself be.

She moistened her lips. "No. And that's why your suicide theory doesn't make any sense. Paul didn't know I'd turned the murder weapon over to you. So why would he panic and kill himself?"

"He knew he was the principal target of the investigation."

His neutral tone steadied her. Maybe that's why he used it. Easier not to think about how she had jumped his bones in his mother's kitchen when he spoke in that formal, dispassionate voice.

"Which is why he set me up." She took a deep breath. How much more humiliating could this be? "I think he wanted Regan to see us together. You said it yourself last night."

A wealthy wife. A willing, adoring assistant. All he has to do is convince the police you were pressing for more and he told you no. Then, when the weapon is found in your possession . . .

For a second she thought she had him, before his shoulders relaxed and he settled one hip against the table. "You've been spending too much time coming up with crazy theories for your boss's books."

She gaped at him. And then she got mad. Crazy theories? She knew how to do research. How to organize facts. How to fit disparate bits and pieces together to make a coherent sentence or a cohesive case.

"At least I don't ignore facts," she said.

"You want facts?" Was it her imagination, or did he raise his voice slightly? "The fact is, Ellis killed his wife. And if he killed himself, it makes things easier for everybody. Including you."

"Paul wasn't into making things easier for other people."

Steve shrugged. "So he could have had reasons you don't know anything about. Grief makes a man do funny things." His voice was grim. His eyes were bleak. "So does guilt."

She felt a flutter of sympathy, a tug of curiosity. But she couldn't let herself be distracted. "Did he confess?"

"What?"

She was onto something. She was sure of it. Her heart banged against her ribs. "In his note. Did Paul confess to killing Helen in his suicide note?"

Steve met her gaze squarely. "I can't discuss that with you."

Disappointment stole her breath. *Can't discuss . . . ?*

She opened her mouth to argue and caught the quick flicker of his eyes to the door.

Can't discuss. *Oh.* Understanding and relief bloomed in her chest. She hugged her arms tightly to hold them in.

"Well, that's just the most unfair, ridiculous thing I ever heard," she complained.

"Tell me about it," Steve said. "Later."

Her heart skipped. She raised her chin, playing along for whoever might be listening. "Tell you about it? I'm not even speaking to you now."

BAILEY escaped into the hot, bright sunshine. After the cigarette- and coffee-tinged chill of the police station, the scent of sweat and pine cleaner and industrial carpet, even the air of the municipal parking lot was a relief. The ice encasing her was gone, leaving her an emotional puddle.

But she wouldn't wallow. At least, not much.

She walked to the street corner. She wanted closure. She needed answers. As soon as she understood what had happened, she could begin to put it behind her.

Sinking onto a bench under one of the mayor's new street lights, Bailey fumbled for her cell phone.

"Need a lift?" Steve drawled.

And there he was, his big black truck idling at the curb beneath the stoplight.

Her heart sped up, treacherously glad to see him. "I thought you'd gone."

"I parked out back. There's a reporter from *The News and Observer* camped in the lobby."

She nodded. She, too, had been warned against discussing Paul's death with reporters. "At least the news van is gone."

"TV crews are at the house."

Wonderful.

Steve climbed from his cab and held the door open for her.

Gabrielle waved from the shadowed interior of the truck. And Bailey's heart, which had been thumping pleasantly, sank to her flip-flops. Had Steve made his daughter wait for her all this time?

"Hey, kid. What have you been up to?"

"Dad took me to see his office. It was cool. He has games on his computer. I played hearts while you were in fingerprinting. Dad let me get printed, too. And the red-haired lady keeps M&Ms in her desk."

Bailey had hated being printed. Even though Sherman told her she was not being detained, even though she told herself the process would help eliminate her as a suspect, it made her feel like a criminal. Smirched. Dirty, inside and out.

Obviously, Gabrielle didn't feel the same way.

"Kid's made more friends in the department than I have." Steve didn't sound upset about it. More amused. He jerked his head toward the truck. "Get in. We'll give you a ride home."

"Actually . . ." She hesitated. "I have to go to my sister's. I'm baby-sitting this afternoon."

Fascinating to watch the little lines of temper jump between his brows, the swift compression of his mouth. Intriguing to imagine what he would be like in the sack, all that passion, all that control.

Bailey flushed hotly. Not that she was imagining any such thing.

"Don't you ever take time off?" he demanded.

"This is time off. Leann and my mother are going shopping. I can either go with them and try on beaded sweaters and listen to questions about what I'm going to do now that I've wasted two years of my life on a dead man, or I can watch the kids." She gave up fiddling with the strap of her purse to flash him a grin. "I'll take my chances with the kids."

"Why doesn't your brother-in-law watch his kids?"

"It's his golf day. Anyway, I volunteered. I haven't seen much of them since Rose was born, and I-Heart-New York T-shirts only go so far in building a relationship. I told them I was coming. I don't want to let them down."

She knew now that Steve's lack of expression usually meant he was feeling something. "What?"

He shook his head. "Never mind. Hop in."

He didn't want to talk to her, fine. They had to talk sometime. But they couldn't discuss Paul's death in front of Gabrielle or Leann or Leann's kids any more than they could in front of Steve's fellow detectives. And he had made it pretty obvious they weren't going to talk about anything else.

"I don't want to take up any more of your time."

He shook his head. "Not an issue. We're not doing anything special this afternoon."

Gabrielle rolled her eyes. "Or, like, ever."

Bailey choked back a laugh.

"She misses her friends," Steve explained.

"It'll be better when school starts," Bailey offered.

"That's what Dad always says." Gabrielle eyed her speculatively from the passenger seat. "How old are your sister's kids?"

Bailey looked at Steve, expecting him to say something helpful like, "Oops. Got to go." His eyes were half closed, and he was . . . Was he smiling?

"Um, well, Rose is a toddler."

"Oh." Gabrielle looked polite.

"Bryce is only seven. But he's got lots of video games." She twisted her purse strap. Okay, this was a bad idea. *Shut up, shut up.* "And a trampoline in the backyard."

Gabrielle perked up. "A trampoline?"

"It's not safe," Steve said.

"Da-ad."

Bailey shrugged. "It seemed okay to me the last time I was on it."

"You jumped on it?" Gabrielle grinned. "I'd like to see that."

"So would I," Steve murmured.

At least, that's what she thought he said.

Thoroughly embarrassed, she said, "I just thought—if you're not doing anything—Gabrielle might like to come along and check it out. Just for a little while," she added hastily. "Since you're dropping me off anyway. What do you think?"

"I think it sounds cool," Gabrielle announced. "Can we, Dad?"

He met Bailey's gaze, and her breath backed up in her lungs. He'd say no. Of course he'd say no. He didn't mix sex with the job, and she was sure he was every bit as good at compartmentalizing his personal life.

"Why not?" he drawled.

FIFTEEN

STANDING in her sister's *Southern Living* sunroom, Bailey watched her mother flutter around Steve and thought this was one of the worst ideas of her life.

Not *the* worst.

Not as bad as giving up her job at Paragon Press to work for Paul or giving up her little apartment to move in with her parents. But definitely up there with, say, trying out for the basketball team or letting Alicia in marketing convince her to include "likes to try new things" in her on-line dating personality profile.

Taking a deep breath, Bailey said, "And of course you remember my sister, Leann."

Nobody forgot Leann. *Blond, right? Cheerleading squad?*

And too young for him. Which meant he must consider Bailey in the same league as Gabrielle.

"Why, Steve Burke. It's been ages." Leann pressed her cheek to his, enveloping him in charm and a cloud of

Beautiful by Estee Lauder. "It's nice to see Bailey's taste in men is finally improving."

"Nice to see you, too," Steve said blandly, which wasn't quite the same, but her sister didn't notice.

He stepped back, so that his hip nudged Bailey's, and drew his daughter in front of him. Bailey's heart bumped. To someone who didn't know any better, they must look like a unit.

"And this is Gabrielle," he said.

Leann blinked at Steve's black-eyed, honey-skinned daughter. "Aren't you just the sweetest thing. Was your mama from around here?"

Bailey gritted her teeth. "Trampoline," she said. "Out back. I'll show you."

"Okay."

Steve's hands cupped his daughter's shoulders. "Gabrielle's mother was from Brazil."

"Like the nuts," Dorothy said.

"More nuts in Stokesville," Bailey muttered. "We're going out back. Come on, Bryce. Gabrielle?"

Collecting the older kids, she retreated to the backyard, leaving her sister in possession of the field. *Running away again.* No, not running away. She'd made a choice to protect this amazing kid. Looking at Gabrielle's bright face as she climbed on the trampoline, Bailey thought their escape felt less like a rout and more like victory.

THAT little bitch Regan thought she controlled him. That she was using him.

But Macon prided himself on his control. And he had every intention of using her.

She huddled in a kitchen chair clutching a mug of coffee. She had received him and the police in a skimpy top and shorts Macon would never have allowed his own daughter to wear out of the house. Her layered blond hair was dragged into a ponytail. Mascara smudged her eyes.

Macon liked a woman to be put together. Marylou didn't go to the grocery store without fresh lipstick and a tennis bracelet on. But the trashy look turned him on. Always had. He'd like to bend little Miss Regan over the kitchen table and fuck her hard from behind.

Later for that.

"You'll need help with the final arrangements," he said smoothly. "Did Paul leave any written instructions?"

"I don't know. I'm not his fucking secretary."

Macon hid his impatience. "In his office, maybe?"

"The police took everything in his office."

Macon's gut tightened. "Everything?"

Her manicured nails tapped her cup. "Well, almost everything. His computer and notes and stuff. It's all listed on the search warrant."

"He might have videotaped a will," he said craftily. "Or audiotaped it. I've had clients do both. I could look for you."

"Why?"

That cool gaze from those Barbie blue eyes unsettled him. He had to think before he spoke. "I'm sure your mother's life insurance reverts to you and your brother on Ellis's death. But it would be good to know how the rest of his estate is disposed."

"Yeah, because it would be so great if I could tell the police I had another motive for wanting the son of a bitch dead."

Her crudeness offended him. Aroused him. Who would have guessed a girl from Regan's background would have such a mouth on her? But the Poole side of the family had always been a little common.

"Or you might convince the police you had no motive at

all," he said easily. "All the evidence suggests Ellis killed himself anyway."

"Or Bailey did." Regan rested her head on her hand. She was pale this morning. "I told Detective Sherman the two of them were screwing around on my mother."

And wasn't that lucky?

Macon rubbed his chin. "Might be interesting to see if he left her anything in his will. Would she have a copy?"

"I don't know. She took some boxes with her when I kicked her out. But I think it was mostly work stuff."

Nerves tingled. "Do the police know?"

"Don't think so. It was before they searched the house."

Better and better.

"Where's she staying? In case I need to be in touch with her about the estate."

"Not here, that's all I care about." Regan's mug clunked on the table. "With her family, I guess."

Family could be a problem. Or not.

On a Saturday afternoon, George Wells would be behind the counter at the hardware and tackle store, dispensing bloodworms and advice to weekend fishermen. The mother would be . . . Macon tried to remember how his own wife spent the afternoon. Tennis? Grocery shopping?

The Wells girl was probably still at the police station.

He rubbed his palms on the thighs of his slacks. Everything would work out. With a little planning, a little luck, everything always worked out.

FIFTEEN-MONTH-OLD Rose fussed at being separated from her mother.

"She'll settle down as soon as I'm gone," Leann said, pausing to check her lipstick in the mirror. "You sure you don't mind?"

"We're fine," Steve said shortly. "I know what to do."

He could handle a toddler. Now, if he could just get her mama and her grandma out the door . . .

Hoisting the kid in his arms, he handed her a toy from the floor. Pouting, she tossed it back down.

"Nice throw," he told her, and repeated the process until Leann and Dorothy realized he wasn't going to play with them anymore and left.

The front door banged.

Rose's eyes widened. Her lower lip stuck out.

"You want to find your Auntie Bailey?"

She stared at him mistrustfully.

"Let's go." He hitched her on his hip and walked through the empty house. "She said the backyard. So we'll just—"

He glanced through the back window and his mind blanked.

Bailey was on the trampoline, flushed and laughing. Bouncing. Her feet were bare. Her hair flew. Her breasts . . . Jesus, had he ever thought her breasts were too small?

She was holding hands with his daughter, coaxing Gabrielle to laugh and jump with her while her nephew bounded around them. Gabby looked as giggly and relaxed as a nine-year-old should. And Bailey . . .

He should be ashamed of himself, ogling her while he held a baby in his arms. But Bailey looked amazing, her slim shoulders and delicate collarbone exposed by that skinny black tank top, her breasts . . .

Steve blew out a short breath and thanked God for gravity and summer. Bailey looked hot.

And he was getting hotter by the second.

He jerked the back door open to get some air. Hot air. It rose from the grass like a breathing beast and gripped him in a sweaty fist.

Bailey's head turned. She widened her stance, finding her balance on the shifting trampoline as the kids jumped around and behind her.

"Hey." She smiled, pushing her hair back from her face, and everything inside him quivered and went still. "Are they gone?"

"Yeah," he said hoarsely.

He couldn't take his eyes off her. She didn't look like a skinny, slightly neurotic New York publishing professional. She looked glowing. Vital. Pretty pink cheeks, pretty naked feet. She wore a silver toe ring. Now why the hell did that turn him on? He was thirty-eight years old. Too damn old to discover a sudden foot fetish.

Her smile faded. "Is everything all right? You look—"

"Daddy! Watch me! Look what Bailey taught me."

His heart, which had been pounding in his chest, catapulted into his throat as his daughter grabbed the side of the trampoline and flipped over and off.

She landed on her feet and came up grinning. "Isn't that cool?"

He cleared his throat. "Very cool."

Bailey frowned. "I told you not to do that without a spotter."

Unabashed, Gabrielle switched the smile to her. "Sorry. I forgot."

She flipped back on the tarp, and Bailey slithered off.

Desire slapped him. Her skinny little shirt clung to her breasts and ribs. Her pants rode low on her hips, exposing a pale line of smooth stomach. With the sun on her hair and a sheen on her skin, she smelled like every summer he'd spent experimenting with sex behind the bleachers of the football stadium.

He forced his gaze to her face. "Thanks for watching out for her."

"I really did tell her to use a spotter," Bailey said.

"I meant before. With your sister."

"Oh." Her already pink cheeks got pinker. He wanted to test their temperature with his thumb. "Leann didn't mean anything by it. Sometimes my family can be a little . . ."

Tactless?

Prejudiced?

Self-absorbed?

"Oblivious," she said.

"Tough on you," he observed.

"Oh, no." Her protest was automatic and, he thought, sincere. "I'm used to it."

He smiled at her. "That's what I meant."

The moment stretched between them, shimmering like the heat rising from the grass.

Rose snapped it, wriggling in his arms. "Jump!"

"No, you don't." He collared her as she flung her small body at the trampoline.

Bailey cleared her throat. "Nice catch."

"This age is easy." He adjusted the toddler on his hip as his gaze sought Gabrielle, laughing and chasing Bryce around the trampoline. "The hard part comes later."

"Jump!" Rose demanded.

"I can take her," Bailey said. "It's almost time for her nap anyway. Hey, munchkin. Want some juice?"

He transferred the squirming toddler to her hold, his gut tensing as her hair brushed his arm, as the back of his hand pressed against her breast.

Stepping back hastily, he hooked his thumbs in his back pockets. Rose patted Bailey's face with starfish hands, poking tiny fingers into Bailey's mouth, giggling when she pretended to bite.

Steve appreciated the picture they made, the blond, plump-cheeked toddler in the arms of the dark, thin-faced young woman. They had the same eyes, dark brown, wary, and nearly identical smiles.

Yearning raked his heart.

He'd wanted more kids.

An only child himself, he had dreamed of a brother or sister for Gabrielle.

We're too busy, Teresa had protested. *Your job, mine, the house, the baby . . .*

He hadn't pushed. They had plenty of time.

"You ever want kids?" he asked.

Bailey blinked, removing Rose's fingers from her mouth to answer. "I guess. But there were other things I wanted more. Or wanted first. I always figured there'd be time, you know?"

Plenty of time, they told themselves.

And then Teresa was diagnosed with cancer, and there was no time at all.

"Yeah."

"Yeah." She smiled ruefully as she met his gaze. "Only now I'm twenty-six-years old, and I haven't been on a date in six months, and I'm beginning to wonder if my mother is right about my biological clock."

He glanced—he couldn't help it—at her pale, flat belly above the black drawstring of her pants. She was worried about her biological clock?

"So you should start dating."

That was smooth. Almost as smooth as his suggestion last night that they make a fresh start.

"It's not that easy."

He raised his eyebrows. "There are no men in New York?"

"Plenty of men. Even straight, single men. And lots and lots of women. And everyone is concerned with where you live and how you get to work and whether you accessorize well with their job or their friends or their image. Do you put out? Do you fit in? Do you measure up? Because if you don't, they cut their losses and move on."

"You're describing boys. Not men."

"Oh, right, like you don't feel the same way."

Her accusation was true enough to sting. "I sure as hell never considered you an accessory."

"Except maybe to murder."

Their eyes locked.

"That's not the same thing," Steve said evenly, "and you know it."

Bailey's gaze dropped. "You're right. I'm sorry."

She turned toward the trampoline. "I'm putting Rose down for her nap," she called. "Be good."

"Okay," her nephew promised.

Bailey looked at Gabrielle. "And no—"

"—flips!" Gabrielle finished for her.

Bailey headed for the house, the baby on her hip.

Steve watched her go. He was doing his job, damn it. He didn't owe her anything. She hadn't asked for anything—not an apology, not an explanation.

It pissed him off.

He caught up with her at the back door and held it open. "Cops learn to compartmentalize," he said. "Depersonalize. It's part of the job."

"And you don't mix sex with the job. I got it. I'm fine with it." Bailey maneuvered the baby's fat little legs into the high chair and strapped her in. "The fact is, you don't fit into my life any better than I fit into yours."

She wasn't saying anything he hadn't thought himself.

They weren't simply on opposite sides of a case. They were at completely different stages in life. The twelve-year gap in their ages might as well be twenty. He had no business lusting after a bright, ambitious girl like Bailey. His best years were behind him.

She had the rest of her life in front of her.

Assuming he could get her out of this mess.

He watched her pour juice into a sippy cup. "I met my wife Teresa on the job."

Now why the hell had he said that?

Bailey snapped on the cup lid. "What did you do, arrest her for jaywalking?"

He leaned against the counter, enjoying her nervous energy as she moved around the kitchen. "Her family owned—owns—an import/export business specializing in furniture and antiques. Gang broke into their Georgetown showroom one night. It was my case."

Bailey handed her niece her juice. "But she wasn't a suspect."

"Not once I ruled out insurance fraud as a motive for the break-in," he said blandly.

Bailey's chin tilted. "You make a habit of getting involved with women you've cleared from criminal charges?"

He fought a smile. "You're the first."

"Second. And I'm not cleared yet."

He sobered. "You will be. Walt Clegg believes Ellis committed suicide."

"I don't think he did."

His attention sharpened. "So you said."

She faced him, crossing her arms under her breasts. "Are we going to talk about it?"

It was a line drawn in the sand. On the one side was the honesty he owed her. On the other was his integrity as a cop. He had never blurred the boundary between public service and his private life. He never crossed that line.

"Now?"

"You said 'later,'" she reminded him.

He liked her. He was worried about her. But this information sharing thing could only go one way. "I do have a few questions. After you put the kid down for her nap."

"I've answered a lot of questions today. I've had enough questions." She bent to unstrap her niece from the high chair, exposing the long, lovely line of her back, the small, vulnerable bumps of her spine. Straightening, she turned with the child in her arms. Her chin raised. "I want answers."

Desire and regret churned inside him. "I can't give you what you want."

"Yeah, you made that clear last night."

A muscle twitched behind his eyes. *Vulnerable?* She was killing him.

"So I'm offering you a trade," she said. "I'll give you what you want if you give me what I want."

His throat went dry. She didn't mean it. Not like it sounded. *I'll give you what you want . . .*

"I can help you," she continued earnestly. "I know Paul. I'll tell you anything you want to know. But in return, I want to know how he died."

She was offering to trade *information*. Steve wanted to laugh at himself, but relief and disappointment made him dumb.

"Well." She shifted the baby on her hip. "You think about it."

"I will," he promised.

It was a damn sight safer than thinking about what he'd do if she actually offered him sex again.

FUCKING dog wouldn't shut up.

The barking started as soon as he emerged from the trees. He had cut through the woods at the back of the lot, leaving his car parked in the shade at the bottom of the Pritchard's pasture a quarter mile away.

Thank God the neighbors had a fence.

The dog quieted some when he let himself in the back door. But then it started up again, deep, aggressive barks that might have scared off an ordinary intruder.

Around these parts, a barking dog was as common as fried chicken on a Sunday. Still, it was a nuisance. If he were caught, there would be questions.

He couldn't afford to get caught.

Too bad he couldn't shoot the dog the way he'd gotten rid of Ellis. The thought almost made him smile.

Kneeling on the floor of the upstairs bedroom, he lifted the lid of the last box. Sweet Jesus, what was that? He took it out, flipped it open, his heart pounding.

Not what he was looking for. But potentially damning, all the same. He stuffed it in his shirt.

Another burst of barking made him jerk. Damn *that dog*. Crossing to the window, he glanced out.

And saw a car sitting in the driveway. A car that hadn't been there fifteen minutes ago.

He froze, panic icing his veins. Somebody was home. He wasn't alone anymore.

He forced himself to be calm. To think. He had to leave before he was found. Before—*fuck!*—before he found what he was looking for.

A heavy lamp stood by the bed, brass, with a white shade. Taking the shade off, he hefted the base like a club. He had to protect himself. A man had a right. It wasn't his fault.

In the hallway, he could hear the muted voice of an ESPN announcer coming from the living room. He crept down the stairs, his breathing fast and shallow.

BAILEY was fading fast, and she wasn't any closer to getting what she wanted.

She frowned at Steve, big and masculine and reassuring in a floral print chair—her sister spent more on sunroom furniture than Bailey earned in a month—and thought she never got what she wanted.

Maybe it was time to do something about that.

"You need to let the police do their job," Steve said for what had to be the fourth time since she'd come downstairs.

"I might if I knew what you all were actually doing." Bailey didn't even try to keep the exasperation from her voice. "That detective—Sherman?—wouldn't tell me anything."

"He wouldn't want to influence your testimony."

She snorted. "Right. Like he believed me anyway."

Outside, the kids sucked freezer pops under the shadow of the trampoline. Bryce had blue stains around his mouth. Gabrielle was smiling. Bailey sighed. So that was one good thing she had managed to do today.

"What did you tell him?" Steve asked.

She pulled herself together. "The same thing I told you. Paul would not have killed himself."

"Not about that," Steve said. Neutral. Patient. "Did you tell him you were with me?"

"Yes." Doubt seized her. "Shouldn't I have?"

"Of course."

"Because I didn't think about whether it would get you into trouble." And she should have.

"It's all right. I told the chief myself. You have an alibi for the time of death."

She wasn't thinking about her alibi. She was glad he was, glad and grateful, but his let-me-take-care-of-that-little-lady routine chafed.

"And if I didn't?"

"You do. Everything's going to be okay."

"You keep telling me that. But I don't know that. You won't talk to me."

"What do you want me to say?"

She wanted closure. She wanted absolution. She wanted . . . more than he was willing to give her, obviously.

She squared her shoulders and met his eyes. "I want to know what Paul said in his note."

He stood there, not saying anything. A muscle ticked at the corner of his mouth.

And she knew.

Pressure built in her chest. "There was no note, was there?"

"Ellis's death is still under investigation. I can't divulge—"

"That's why you won't tell me. Because you know I know Paul would leave a note."

"Not every suicide writes a note."

She was tired of his "Me Cop, You Civilian" attitude. Maybe she didn't have his experience, but she read. She researched.

"The absence of a note is still a marker for homicide. Suicides who don't leave notes tend to be elderly, emotionally isolated, or have lost the ability to communicate." His eyes narrowed, so at least she had his attention. She talked faster, afraid at any moment he would retreat again behind his blue wall. "Paul was a writer. He would have left a note."

"Maybe we just haven't found it yet."

Her breath stopped at his tacit admission. He was telling her—indirectly—there was no note.

"It's not just the note," she said. "Paul never expressed any intention to commit suicide. He didn't make any preparations. He didn't even say good-bye."

"That's a good argument," Steve said slowly. She relaxed in her seat, flushed and vindicated. "But it's just an argument. The crime scene evidence supports suicide."

She sat up again. "What about the medical examiner's report?"

"This isn't like Helen's death. There are no suspicious wounds. No lacerations. I talked with Sherman. Ellis was killed at close range by a .22-caliber bullet."

"But he didn't own a gun. Not that I ever knew about. I told Detective Sherman that."

Steve's eyes narrowed. "You told Sherman."

"Yes."

He paced the bright, narrow room. "He could have acquired one. It's not hard to buy a gun in North Carolina."

"On the day of his wife's funeral? You searched the house Thursday night."

His mouth quirked. "Thought of that, did you?"

Was that respect in his voice?

She flushed. "I'm not stupid. Well, except about men. I was dumb about Paul."

"Then why do you care if he shot himself? It doesn't help you any if his death is ruled a homicide. On the contrary. So what are you after? What are you trying to prove?"

She stared at him, stunned by his sudden attack. "I haven't thought about it."

"Maybe you'd better. Before Regan Poole tells everybody in town you killed your boss because he wouldn't marry you."

She couldn't breathe. She couldn't think. "Is that what she's saying?"

He watched her with flat, black eyes. "Close enough."

Blood buzzed in Bailey's head. "That bitch." She stood jerkily and then sank down again when the floor tilted under her. "If anybody shot him, it would be her. I couldn't. I didn't. I . . ."

"Loved him?"

"No! But I knew him. I worked with him." Her voice

shook. Her hands shook, too. She clasped them together in her lap. "And it's wrong if somebody killed him. How I feel about him doesn't matter. I want . . ."

A void opened in her chest. She teetered on the edge, staring into the chasm that had swallowed all her assumptions, all her plans and dreams.

What did she want?

"Justice," Steve suggested quietly.

She remembered his words that day at the bottom of her parents' driveway. *You do justice to the victims by putting their killer in jail.*

That was it. That was almost it.

"The truth." She seized on the word with relief, held it like something hard and precious she'd found in the mud. "I guess I just want the truth."

Steve stood over her, his hands in his pockets, his face unreadable. "Then we want the same thing."

She looked up, surprised.

And he kissed her.

Soft, like love words whispered in the dark. Warm, like a salute. So good. Confusion and pleasure crashed inside her. His tongue touched her bottom lip, a promise of intimacy, a hint of heat, and withdrew.

He straightened, his breathing rapid and his dark eyes turbulent. Her hands fisted in her lap.

"Dad, can we play video games in Bryce's room?"

Shaken, Bailey turned her head and saw Gabrielle and Bryce standing at the back door.

"For a little while." Steve rubbed the back of his neck. "Don't wake the baby if you go upstairs."

"Okay."

Her nephew galloped through the room.

Gabrielle dawdled, her gaze darting from Bailey to her father.

Bailey's face burned.

"Did you want something?" Steve asked dryly.

His daughter grinned at him. "Maybe."

Gabrielle's convinced herself—or maybe my mother convinced her—that if I had a wife, we could all move back to D.C.

"Then go upstairs," Steve said, and her grin widened.

"Hey, Bailey," she called as she danced past. "Thanks for the freeze pops."

Bailey scraped together her composure. "You're welcome."

The girl thundered upstairs, shouting at Bryce to wait.

But the world she brought in with her lingered in her wake, crowding the narrow, sunlit space, pressing on Bailey like the heat of the afternoon.

Did she and Steve really want the same things?

Aside from the accident of attending the same schools, of knowing the names of the same teachers and streets, what did they have in common?

Born in the same town, they might as well have sprung from different worlds. They were coming into this relationship—not that they had a relationship, exactly—with different expectations. Experience.

Baggage.

He had kissed her. Her belly quivered at the memory of his kiss. And her heart stumbled.

But still, she was way past the age when she could pretend a kiss could make everything better.

She looked at him, his impassive face and dark, hot eyes, and waited for him to say something.

"Guns don't take prints well," he said. "Anybody smart enough to shoot Ellis and set it up to look like suicide will have wiped the gun anyway."

Bailey blinked. "What about . . . um . . ."

Cops learn to compartmentalize, he had said. *Depersonalize.* Could she do that?

"What about the residue tests?" she said. "Won't those at least prove whether or not Paul fired the gun?"

"On *CSI*? Sure. In real life—" Frowning, Steve reached for his cell phone. "I have to take this."

"You go right ahead," she said sweetly. "You want me to go upstairs and play?"

Oh God, she sounded like her mother.

He shot her an annoyed look and flipped open his phone. "Burke."

His body went utterly, unnaturally still, his face wiped of expression.

Her stomach pitched. *Bad news,* she thought.

"Condition?" His eyes were hard. "All right. We'll meet you there."

Her breathing hitched. *We?*

"Not necessary," Steve said into the cell phone. "She's with me."

Oh, God. Bailey swallowed. "What is it?"

"No, I'll handle it. Yeah. Fifteen minutes."

He snapped shut the phone.

"What is it? Was there a—" *Oh, God.* "Was there an accident?"

"No. Your mother and Leann are fine."

"Then . . ."

"There was a break-in at your parents' house," he said gently.

"A . . ." She worked moisture into her mouth. "But she wasn't there, right? You said she was fine."

"Your mother and Leann were still out shopping. But—"

Bailey froze in rejection. "No."

She didn't want to hear. She didn't want to know. She

was a writer. She knew the power of words. As long as he didn't say it, it couldn't have happened.

He said, still in that grave, calm, cop's voice, "Your father was in the house. They think he came home when the intruder was upstairs."

"Is he . . ."

Steve regarded her, a terrible compassion in his eyes. "He's at the hospital. Is there someone you can call to watch the kids? I'll take you there."

SIXTEEN

STEVE hated hospitals.

Teresa had, too, which made it even more unfair she had ended her life in one. But at the end, she was too ill to resist him.

He was sorry for that now. Now that it was too late.

Compared to the chaos of Greater Southeast in D.C., the emergency department at Chapel Hill was almost orderly. The chairs looked more comfortable, too. But on a Saturday afternoon, the waiting area was full of people who couldn't afford doctors or couldn't wait for one. Phones rang, stock carts rattled, and babies cried under the invasive hum of the fluorescent lights. A white-faced teen in shin guards turned his face into his mother's shoulder. An elderly man patted the arm of his mumbling wife, who kept making furtive attempts to stand. The air was sharp with disinfectant, thick with pain and patience and despair.

Bailey braced in a chair, still in the tank top and exercise pants she must have been wearing when Sherman picked her up this morning. The harsh lighting revealed the lines of strain around her mouth and the fatigue like bruises under her eyes.

His instinct was to take her in his arms and comfort her.

But after her first, involuntary protest, Bailey had rallied, calling Leann's cell phone to break the news to her mother and sister, making arrangements with a neighbor to stay with her sister's kids and Gabrielle. Making herself useful. Going through the motions, as if efficiency could hold disaster at bay.

She would have made a good soldier, he thought. *Or a cop's wife.*

She glanced up as he approached from the nurses' station.

"He's conscious," he reported. "They just let your mother go back to sit with him."

"How is he?"

He gave her the best answer he could. "The nurse says he looks good. They're waiting to see the doctor now."

"Can I see him?"

"Maybe later. They only let one family member back at a time."

"Leann?"

"As soon as she heard your father was stable, she went home to be with the kids. We probably passed her in the parking garage."

"You should go get Gabrielle."

And leave Bailey here alone?

Steve had worried Gabrielle might object to being left in an unfamiliar place. But she heard "hospital" and "father," and went into Good Child mode.

"Don't worry, Dad. We'll be fine," she had said before dragging Bryce upstairs for more video games.

Making herself useful. Going through the motions. Just like Bailey.

His heart ached for them both.

"My mom will be back from her trip soon. I'll stick around until the doctor comes out to talk to you," he said.

In case the news was bad.

Bailey frowned. "But he's all right, you said."

"Yeah."

Probably. The triage nurse had thrown around a lot of big words and scary phrases like subdural hematoma and intracranial bleeding. But they didn't actually know anything until the X ray results came back. How much should he prepare her? What did she need to know?

"He's got a headache."

"A headache? Or a concussion?"

Steve shrugged. "He was out for a while."

"What does that mean?"

"You lose consciousness, you probably have a concussion." Probably, his ass. For sure. "Happens to football players all the time."

"My father wasn't playing football," she said sharply.

"No," he admitted.

"Somebody *hit* him," she said, like she was trying to make sense of it, to make what had happened fit the world she knew.

He knew how she felt. He'd felt that way, too.

It was his job to find answers, but explanations had failed him when he needed them most.

It was the sheer ordinariness, the unexpectedness, of tragedy that took your breath away, the accident on the road you drove every day, the bullet that shattered a window and killed the child sleeping in her crib, the cancer discovered during a routine physical appointment, the plane coming out of the clear September sky.

Random, senseless, unavoidable loss. You couldn't stop

it. All you could do was sort through the wreckage, searching for clues to comfort the survivors.

"We'll find whoever's responsible," he said.

Her eyes, her wonderful, expressive eyes, focused on his face. "What happened, exactly?"

Maybe talking about the case would take her mind off whatever was going on beyond those double doors. Or maybe it would only help him.

"Near as we can tell, somebody walked through the back door while your father was at work. He left the hardware store about three o'clock. Neighbor heard her dog kicking up a fuss sometime around then, growling and barking. She finally looked out a back window, saw a man running away from the house toward the woods, and called 911. Chief Clegg was right around the corner, so he stopped by to check things out. Found your father's car in the driveway and the back door unlocked."

"The back door is always unlocked," Bailey said.

"Sugar, in Stokesville everybody's back door is always unlocked. Which is probably what the intruder was counting on. Anyway, when nobody came to the door, Clegg let himself in. And found your father on the living room floor."

"It couldn't have been . . . I don't know." Her hands rose and fell in her lap. "A stroke? A fall?"

"Not unless he fell and hit the back of his head with a bedroom lamp."

The words lay between them, heavy and stiff as a corpse.

Bailey exhaled. "Okay, not a fall. So, what happened?"

"Our best guess is your father came home and surprised the intruder upstairs."

"What was he doing upstairs?"

"Probably looking for cash. Jewelry. Anything small he

could turn into a quick fix. Your mother will have to go through the house, see what's missing."

She shook her head. "This is Stokesville, not D.C. We don't do junkie burglaries."

"The whole county has a growing meth problem. And you've got gangs moving in from Raleigh and Durham. Of course, it's possible your father spooked the guy and he ran off without taking anything."

"Did Dad see him? Could he identify him?"

"The chief tried to get a description when your father came to. But he doesn't remember anything. He was watching TV on the couch when he was struck from behind. He probably didn't see anything."

"Not if ESPN was on," Bailey said ruefully. "What about the neighbor? What did she see?"

"Not much from the back. White male, medium build, wearing jeans and a ball cap."

"That narrows it down to, what? Half the population of Orange County?"

"Maybe a third." Frustration stuck in his throat. "We'll do our best."

Bailey took his hand and squeezed. As if this time his best would be good enough. "I know you will."

Surprise held him speechless. She had pretty hands, long fingered, with neat, unpolished nails. He'd indulged a few private, inappropriate thoughts about those hands on his body.

But Bailey had never before initiated any physical contact between them, never touched him the way a woman does when she wants a man's attention, never patted his arm or brushed his shoulder or touched her fingertips to his chest to make a point.

It felt . . . nice.

He tightened his hand on hers.

A baby wailed. A nurse called the limping teenager back to an exam bay. Patients walked or were wheeled through the sliding doors. An hour passed, bringing another nurse. A different baby.

"You must be used to this," Bailey said.

"This?" he said cautiously.

She flapped her free hand at the shifting population of the chairs. "This. The waiting. It sucks."

She'd been up almost all night. She must be exhausted. "You want something? Water? A magazine?"

"No, thank you. Was she sick a long time?"

I want answers, she'd said. *I'll give you what you want if you give me what I want.*

"Who?" he asked.

"Your wife. You said she had cancer."

He didn't talk about it.

"You want a story, I'll buy you that magazine. Hell of a lot more entertaining."

Her gaze was warm and level. "I'm sorry. This must be hard for you."

"I'm fine."

"You probably spent a lot of time in hospitals."

She was harder to fool than the grief counselor. Or maybe just harder to shake.

"Not really. By the time we knew Teresa was sick, it was already too late."

"You didn't have any . . . warning?" Her quiet voice pulled at him, plucking at memories like loose threads in a tapestry.

"She'd gained a little weight. Lost her appetite. We thought . . . I hoped she might be pregnant. But she kept saying no. So after the second home pregnancy test turned up negative, I finally talked her into seeing a doctor."

Bailey squeezed his hand. "And?"

"She had stage-four epithelial ovarian cancer." He could say it. He could say the words. "She had the first surgery, for the diagnosis. But after that . . . There are treatments. Chemo. Radiation. More surgeries, to debulk the tumors and clear the blockage of the intestine. But she wouldn't . . . She didn't want . . ."

He stared very hard at the clock on the opposite wall until the numbers blurred.

"I'm sorry," Bailey said again, softly. "I didn't know."

"Palliative treatment, they call it. Drain the fluids, to relieve the pressure. Pills, for the pain. We fought about it all the time. I didn't want her to suffer. I just . . . Christ, I wanted her to live."

"Of course you did."

"At the end, she couldn't make decisions herself anymore. I took her to the hospital. Hell, I dragged her to the hospital. Only by then . . ." He drew a harsh breath. "She couldn't eat. The doctors—they wanted to feed her through a tube. She could live a little longer that way, they said."

"Is that what she wanted?"

"No." He rubbed his hands over his face. "No."

"What did you do?"

He dropped his hands. "I told them no." He stared again at the opposite wall, not seeing it, not seeing anything but his wife, begging him with her eyes. "I let her die."

He wasn't asking for pity. He had no right to her sympathy or her understanding. But maybe that wouldn't matter to her.

She blinked those big brown eyes at him. Intelligent eyes. Compassionate eyes.

"That's crap," she said.

His jaw slackened. He clenched it tight. He should never have opened his mouth. "Forget it."

But Bailey wasn't finished with him. "You're not responsible for your wife's illness. Or her treatment plan. Or her death."

"I don't want to talk about it."

"Maybe you should. Maybe then you could deal with this misplaced sense of guilt instead of brooding about it."

Something like panic kindled inside him. He blew it into rage. Anger was cleaner, easier to handle.

"You don't know what the hell you're talking about."

She touched him again, her fingers light on his bare arm, stirring him in ways he thought he was done with. He wanted her touch.

And he didn't, because he was sitting here talking about his wife the way he never talked about her to anybody, missing his wife, cheating on his wife by lusting after Bailey.

"So explain it to me," she said.

"You wouldn't understand. I let Teresa down. I let Gabby down."

"You did your best."

"It wasn't enough."

He had always been able to protect them. The big, tough cop. The competent male. *My hero,* Teresa used to tease, watching him slide off his shoulder holster before joining her in bed.

But he hadn't protected her, he hadn't been there for her, when it mattered most. He lost her.

And he'd lost himself.

"Miss Wells?" A tall young man in nurse's scrubs with a single diamond stud in his ear claimed her attention. "You can come back now. Only one of you," he added when Steve stood with her.

Steve was in no mood to argue. He flashed his badge instead.

The nurse looked unimpressed. "Right. Another one. Well, come on. Maybe you can talk your boss into getting out of my worklane."

Bailey clasped her hands in front of her. "Has the doctor seen my father yet?"

The young man smiled. "Seen your father and talked to your mama. They're both going to be just fine."

"When can he go home?"

"Doctor wants to keep him for observation overnight." The nurse pushed open the swinging doors, moving like a sprinter in his white athletic shoes. "But his films look good."

Fighting off temper, Steve followed them. He was here to provide escort and support, he reminded himself. But he was still stirred up inside. His feelings churned like water released from ice, threatening the detachment he had hidden behind so long.

In the lane on the other side, Walt Clegg made his way down the row of curtained beds like a politician working a Fourth of July picnic.

Steve stopped. *Shit.* The last thing he needed now was to go another round with his boss.

"You all take care," Walt said to a patient. "This heat's killer . . . Margaret, how's that grandbaby of yours?"

He saw Steve with Bailey, and his expression hardened. "Miz Wells." He nodded. "Sorry about your daddy."

"Thank you. Is he—"

"This way," the nurse said.

Walt's gaze cut to Steve. "Stick around a minute."

"Later."

"You go ahead," Bailey said. "I'll be fine."

Steve didn't want to leave her. But she wasn't asking for his support, was she? On the contrary.

He let her go.

"Pretty girl," Walt observed as she followed the tall black nurse down the curtained row. "But damned if she don't remind me of that L'il Abner character. You know the one? Little guy in black with the bad luck cloud following him around."

"Before my time," Steve said tersely.

Walt shook his head. "Seven years I've been chief, and only one homicide. She comes back to town, and within three weeks I've got two dead bodies and a felony assault on my hands."

Unease slid through the temper. "That's not her fault."

"Maybe not," Walt said. "In fact, she did us a favor last night."

Steve balanced on the balls of his feet, waiting for the punch.

"Just got off the phone with SBI. Their lab boys found traces of the deceased's blood in the crack of the base. I'd say we have ourselves a murder weapon."

Steve didn't think Walt had pulled him aside to tell him he was right all along.

He struggled to get his head back in the job.

"Prints?" he asked.

"Wiped."

He expected that. Paul Ellis was too smart to plant the weapon on Bailey without carefully wiping his prints first.

"So we still can't prove Paul Ellis killed his wife," Steve said.

Or that Bailey didn't.

Walt rubbed his jaw with the back of his hand. "Well, now, I talked to Jim in the DA's office. We know Ellis had the opportunity. He had the financial motive, and now we've got the means."

"But it's all circumstantial."

"I'm not saying I wouldn't have liked to get Ellis's

confession. But him killing himself like that . . . it's damn near the same thing. If Miz Wells will cooperate, we can make this whole thing go away. I'm asking Jim in the DA's office to rule the deaths a murder/suicide."

Which would leave Bailey cleared, both cases closed, and everybody happy.

Except Steve.

And Bailey, who was too damn honest for her own good.

He should let it go. He had come home to Stokesville to make a better life for his daughter. He wasn't here to make news, to make waves, or to make enemies. But something about this whole setup nagged at him like an open window in a ground floor apartment.

He jammed his hands into his pockets. "What else did the lab boys tell you?"

"About what?"

"About Paul Ellis. Sherman did swipes on his hands. Did you get results yet?"

Walt pulled in his chin. The corners of his mouth pulled down in displeasure. "I told you I'm making my recommendation to the DA. I'll have your case file on my desk Monday morning."

He didn't add, "If you know what's good for you."

He didn't have to.

"AND behind curtain number three . . ." The nurse winked at Bailey and slid back the striped curtain around Frank Wells's bed. "Mr. Wells, your daughter's here to see you."

Bailey caught her breath, her already raw emotions scraped by the sight of her father under the harsh hospital lights. His bluff red face was all eyebrows and nose, his skin slack and gray. His big frame seemed shrunken under the white sheet. Even his hair seemed thinner.

"Hey, Daddy," she said softly.

His mouth curled. One big hand lifted before it fell again to his lap. "Hey, Bailey girl."

Her eyes welled. Her throat clogged with snot and tears.

They had never had much to say to one another. Now she was speechless.

Her mother wasn't.

"Doesn't he look good? You should have seen him before. I thought he'd never stop bleeding. Dr. Andrews says head injuries do that. And he has staples, actual metal staples, in his head. Like Frankenstein. Show her, Frank."

"Girl doesn't want to see my staples, Dotty."

"Well, but it was very interesting. I thought they'd use stitches. But Dr. Andrews put in those staples with me sitting right here. Pop, pop, pop." Her voice shook slightly. She twitched the rough white sheet over her husband's chest, smoothing it with trembling hands.

"Don't fuss," Frank grumbled. But he patted her hand as he said it.

Dorothy turned her palm over and clasped his hand compulsively.

Bailey felt as though she'd caught her parents kissing. She cleared her throat. "Can I get you anything?"

Her mother blinked rapidly. "I need a few things from home. Dr. Andrews wants to keep an eye on your father overnight because he was unconscious for so long. But I can spend the night with him."

"Damn fool idea," Frank said. "You should go home. Go to bed."

"I wouldn't sleep a wink. I'd be too worried about you."

Frank harrumphed. "You won't sleep here, either. Not in that chair."

"Do you want me to stay?" Bailey offered. She was already so tired it was an effort to stand, let alone think straight. But her mother vibrated on the edge of exhaustion. "You could go home and change, maybe get something to eat."

"They have a cafeteria here," Dorothy said. "*And* a gift shop." She sounded pleased.

Bailey looked at her father.

"You go on. You've got better things to do than stick around here." He smiled at her crookedly. "You always did."

"Oh, Daddy." The tears escaped. Dripped.

"Go on," he repeated. "We'll be fine."

"But bring me my toothbrush and a sweater," Dorothy said. "The blue one, in my middle dresser drawer. And I could use my back pillow."

"I'll take care of it, Mom."

"That's my girl," Frank said.

Startled, she met her father's gaze. And he smiled.

"YOU don't need to wait," Bailey said to Steve on the porch of her parents' house.

She could handle this herself. She could handle anything.

She sighed. Except, apparently, him.

Ever since she had trespassed onto his personal emotional territory, he had retreated into Robocop mode. Professional. Polite.

Dangerous.

Under his mechanical courtesies, temper radiated. He hadn't forgiven her for calling him on his little guilt trip.

Brooding again, she thought, but the sneer didn't make her any less miserable.

"I'm just going to grab a few things and go back to the hospital. I can drive myself," she said.

Steve ignored her, plucking the keys from her hand to unlock the door. "You're too tired to see straight. I'm not letting you drive."

Let her?

"Look, I appreciate everything you've done. The ride home and . . . and everything. But you can't chauffeur me around indefinitely like a drunk in the back of a squad car. You need to get home to your daughter."

"My daughter is fine. My mother picked her up from your sister's an hour ago. I don't need you to lecture me about my obligations."

Ouch.

"Maybe not." Bailey stuck out her chin. "But I don't have to put up with being treated like one of them, either."

His head snapped around. "You are not an obligation," he said through his teeth.

Her heart thundered. "No? What am I, then?"

"You're a damn nuisance."

Disappointment swelled her chest and closed her throat. When she could speak again, she said, "Thank you. Another magnificent nonanswer from the king of emotional evasion."

He glowered. "Damn it, Bailey, what do you want me to say? We've known each other less than a week."

She was shaken. He was right.

But she was tired of investing herself in no-yield relationships, sick of holding back, of saying nothing, of playing it safe.

"I want you to talk to me. I need to know what you're feeling. I don't want to get into another relationship knowing from the beginning that it's not equal and it's not going anywhere."

Not again. Not ever again.

"I'm not Paul Ellis."

"No, you're not," she agreed readily. "You could hurt me more than he ever did."

"Shit. All right. All *right*." He didn't look lover-like. He looked annoyed. "You want feelings? You make me feel . . ." He stopped, apparently at a loss for words.

Bailey held her breath as he tottered on the brink of real disclosure. All it would take was one word, one push, from her.

And God help her, she couldn't do it.

Maybe she didn't want to know how he really felt.

Maybe hope and cozy self-deception were preferable to rejection after all.

"After Teresa died, I shut down," Steve said. She watched him with painful attention, as if she could find her way by the light of his expression. His eyes were dark as night. "I had a job to do, and a kid to raise. I figured that was it for me. But you make me feel . . . You. Make. Me. Feel." He repeated it slowly, emphatically. "Is that what you wanted to know? Is that enough for you?"

Bailey moistened her lips. "I don't know," she said honestly. "I haven't decided."

His expression changed. Excitement shivered along her nerves. He didn't look like a frustrated father, a grieving husband, a laid-back Southern lawman anymore. He looked like the cop he must have been in D.C., his eyes sharper, his mouth harder.

"Let me help you make up your mind," he said and reached for her.

SEVENTEEN

STEVE jerked her toward him.

Bailey lost her balance, grabbing at him, before she fell flush against his big, solid body. He kissed her, deep and slow and long, until her mind spun and her fingers flexed on the muscle of his shoulders. His hand fisted in her hair, holding her head for his kiss, while the other slid down her back and pulled her hips to his.

His mouth was hot, hard, and hungry. His hands gripped and took. Temper and need pumped through him, fueling his desire, feeding hers. Her nerves jangled. Her brain shut down. His earlier testing, tasting, exploratory kisses hadn't prepared her for this.

Nothing in her life had prepared her for this.

Yearning shuddered through her. His hand slid over and around her body, closing on her breast. He palmed it, shaped it, found the nipple and rubbed it to a tight, aching point. She made a choked sound—not a protest—into his mouth.

He tugged her hair, forcing her head back. Their faces

were inches apart. Their lower bodies pressed together, belly and sex. He was hotly, heavily, gloriously aroused.

"Is that enough for you?" His voice grated.

She blinked and licked her swollen lips. "No."

The hand on her breast stilled. Could he feel the crazy thump of her heart? "No?"

"I meant . . ." She tried to get her mind and lungs to function. Raising her hand, she skated her fingers over his rough jaw and soft lips, the smooth, flushed skin high on his cheek, and the tender corner of his eye. Inside her everything clenched and then loosened. Softened.

"More," she said.

Steve's gaze narrowed dangerously. "I'll give you more."

His mouth descended, crushing out thought, blanketing her in sensation. He took her over, his strength supporting her body, his breath supplanting her breath, his tongue possessing her mouth. Bailey clung to him, buffeted by emotion, swamped by craving.

It was too much.

It wasn't nearly enough.

Desperate to touch him, to feel skin, she ran her hands down the solid muscle of his back, working her fingers under his belt, reaching for the hem of his shirt.

He started at her touch and broke away. "I'm too old for this," he muttered.

Her jaw dropped. Her heart failed. "Not again."

He scowled. "Not again, what?"

She was shaking, scared of the way he made her feel, afraid of the things he made her long for. Terrified he wouldn't give her what she wanted. Needed. Now.

"I am not going to let you turn this into another I-don't-mix-sex-and-the-job moment. I don't care if—"

He stopped her with another kiss that made her raise on her toes and clutch him.

"I am too damn old," he said, "to take you on the stairs. Where's your bed?"

Speechless, she pointed toward her room. And gasped, thrilled and off-balance, when he hauled her off her feet and carried her up the stairs like Rhett Butler making off with Scarlett O'Hara.

The door was open.

He strode with her into the blue flowered bedroom with the girl rocker posters on the walls. Shifting his grip, he let her slide down his broad, hard body onto her feet. His erection dragged against her, nudging the bare skin of her belly. They both shuddered.

But the transition had given Bailey time to think, time to second-guess her instincts and his intentions.

Glancing at the narrow white bed, she bit her lip. "It's kind of small."

Steve's mouth quirked. "I sure hope you're talking about the mattress, sugar."

Startled, she chuckled. "I was. I was worried how we would, um . . ."

"Fit?" he suggested, his eyes wicked.

She nodded.

"Let me show you."

He bent and nuzzled the curve of her jaw, the line of her throat, while his hands grasped the hem of her tank top, working it up and over her head.

She reached to help him. Gently, he lifted her hands away and stared down at her breasts in their black demi-bra.

Her mouth dried. Her nipples peaked.

With one finger, he traced the swell of her breasts along the line of plunging black nylon. Sliding his thumbs into the satin cups, he dragged them down. Her breasts popped free.

Bailey closed her eyes, turned on and embarrassed. And jolted with shock and need when his hot mouth closed on one breast. He suckled her, hard. She squeezed her eyes shut, overwhelmed by sensations: the brush of his hair, the scrape of his beard, the hot, sweet suction of his mouth. Fever and chills chased over her body. She swayed on her feet.

His fingers fumbled with the drawstring at her belly before he slid her pants over her hips and down her legs.

His breath hissed. His hands stilled.

Bailey opened her eyes, misgiving dancing in her stomach. "What is it?"

"I didn't figure you for the thong type."

What was he expecting? Granny panties?

"They're actually very practical," she said defensively. "They don't show under my clothes, and they're—"

"Sexy as hell."

He took two fingers and rubbed them slowly over the tiny satiny triangle. It was already damp. She sucked in her breath. Her knees wobbled.

"Very sexy," he said.

He stripped rapidly, T-shirt, shoes, belt, jeans. She watched, nervous and enthralled, as clothing hit the floor and his body was revealed. Powerful, hairy chest. Broad, smooth shoulders. Strong, hairy thighs. He left his underwear on, navy briefs that clung and stretched over his very male, very aroused body.

Oh, wow.

"This is a first for me," she said brightly.

He froze stepping over his jeans on the floor. "What are you talking about?"

"I'm twenty-six years old, and I finally get to have sex with a football player in my bedroom while my parents are out."

"Ex–football player. But if you have some high school fantasy thing going, sugar, that's fine by me. I was afraid you were going to say I was your first, period."

He wasn't. Not by a long shot. But she was hurt all the same, for reasons she couldn't put a name to. "Would that be a problem for you?"

"Frankly, yes." With his thumb, he smoothed the tension building between her brows. "I haven't been with a woman—any woman—in three years. I don't want to go too fast for you."

She was appeased. Aroused. And more moved than she would have believed possible. This vital, virile man had gone without sex for . . .

"Three years?"

Since his wife died. Since before his wife died.

He raised his eyebrows. "Is that a problem for you?"

Yes. No. Yes.

Why now? she wanted to demand. Why me?

But she was afraid to hear the answer.

"I'm impressed," she said.

He shook his head, his expression wry. "Sugar, I'm not looking to impress you with my lack of experience. More like warning you about my lack of control."

Daring, she let her gaze drop to his navy briefs and then smiled into his eyes. "I don't see anything lacking."

Warm humor lit his gaze. "Maybe you need to examine the evidence more closely."

He freed himself from his briefs and let them drop. Her insides clenched.

Naked, he sat on the edge of the bed. His long legs stuck out in front of him. His erection jutted up. He pulled her to him, guiding her with firm hands on her waist, her thighs, her hips to straddle him, her knees on the mattress.

"That's it." He stroked her. Opened her. Stretched her. "Just like . . . Oh, yeah, sugar, like that."

She let herself sink down, down, entranced by the

shuddering power of his body under hers, the play of muscle beneath her hands, his sudden catch of breath.

"Bailey." His jaw was set. His voice was strained.

"Mmm." She experimented, gliding over him, easing down on him, her senses humming. *Hot.* He was so hot.

"Birth control," he said hoarsely. "Do you have any?"

"Oh, God." She scrambled off him so fast she almost fell on her ass.

He caught her. "Easy."

"Oh, God." She was horrified. She was always so careful. "I can't believe I forgot."

"Easy," he said again, supporting her. Soothing her. "It's not a disaster. Unless you don't have anything and I've got to go lights-and-sirens to the nearest drugstore."

"No, I have . . ." She struggled to get away. "In my purse."

He kept hold of her until he was sure she could stand. She stumbled across the room and dug in her bag, aware of his gaze on her bare ass. Tissues, Tic Tacs, tampon, mace . . . condoms.

Face burning, she crossed the room again and handed the foil packet to him.

"You don't mind?" she asked.

"Hell, no. You're practical. That's part of what I like about you."

"You like me because I'm practical," she repeated, trying not to feel insulted.

"Yeah. Plus, you're naked." His eyes gleamed. "I really like that."

"Practical and naked." She nodded. "Anything else?"

STEVE looked at Bailey, pale, slim, and burning like a candle in the cool, blue room. Her eyes were mistrustful. Yearning. Their impact knocked a hole in his chest.

Christ, she got to him.

He liked the puzzle of her, her smart mouth, quick mind and slow smile. Beneath her sometimes brittle defenses, she was solid and warm and real.

And naked, or nearly so.

Blood pounded in his head and pooled heavy between his legs. His gaze traveled down her beaded breasts, the shadowy indentation of her navel, the tiny scrap of fantasy between her pale thighs, and he wanted her under his hands. Under his mouth.

He shook his head. "I can't explain it to you, sugar. Hell, you wouldn't believe me anyway." Rising, he cupped her face in his hands. Her skin was cool and smooth as porcelain. He could feel the heat inside her, like coffee warming a cup.

"So I'll have to show you," he said, and laid his mouth on hers.

She gripped his wrists, but under his lips, her lips softened and parted. She swayed into him, the points of her breasts brushing his chest, the smoothness of her belly teasing his erection, and he almost exploded.

He licked into her mouth and felt her soften and yield, felt her quicken and sigh. Satisfaction beat in his blood. He wanted her willing and with him, wanted her open and under him.

Now.

He laid her on the twin-sized mattress and followed her down.

Take it slow, he warned himself. *Make it last.*

He took her mouth, and now she was kissing him back, sweet, deep, long kisses, her body arching and her tongue chasing his. He slipped his hand between their bodies, dying to touch her, eager to strip that bit of black nothing off her and feel her shudder and respond. But she wrapped her arms and legs around him, her hips rising, urging him on, pulling him in, guiding him home.

He pushed himself just a little bit inside her, and she reached around and grabbed his ass.

Sweet God in heaven. He was buried to the hilt, and she was slick and sweet, hot and tight around him, making these little whimpers in her throat that destroyed him.

He was still in control. All he had to do was not move. *Yeah, right.*

Not breathe. *Entirely possible.*

Not feel.

She tightened around him, a velvet fist, and blew his world and his control to pieces. Every time he tried to take it easy, to take it slow, to make it good for her, to make it last, she tugged at him or gasped or bit.

He was losing it. Losing himself in the slap of flesh on flesh, in the scent and sight and feel of her, wet and aroused.

Losing himself.

Heat built in his balls and the base of his skull like fury, blinding him, driving him, making him pound into her, heavy, hard, hammering faster, harder, into her.

She cried out and came, her short nails digging into his back. Her internal muscles clamped him. Milked him. She wrung from him every bit of response, wrested from him every pretense at control. He groaned and gave it up, gave everything up, emptied himself in her slim, pale body on her narrow white bed.

Home.

BAILEY lay stunned, her body in satisfied languor and her mind and emotions rioting.

Steve had shifted their positions so that she sprawled over him. She had to, to avoid falling out of bed. Her thigh nestled between his hard, hairy thighs. Her arm stretched across his broad, damp chest.

What was the old saying? Be careful what you wish for because you just might get it.

Sexually, Steve had given her everything and demanded everything she had to give in return. She had never felt this way before. Smug. Sore. Confused.

Her fingers curled.

"Ouch," he said mildly, and removed her hand from his chest hair.

He kissed her palm and laced his fingers with hers, holding their joined hands against his heart. The tenderness of the gesture made her melt.

"So, now that we've gone all the way," he rumbled, "will you wear my letter jacket?"

She smiled against his shoulder. He smelled so good, sweaty, sexy, and male. "You're too big. It wouldn't fit."

"Let's see." He rolled with her. Pressed against her.

She gasped with laughter and renewed desire. "We were talking about your jacket!"

"I wasn't." He rocked against her, his eyes dark and heavy lidded. "Got another condom?"

HE went into his office, where he could appear to be working and no one would disturb him, and closed and locked the door.

He was annoyed to notice his heart was still racing.

He had hoped to solve one problem, and now he had two. Taking out his find, he set it on his desk. It looked tacky and out of place against the brown leather blotter, a reminder of a tawdry episode from another time. Another life.

He sank into his desk chair. He'd thought . . . he'd really believed Billy Ray's death would be the end of it.

But then Ellis had come, prying into things that were none of his business, bragging about things he didn't understand. Frank Wells had barged home at the worst possible moment. And he'd seen his carefully constructed life, his plans and his reputation, shift like a house built on shaky ground.

He had done his best to shore up the damage. Nobody had questioned his arrival at the Wells place. That was the beauty of a small town, and the advantage of his place in it. He had made the appropriate noises about kids and drugs and why a good dog beat one of those newfangled alarm systems any day.

And he'd plotted his next move. He hadn't gotten where he was today by leaving things to chance or other people.

He had to make this go away.

He had to find those tapes.

They weren't in Ellis's study. He'd searched.

And they weren't in the Wells girl's bedroom. Unless that skinny bitch had hidden them. What exactly did she know, or suspect?

If the tapes had been packed up with the rest of the evidence Burke turned over to the lab in Raleigh, he might already be too late. Unless he pulled strings at SBI the way he had at the prison. Something to consider for the future.

The important thing was not to panic. As long as he kept his head, as long as he kept control, everything would work out. Everything always worked out. Pulling his find toward him, he skimmed the pages, searching for the mention of his name.

"YOU can't stay here alone tonight," Steve said in his cop voice. Detached. In control. As if nothing at all had changed.

And maybe, for him, nothing had. *You make me feel,* he'd said. *Is that enough for you?*

Bailey wiggled her jeans over her butt. She would be happy for his company, but she wouldn't accept his protection as a present. Not if it came wrapped in that patronizing, "all part of the job, ma'am," attitude.

"I'll be fine. Besides, I don't have anyplace else to go."

"Then stay with me."

Stay with him, sleep with him, be with him . . . She flushed all over at the thought.

She fastened the button at her waistband, resolutely not looking at him. "For how long?"

Steve prowled her bedroom, his hands in his pockets, already fully dressed. She saw him glance from her Lisa Loeb poster to the romance novels on her bookshelves and felt even more exposed. "Your father's discharged tomorrow."

Tomorrow. So his offer was a totally temporary thing. Which was fine with her, because there was no way she was staying in Stokesville. Although what was waiting for her in New York?

She bent to retrieve her bra from the floor. "Stay with you in your mother's house? I don't think so."

"We're not teenagers." He sounded amused. "She'll be thrilled."

"Uh huh. And your daughter? I don't know much about raising preteen girls, but I'm pretty sure flaunting overnight guests isn't in the parenting manual."

He raised his eyebrows. "So you can have my room. I'll grab some pillows and take the couch."

She was tempted. Too tempted. "Such a sacrifice."

"Not really." His eyes gleamed. "I don't plan on actually sleeping there."

Instant sexual meltdown.

She was in so much trouble here.

Ignoring the thrill his words gave her, the treacherous softening of her body and heart, she yanked her shirt over her head. "Thank you for your very attractive offer, but no. As you said, it's only for one night. I'll just . . ."

Her heart tripped in her chest. She felt a second's unbalance, like the pause at the top of the stairs.

"What is it?" Steve asked quietly.

Nagged by a subtle sense of something wrong, she surveyed the familiar items scattered on her nightstand: a box of tissues, an empty water glass, a pencil. Two condom wrappers.

Her breath hissed out. "Where's my lamp?"

His gaze narrowed. "Your lamp?"

"My father was hit with a lamp, you said. A brass lamp? With a white shade?"

"They took the shade for prints," Steve said.

"He was in my room." She found her confirmation in his eyes. "Whoever hit my father was in my room. But I don't have anything valuable, I . . ."

She spun toward her desk, where the evidence boxes were stacked in random order, and counted. Everything was there. Wasn't it?

She jerked the lid off the nearest carton and looked inside. She had never actually inventoried the contents. How would she know if anything was missing? But her feeling of being off balance, that breathless moment before a fall, grew.

"What is it?"

She opened another box and another.

"What are you looking for?"

She hardly knew. Until she flipped the lid of the last

carton and realized it wasn't there. Not on her bedside table, not on the floor, not in any of the boxes.

"Tanya Dawler's diary." She sank back on her heels, looking up at him in dismay. "It's gone."

EIGHTEEN

STEVE rocked on his heels, hands in his pockets. "Why? Fear of exposure? Blackmail? Did she do like that Hollywood madam and write about her johns?"

Bailey released a breath she hadn't been aware she was holding. "Heidi Fleiss never actually divulged the names of her . . . All right, no," she said, when he looked impatient. "Tanya wrote about ordinary stuff—fights with her mom and how much she hated school and which boys she had crushes on. She hardly ever wrote about her clients. Not by name."

"Whoever took the diary wouldn't know that."

"Still . . . it seems a big risk for a little return. Who cares who visited a prostitute twenty years ago?"

Steve shrugged. "An underage prostitute. Statutory rape's a crime."

"So is murder."

His gaze sharpened.

Encouraged, she continued. "Paul always argued the

police missed something important in the Dawler case. No one was threatening to publish a list of the women's clients. Paul was writing about their deaths. What if Tanya's diary was stolen because it implicates someone else in her family's killings?"

"Billy Ray confessed."

"Billy Ray is *dead*. He talked to Paul—"

"And Ellis is dead," Steve finished for her. "I got that. What I also have, aside from your twenty-year-old crime, are three isolated deaths in two separate jurisdictions with plausible, unrelated explanations for each."

"Three deaths?"

"Helen Ellis was killed, too." His eyes were dark and weary.

Bailey felt an instant's shame. In her focus on Paul and Billy Ray, her worry over her father and her excitement over the diary, she had forgotten Helen.

"Do you think . . . Could her death be connected, too? She's from Stokesville. Maybe she knew the Dawlers."

"I don't see Helen and Tammy Dawler moving in the same social circles," Steve drawled.

"Her husband, then. Jackson Poole. He could have been a client."

Steve shook his head. "What if he was? You still have to make a case based on motive, means, and opportunity. Paul Ellis was in debt. He stood to benefit from a four-million-dollar life insurance policy. The murder weapon was from his study, and he tried to frame you for the crime."

She was shaken, her conviction and her confidence fading under the force of his attack. "Well, if you're going to put it that way . . ."

"It's my job to put things that way. We need to look at this rationally."

His job. This was all a job to him.

She should be grateful for his expertise. But she couldn't escape the unwelcome feeling that maybe she was a job to him, too.

Squash that thought.

"I'm rational. I'll be as rational as you want. But I can't compartmentalize the way you do. I can't be impersonal." She pulled herself to her feet. "Somebody was in my room. Somebody attacked my father. That makes it personal for me. If there's a link to the Dawler case, to my work for Paul, then this is my fault."

"No, it's not. You can't make yourself responsible for this the way you do for everything else that goes wrong."

Fatigue and frustration made her unwary. "Look who's talking," she snapped.

Steve looked like she'd hit him in the face with a fish.

Oh, God.

She couldn't believe she'd said that, that she could throw his admission of guilt over his wife's death into his face like that.

"I'm so sorry," she said. "That was rude."

His mouth twisted. "But true."

"No, I—"

"You want the truth? The truth is, Paul Ellis murdered his wife. I don't know about the rest of it. I don't understand why anybody would steal Tanya Dawler's diary, and I don't like the idea that somebody was in your bedroom any more than you do. But I can't go to the DA over my boss's head and demand he reopen two cases based on a theory."

"And the diary," she reminded him.

"Sugar." His voice was gentle. "We only have your word for it that the diary's even missing."

She stared at him, stricken. "My word isn't enough?"

He shot her an impatient look. "For me, yeah. Not for

the DA. It doesn't matter what I believe. What matters is what I can prove. And I can't prove any of this."

God, she was exhausted. If only she could *think.*

"Unless Paul didn't kill himself," she said.

Steve's gaze narrowed.

Her chest expanded with sudden hope. "If somebody killed him and staged it to look like a suicide, that would be proof, wouldn't it?"

"Not proof," he said. "But it sure would be something."

Bailey held his gaze, breathless.

"I'll make a call," he said.

THE guys who have sex with you at a party on Saturday night won't even talk to you at school on Monday morning. But they'll talk about you, Tanya had scribbled in her childish, rounded handwriting. *Bet they wouldn't like it if I talked about them. Or their daddies.*

He could almost smell the vivid pink ink rising above the faded paper, a whiff of strawberry or bubble gum.

Or maybe it was only Tanya's ghost, trashy, cloying, and eternally young.

Thumbing through her diary, he felt almost nostalgic. Not for her. She was, after all, a slut. But for the way he had been back then, the image of himself in her eyes.

He is so cool. Sometimes when he comes by to pick up Billy Ray, my knees get weak. I think I'll just die if he doesn't notice me. And then I think I'll die if he does.

"LOOK, I already told your chief what I think." The evidence tech's exasperation traveled clearly over the line. "Talk to him. I'm not getting in the middle of some department bullshit."

Steve rubbed the back of his neck. The tech was under no obligation to talk to him—Paul Ellis wasn't his case—and probably had better things to do with his Saturday night than repeat results over the phone to a rural detective. Because the two state labs, one in Raleigh, one in Asheville, served law enforcement all over the state, most evidence sat for weeks or months before processing. The state boys must feel they'd already gone above and beyond in complying with the DA's rush request.

"Sure. No bullshit. Guess I'm just bummed the bastard offed himself before I could serve a warrant for his wife's murder. You do the actual testing?"

Bailey stopped fussing with the covers of her bed to give him a long look. He wasn't sure how much she could pick up listening in on his end of the conversation.

The tech sighed. "Disks and swipes," he confirmed. "Both turned up negative residue on the left hand and equivocal residue on the right."

"Equivocal, how?" he asked.

"What am I, CSI? I don't talk for your entertainment."

"How about a bottle of Scotch?" Steve suggested.

"Is that how you all get things done in Stokesville?"

"I don't know about Stokesville," Steve drawled. "But in D.C., Johnny Walker does the job."

"In these parts, it's Jimmy Beam."

Steve grinned sharply. "Jim Beam works for me. One bottle of Black Label?"

"What do you want to know?"

He pulled out his notebook. "Tell me about that right hand."

Lubricated by the promise of bourbon, the tech became downright chatty. Steve ended the call satisfied.

But he was far from happy.

Bailey sat on the edge of her bed, the bed where she had

recently shorted his control, blown his mind, and ended his three-year sexual drought, thank you Jesus.

The possibility that she could be in danger, that she would willingly put herself in danger, tightened his chest.

He cleared his throat. "Looks like you were right about Ellis."

"How do you know?"

Steve hesitated. He never discussed cases off the job. But all he had to protect her was the truth. "What do you know about residue testing?"

"Only what I've researched. Residue testing is notoriously unreliable. But when a gun is fired at close range—say, under twelve inches—the discharge from the barrel creates a smudge around the wound. And, of course, the discharge from the chamber deposits gunpowder soot particles on the shooter's hand."

She must have caught him staring, because she broke off. "What?"

He shook his head. "Nothing. I just think it's cute when you get all technical."

Her eyes narrowed. "Cute."

"Hot," he corrected. "It's very hot."

"Really? Projective particles," she said experimentally. "Stellar bursting. Carbon tattoo."

He grinned. "That's done it. Come here."

"Uh uh." She slapped her hand in the middle of his chest. "You were telling me about residue testing. Did the lab find powder deposits on Paul's hand?"

He sobered. "Yeah, they did. But if Ellis fired the gun himself, you'd expect to find most of the residue on the back of his hand, with a smaller amount on the palm. The lab found trace amounts on both sides of Ellis's hand, with slightly higher deposits on the palm."

He watched her brows draw together as she worked it

out. "But if Paul didn't fire the gun, how do you account for the residue on his hand?"

"Say there was another shooter."

"The murderer," she said flatly.

He inclined his head in acknowledgment. "The murderer. He fires the gun, puts it in Ellis's hand." Steve wrapped his own large hand around her much smaller one to demonstrate. "Ellis's palm picks up residue from the butt. And the back of his hand . . ."

Her face turned to his. "Would be contaminated by residue from the shooter's palm."

He stared down at her, dry-eyed, determined and achingly vulnerable, and his heart lurched in his chest. For a moment he couldn't think. Couldn't breathe.

This was why it was a mistake to mix sex with the job.

She turned to face him, slipping naturally out of the protective circle of his arm. "What are we going to do?"

Fear for her made him harsh. "You don't do anything. You let the police do their jobs."

"The police want to treat Paul's murder as a suicide. Isolated deaths, different jurisdictions, you said. But if the cases really are connected, they'll never be solved by investigating them separately. And if the connection is the Dawler case—"

He couldn't let her go there.

"I'll go to the chief," he said, in his best public relations voice. Never mind that Clegg wanted the Ellis file on his desk on Monday, and probably Steve's resignation, too. "I'll tell him we need to look into it."

"He won't listen to you. That's not what he wants to hear."

The hell of it was she was right.

Steve didn't know if the chief was bent on preserving the town's reputation or on protecting his own ass. But it was obvious that Walter Clegg wanted this case and the resultant media attention to go away.

Too bad. Because now there was more at stake than Stokesville's low-crime, small-town image.

"I'll make him listen," Steve said grimly.

"Not without evidence. You were right. We don't have proof. I don't think a missing diary is enough to convince him."

The tension in his jaw radiated outward like the pain from a bad tooth. "Then I'll dig until I find something else. Something he can't explain away or ignore."

She nodded eagerly. "I can help. I can—"

"No."

She drew in on herself, shoulders hunched, brows together, mouth a little tight. And then the chin came out. "What do you mean, *no*?"

"You're not investigating. Your father interrupted an intruder. What if he decides to come back?"

"Why should he come back? He has the diary."

"And what if that wasn't all he was looking for? You can't make yourself a target."

She flushed. "I'm already a target. The only way I can protect myself is to figure out why."

"The best way to protect yourself is to move in with me."

"That's sweet." She pressed his arm. "And I do appreciate the offer. But if we're right, if somebody could be after me, I won't put your mother and daughter at risk."

He leveled a look at her. "I can take care of my family. And you."

"I don't need you to take care of me."

"You can't stay here."

"I know," she said, surprising him. "I don't want to put my family at risk, either. I'll go to a hotel."

His teeth ground together. "What happened to, 'I don't want to be the dumb dead girl'?"

"You know what would be dumb? Refusing to acknowledge that as Paul's assistant I have the best chance of figuring out what he knew that got him killed."

Steve wanted to argue. But in his gut, he knew she was right.

It was his heart that kept protesting.

"If you had access to his files, maybe. But we emptied his office. I turned his computers over to SBI."

"Yes, well . . ." Suddenly she wasn't so eager to confront his gaze. "I backed up everything on my flash drive."

"You backed up . . ." He was dumbfounded. Irritated.

"Everything. Before I moved out, so I could work from here."

"You've been holding out on me, sugar."

"Oh, and you tell me everything."

Wisely, he ignored that. "You can go through Ellis's files?"

She nodded. "All I need is a computer."

"First we get you into a motel," Steve said grimly. "Then we worry about a computer."

Still, she hesitated. "What about my parents? I mean, they're all right tonight, but Dad should be released tomorrow. If you're right, if this guy comes back, they could be in danger whether I'm here or not. Dad's already injured. And my mom can be scary, but she's no match for an intruder."

He hated that he couldn't reassure her. That he couldn't protect her or her family. "I could request additional drive-by patrols for the house. But this might be a good time for your parents to take a little vacation."

"My parents don't take vacations."

"A family visit, then."

"My aunt Grace lives in Kinston. But I don't see my

parents making a road trip while Daddy has a concussion. He does all the driving."

"Let me talk to your father's doctor. Maybe I can persuade him to admit him to the hospital, keep him for another day."

"And leave my mother all alone in the house?"

"She could stay with your sister. Leann lives closer to the hospital anyway."

And after a trip to the hospital to drop off Dorothy's car and back pillow, it was all arranged.

THE Pinecrest Motor Lodge off Highway 85 lay just beyond the tangle of off-ramps at the city limits. It boasted cable TV in all the rooms and a diner across the parking lot that served breakfast twenty-four hours a day.

Steve chose it because the doors were reinforced steel and some of the rooms faced the back. Bailey accepted it because it was only forty-nine dollars a night and she was tired enough to sleep standing up.

She waited in his truck with the doors locked and the motor running while he registered her.

"Won't they think it's suspicious if I don't come in?" she had asked before he climbed from the truck.

"Not if we register as Mr. and Mrs. Smith."

"Gee, I've never checked into a cheap motel under an assumed name before," she said, trying to make a joke of it, trying not to reveal how much his precautions scared her.

His eyes warmed, but the set cast of his face didn't change. "Another first," he said.

He entered the room ahead of her, carrying her hastily packed bag and some essential groceries: bread, peanut butter, a paperback romance.

Bailey watched as he set the groceries on the minifridge,

checked the windows, and closed the blinds, tempted to ask if he was going to look under the bed for monsters, too. But there was nothing remotely funny about the hard line of his mouth.

"I can't assign an officer to watch you," he said. "Even if I could convince Clegg you're in danger, the department doesn't have the manpower."

"I'll be fine."

"I could stay," he offered abruptly.

She looked at him, big and tough and ill at ease in the middle of her shabby motel room, and her heart stumbled.

She wanted him to stay. And felt guilty she had unintentionally forced him to a choice.

"No, you have to get home to your daughter. I'll see you tomorrow."

"I don't know what time," he warned.

She forced back her instinctive protest. He had other duties, another life, away from here. She had no real claim on him at all. Somehow, sometime during the past twenty-four hours, she had begun to turn to him, to depend on him. That didn't mean she had to make things more difficult for him because he had a job to do and a daughter to raise.

"I'll be here," she said.

It wasn't like she had a car. Or much choice.

But he still didn't leave her. "You want anything before I take off?"

She smiled wryly. "Something to do?"

To her surprise, he took her request seriously. "There's an evidence box in the truck. You could look through that."

"What am I looking for?"

"The missing link."

"You want me to solve the mystery of evolution?" she teased.

Steve didn't smile. "I want you to figure out who had a reason to steal Tanya Dawler's diary."

Right.

She stood by the door as he went out and came in bearing the box. He was wearing his cop face again, the one that said he had already gone away from her in his head.

"You lock up behind me, and don't answer the door for anybody else. Here's my cell phone number and the department number. My home number's on the back."

"You forgot the number for the poison control center and my pediatrician."

She appreciated his concern. She ought to be grateful for his willingness to take charge of a situation that was totally beyond her expertise. But she didn't like being treated like one more detail he had to take care of.

His mouth quirked. "Funny. Just be careful."

"You, too."

"Excuse me?"

Her chin angled up. "If somebody out there is targeting anyone who investigates the Dawler case . . . I'm just saying you should be careful, too."

He kissed her then, hard and slow, leaving her shaken and clinging to him.

The thought made her uncomfortable. Her clinging days were over, she thought, as she locked the door behind him and flipped the security bolt. She wasn't putting her trust and pinning her future on another man. This time was different.

Steve was different.

She was practically sure of it.

NINETEEN

STEVE nudged Gabrielle into a pew at the back of Saint Mildred's Catholic Church. The nine o'clock mass was crowded with old folks anxious to escape the day's heat and young families who couldn't afford to miss nap time, with women with an eye on Sunday dinner and men with their minds on the afternoon ball game.

The homily was short and the choir's ranks decimated by summer vacations. But the order of the mass was the same.

Lord, have mercy . . .

Lamb of God, who takes away the sins of the world . . .

I am not worthy to receive you. Only say the word, and I shall be healed.

Standing and kneeling beside his daughter, Steve waited for the familiar litany of guilt, the self-disgust that rose from his soul like incense. But it didn't come. Today, the memorized rituals brought comfort, not shame.

You're not responsible for your wife's illness. Or her treatment plan. Or her death.

Looking down at Gabrielle's smooth, dark head and the gold hearts dancing at her ears, he felt an unexpected peace. A profound thankfulness.

For Gabrielle.

And for Bailey.

Bailey, solid, bright, straightforward, had stolen into his disciplined life like the light through those stained glass windows. Making him feel again. Making him believe again. Waking him to painful hope.

He stood for the final hymn, his heart pumping in an urgent rhythm that had nothing to do with the pounding of the organ in the choir loft. Because along with renewed life came renewed fear.

Somewhere out there, somebody hunted to keep a secret. Somebody who had killed and might kill again.

And until Steve caught him and put him away, that bastard threatened Bailey.

He steered Gabrielle from their pew into the stream of departing churchgoers. He needed to review the Dawler case again. Beyond the headlines and court reports, there had to be something that had sparked Paul Ellis's interest . . . and his murder.

The congregation spilled into the sunshine and down the broad, flat steps. Under a stand of tall pine trees, children, released from church and careless of the heat, whooped and ran around some aging playground equipment.

"Lieutenant?"

Steve turned as Darian Jackson emerged from the shadow of the church porch, sweating and uncomfortable in his Sunday suit. Beside him, a handsome woman in a floral print dress chatted with the pastor.

Jackson came down the steps alone. "Welcome to Saint Mildred's. I didn't know your people were Catholic."

"Her mother was."

"Ah."

Sensing an opportunity, Gabrielle tugged on his arm. "Can I go play?"

Steve was restless, angry, jumping out of his skin with the need to do something, to protect Bailey. He looked down at his daughter's hopeful face and drew a deep breath.

"Ten minutes."

"Okay."

She ran off.

"Must be tough," Jackson observed. "Starting over in a strange place with new people."

"We manage," Steve said.

"I'm sure you do. Sure you do. Still, it takes a while to find your feet."

Were they still talking about Gabrielle?

"There's always prejudice against the new kid," Steve said. "You can't let it get to you."

Jackson grunted. "Twenty years ago I was the only black officer in this department. There's not much you can tell me about prejudice."

"Guess not," Steve said.

The children ran and played in the sunshine.

Something Jackson had said nagged at Steve. "You were here twenty years ago?"

Jackson nodded. "Fresh out of the army."

"You work the Dawler case?"

"I was the responding officer. Although Chief Clegg—he was Detective Clegg back then—pretty near beat me onto the scene. Shit, every man on the force, seven of us, turned out that night. Never saw anything like it." Jackson shook his head. "Never want to see anything like it again, either."

Steve fought to contain his rising excitement. This couldn't be the break he'd been praying for.

"Domestics are always the worst," he said.

"He did them with the kitchen knives," Jackson said. "Murdered them in their beds. Blood everywhere. Grandmother went down pretty quick. Sister, too. But the mother, Tammy, she must have woke up. She fought him. Fought her own son for her life. We found her in the hall."

"And Billy Ray?"

"Curled up in the garage with a bottle of bourbon, drinking and crying and covered in blood. Most of it theirs. Kept talking about how he had to do it, how his life was worthless anyway because his family was all whores. How everybody was laughing at him and he had to be a man and stop their whoring. Nothing to do but bring him in."

There was no satisfaction in his voice.

Steve raised his eyebrows. "You ever consider other suspects?"

Jackson stared across the playground. "Men were in and out of that house all the time, Lieutenant. We could have hauled in every migrant worker and trucker in the state for questioning along with a good number of married men in this town. But everything pointed at the boy. We had his confession. We had his prints, and only his prints, on the knives. Most folks just figured the boy couldn't take it anymore."

"That made it easy," Steve remarked.

"Didn't make it wrong. A lot of folks—a lot of men— were already nervous. A lot of wives were upset. Clegg didn't see any point in stirring things up by dragging out the investigation."

That sounded like Clegg.

"And you agreed with him." His voice carefully neutral.

"I was new on the force. Still on probation." His gaze slid sideways to meet Steve's. "It wasn't my place to agree or disagree."

Justification or warning? Steve could sympathize with the first. He chose to ignore the second. "And now?"

"Now I'm close to retirement. Pretty soon I'll be living off my pension with an attic full of notebooks."

Casual words, casually delivered.

A lot of cops kept their case notes. Steve did himself. Like high school yearbooks or empty liquor bottles on a dormitory windowsill or a serial killers' trophies, the notebooks reminded you who you were and what you had done and sometimes what you had to atone for.

Given the subject, Steve didn't think their mention was an accident.

"Must make interesting reading," he said, equally casual.

"Interesting enough."

"Maybe I could take a look."

"I'll be home all afternoon," Jackson said. "You should drop by. Meet the wife."

His wife, unless Steve was very much mistaken, was still on the church steps above them, talking to the pastor.

He nodded. "I'll do that. Thanks."

IT was hard to feel in control of your destiny when you were stashed in a cheap twelve-by-twenty motel room without room service or transportation.

Bailey couldn't even control the temperature. The unit's air conditioner had two settings: brain-rattling and freezing or ominously silent and hot.

She settled for steamy, stripping to athletic shorts and a black cotton tank top to work her way through the evidence box. Outside the sun was shining, but she kept the blinds closed, as instructed. The darkness didn't do a damn thing to relieve the heat. Or the creepiness of her task.

She didn't touch the plastic bags and paper-wrapped

packages except to move them out of the way. The case summary alone was enough to give her chills, even in this sauna of a room. Wet splotches and bloody footprints, used condoms and an unopened pregnancy kit . . . Bailey pushed her hair out of her eyes and painstakingly noted them all. She turned hastily through the photos.

No wonder Steve was so good at dissociating.

He had to, to keep his sanity. To keep his humanity. She had a new appreciation for his job, and its cost. After only a couple of hours, she felt on edge, depressed, and not one bit closer to finding an angle, an insight, or a flaw in the police investigation.

She rubbed her forehead. How could she? Everything she looked at was the result of that investigation. It had already been analyzed, evaluated, and entered into evidence by professionals.

Two years working for one of the best true crime writers in the business, and she still lacked Paul's instincts. Or his ego. She sighed with frustration. Maybe if she had his notes, or his interview with Billy Ray . . .

She straightened slowly. The vinyl arm chair released her skin with a soft, sucking sound.

Or his interview with Billy Ray.

Her heart pounded. Was that what the intruder was after? The interview? But he had taken Tanya's diary. Which meant . . .

Oh, God, she needed a computer. If she could get into Paul's files, maybe she could figure out what it meant.

Think. She had read the diary. At least, she'd read parts of it. She should focus on that.

It was, as she had told Steve, extraordinary for its ordinariness, like a modern teenager's facebook profile of likes and dislikes, crushes and peeves. Tanya Dawler had liked Madonna and the color black, disliked math and—what was that teacher's name? Mr. D.—had a crush on Rick Springfield and her brother's friend Trey, Trace, something like that. She worried about the shape of her nose and the size of her breasts, and she dreamed of becoming a singer, a model, an actress. The details were fuzzy and changed frequently, but the desire to strike out and hit it big stayed constant.

Bailey could sympathize. What she couldn't do was imagine how any of this played into the girl's death or Paul's murder or the attack on her own father.

The knock on her door echoed through the room like a gunshot. She bolted upright in her chair as paper cascaded to the carpet.

Her heart thudded against her ribs. She felt giddy. Terrified or sleep deprived, at this point it didn't matter. Should she answer?

"Housekeeping," a light, accented voice called.

Sheesh.

"I'm fine, thanks."

She was a moron. An idiot.

Still she sat frozen, listening, until she heard footsteps move away from the door, until she saw a shadow cross the blinds.

She drew a deep, shuddering breath. *Okay. Don't just sit there, moron. Do something.*

What had Steve told her? *See if you can figure out who had a reason to steal Tanya Dawler's diary.*

Right. Bailey couldn't even recall any names, only nicknames and initials. But she picked the papers off the floor, bending stiffly like an old woman. She lined her sharpened pencils like soldiers on parade. And she wrote down as many of Tanya's notations as she remembered, frustrated she couldn't even build a database but had to rely on paper and pencil. The point dug into the page.

She had a sudden, sharp memory of Paul demanding his laptop, complaining. *I can't write the damn book on hotel stationery.*

Right there with you, Paul, she thought.

But Paul was dead.

She was alone. She had to figure this out herself, with or without a computer.

She reviewed her pathetic penciled list. Too bad she didn't have a client list for the brothel business to compare it with. Or a school directory. Mrs. Buncombe, the faculty yearbook advisor, used to insist Bailey check all the students' names against the listings in the student directory.

Yearbook.

The idea snapped on like the bathroom light. If she could get her hands on a yearbook, maybe she could match Tanya's abbreviations to names and faces. A male teacher whose last name began with D; an upperclassman named Trey—no, Trip, that was it; an S.W. with a blond ponytail. People who knew Tanya or her brother.

It was a place to start.

It was something to do.

Nineteen years ago, Tanya had been a freshman in high school. If she had lived, she would be thirty-five now, older than Bailey, almost as old as . . .

Bailey caught her breath. Digging for her cell phone, she punched in her sister's number.

Leann answered the phone against a babble of background noise. Bailey could hear their mother, apparently fixing lunch for Rose in the kitchen. "Bailey? Where are you? We missed you in church this morning."

"I'm fine. I'm . . ."

Hiding out under an assumed name in a sleazy motel by the highway. Her hand tightened on the phone.

"Doing research," she said.

"For that book? Hang on. The apple juice, Mom. On the second shelf."

A sudden wave of love for her family swamped Bailey, swelling her throat. "How's Daddy?"

"Oh, you know. He's grumpy because his doctor admitted him to the neurology floor, and then Mama told all the nurses he had brain damage, which of course he doesn't. But basically they're fine."

Bailey caught herself grinning. "Listen, can I ask you a favor?"

"*Apple* juice, Mama. Behind the pudding." Leann blew out a breath. "Okay, shoot."

Bailey cleared her throat. "Do you still have your old yearbooks?"

She had just ended the call with her sister when her phone chirped. She glanced at the familiar New York area code before she pressed the button. "Hello?"

TWENTY minutes later, Bailey sat cross-legged on the quilted motel spread, her phone clutched in her hand. Her mind whirled. Her stomach churned.

She should be flattered. Nervous. Hopeful. She felt . . . numb.

When the knock on the door came this time, she barely jumped. "Who is it?"

"Mr. Smith."

Steve.

She roused enough to consider running to the bathroom to reapply her deodorant and brush her hair. Stupid. She couldn't leave him standing outside while she primped. Scrambling off the bed, she opened the door.

He scowled at her from the sunlit strip of concrete. "Did you check through the peephole?"

No kiss, no compliment, no hi-honey-how-was-your-day. He was in full cop mode, those double lines cutting between his brows, his mouth hard.

She blinked. "I knew it was you."

"You should still check."

This was what it would be like to be with him: the tension and the terse replies, the sense that his head, if not his heart, was otherwise engaged.

Unless she did something about it.

"I was distracted."

"What's the matter? Is it your father?"

"He's fine. I'm fine. I'm great. Never better."

Steve's gaze narrowed. "What happened?"

She hugged her elbows, suddenly glad she had someone to share her amazing news. Wishing he would take her in his arms. Hoping his reaction would help her somehow to make sense of her own. "Paul's agent called."

"So?"

"So . . ." She drew a deep breath. "She wants me to finish the book."

"Ellis's book," he said without expression.

She nodded, anticipating surprise. Congratulations. Maybe even an argument.

"Are you going to do it?"

His lack of reaction brought her chin up. "I could. I have access to his sources. To his notes. Or I will once I get my hands on a computer."

"Laptop's in the car."

"Oh." That was it? "Well, great. Thanks."

He set a white paper sack on the air-conditioning unit

under the window. "I stopped by Crook's Barbecue. I figured you'd be tired of peanut butter by now."

A man who brought barbecue home could be forgiven almost anything. Even a less than enthusiastic response to Paul's agent.

"I love Crook's," Bailey said. After all, if he was making an effort, so could she. "That's one thing you can get around here you can't find in New York."

His dark gaze collided with hers. "There's lots of things you can get around here you can't get in New York."

She waited, breathless.

But he looked away, shoving his hands deep into his pockets. "Hot in here."

She bit back her disappointment. "You shouldn't have dressed up for dinner."

He glanced down at his rumpled dark suit as if he had forgotten he had it on. "I took Gabrielle to church this morning."

"And you didn't have time to change afterward?"

His expression shuttered. "I had things to do."

What things? she wanted to demand. But he had already retreated someplace she didn't know how to follow. Maybe he wasn't that different from Paul after all, she thought in despair.

And maybe she was the one who hadn't changed.

Who needed to change.

She thought about it as she cleared a space on the brown quilted spread to sit and he pushed the table closer to the bed. She popped the lids from their sweet tea and spooned coleslaw onto paper plates while he shifted the evidence box to the floor.

Like an old married couple, dividing chores without speech. She flushed.

The spicy aroma of good barbecue filled the room. She waited until he had worked his way through half a pile of barbecue before she dragged a hush puppy through ketchup and pointed it like a gun.

"Tell me about your day."

His mouth quirked. "Or you'll shoot?"

Biting the end off the hush puppy, she wagged the stump at him. "You have no idea what I'm capable of."

"Obviously not," he murmured. Now that he'd eaten, he looked . . . not relaxed, she thought. But more approachable. "Tell me about this book deal."

She accepted the change of subject. For now.

"It's not a deal yet." She chewed and swallowed. "I haven't decided whether I want to do it."

"Why wouldn't you?"

"No good reason. The advance would pay my bills. I'd be able to stay in Stokesville while I figure out my next move. Or at least until the sublet on my apartment is up."

"Would it be under your name?"

"What?" Now how had he zeroed in on the thing that bothered her most?

"The book. Would your name be on the cover?"

"Yes." She dug her plastic fork into a heap of barbecued pork. "Somewhere. Paul's agent suggested 'by Paul Ellis with Bailey Wells.' "

"Don't do it."

She felt a flare of resentment. What did he know about it? "It's more acknowledgement than I'd get if Paul had written the book."

"Paul isn't writing the book. You are."

"But his name is established. His name sells. And anything I wrote would be based on his work. His ideas."

"Then write something based on your own ideas. Sell that. I thought you were working on a kids' book."

She scowled. "It's not that easy. Although . . . I did pitch my YA book to her."

"Good for you." His approval warmed her all the way through. "And?"

"And she asked to read the complete manuscript." Impossible to contain the glow of pleasure.

"That's good, right? That she wants to see the whole thing."

She allowed herself a small smile. "It's very good."

"So why are you even thinking about the other job?"

Because she was terrified of failing.

"Well . . . it would pay more."

"In the short term, maybe. You need to think long term. Look at this as an investment in yourself and your career."

"What if she doesn't like it?"

"What if she does?" he countered. "Do you really want to be stuck finishing Ellis's book when you could be working on your own?"

"No-o."

"Then leave it. Put all this behind you."

"I can't."

"Why the hell not?"

"Because even if I don't write the book, I need to go through Paul's files. I have to find what he knew that would lead someone to kill him."

His face was unreadable. "Sugar, there may not be anything. Not if we can't turn up his interviews with Billy Ray."

"I have the interviews."

Steve went very still. "You have transcripts?"

She shook her head. "Paul never gave them to me to transcribe. But I should have the original files."

"You have the tapes." Steve bit the words out. "And you never told me."

"They're not tapes," she hastened to assure him. "They're audio files. On his computer. Paul never went anywhere without his laptop. Most come with built-in microphones now to enable Internet conferencing, but he actually used a microphone jack—you know, like some students use to tape their professors' lectures? He recorded the interviews directly onto his hard drive."

A muscle jumped beside Steve's mouth. He pushed away his half-empty plate. "Let's hear 'em."

He went out to the truck.

So much for sharing the news of their day over dinner.

She was clearing away the remains of their meal when he returned with a slim black laptop.

"I've got this," he said, taking hold of her plate.

Her hand instinctively tightened. She wasn't used to accepting help. Particularly domestic help from a man. "I can do it."

"So can I. What I can't do is access your boss's files. Sit. Work."

She sat. While the computer booted, she retrieved her flash drive from her purse and plugged it into the USB port. The contents flashed on the screen.

"What's this?" Steve stood by the bed, her penciled list in his hand.

"All the names and abbreviations I could remember from Tanya's diary. Not very many, I'm afraid."

"Mind if I copy it?"

"Of course not."

The mattress dipped under his weight. Bailey glanced at the stretch of his suit pants over his thighs and then away. It just figured that the first time she was alone with a man in a motel room, they'd both be doing paperwork.

She hadn't come home to find romance.

She hadn't made love with him expecting to find her happily ever after.

But now that they were here, she wanted to touch him. She wanted to burrow under his cop suit and find the man inside.

Put all this behind you?

She only wished they could. Sighing, she turned her attention to the computer screen. Fortunately, the laptop Steve had provided had a sophisticated sound card.

She searched Paul's files using keywords. *Dawler. Billy Ray. Interview.* Nothing.

She scrolled through his documents, looking for unfamiliar icons or names. Nothing.

She tapped softly on the base of the keyboard. Paul was brilliant and computer savvy, but he wouldn't waste his time with an elaborate retrieval system.

"If I were an audio file," she murmured, "where would I be?"

Music, she thought. She clicked on his music folder. A window opened with a list of song titles, dates . . . Dates.

"Found them," she announced.

Steve leaned over to look. She could smell him, musky and male, and feel him, hard and warm against her shoulder blade. "How many?"

She scrolled. "Three since we moved here."

"Try that one. The most recent."

She clicked. And flinched as Paul's smooth, remembered voice flowed from the tiny keyboard speaker.

It was obvious from the nature of his greeting and the tone of Billy Ray's reply that they had met before. Paul started the interview with simple, seemingly caring questions. *How had Billy Ray been? Did he need anything? Was he sleeping?*

Bailey forgot to take notes. She was helpless to do anything but listen, fascinated and repelled, as Paul wielded his voice like an oyster huckster's knife, prying and sliding, seeking the weak spot that, with the right pressure, would yield the juicy meat inside.

The questions became more pointed.

Did you know your sister was pregnant when she died?

She deserved to die, Billy Ray's voice said. *Whore.*

Bailey bit her lip.

But the child—your nephew—was innocent. Did he deserve to die?

Billy Ray muttered something that sounded like, *Son of a whore.*

That's not his fault, Paul said smoothly. *Any more than it was yours.*

Bailey recoiled from his insinuation. She had never realized before how manipulative he was. Was it death or distance that made her finally hear him this way?

Did you know she was pregnant? Paul repeated.

Billy Ray was silent. Maybe he nodded, because Paul asked, *Who told you?*

Everybody would laugh at me. She'd come to school with her belly sticking out, and everybody would laugh, he said.

Who said?

Silence.

Who told you she was pregnant? Paul pressed. *Tanya?*

No.

Who was the baby's father?

Not me. The words burst out. *He said they'd say it was mine. But it wasn't. I never did. Not with my sister.*

No, of course not, Paul soothed. Only someone who knew him well would hear his revulsion. Or his excitement. Bailey knew him very well. She shivered.

A friend would tell you if your sister was going to have a baby, Paul said. *If she was going to shame you.*

He did. He told me. My only friend.

And so you never told the police.

No.

All these years, you were silent to protect him.

Bailey's nails dug crescents in her palms.

He didn't do it, Billy Ray insisted. *It was me. My responsibility. He understood.*

But he was there.

Not then. Not when I did it. Before.

He brought you the whiskey.

He was my friend.

Who was it, Billy Ray?

Bailey held her breath. Behind her, Steve tensed.

Can't tell.

Can't, or won't?

Billy Ray remained stubbornly silent.

Paul switched tacks. *He told you to do it, didn't he? He told you to kill your sister.*

Because he cared about me.

He didn't care about anybody but himself. Or why are you in prison alone?

He was my friend.

He was the baby's father.

Billy Ray howled, an animal sound. *Nn-oo.*

A scrape, a crash, and the guard's voice, jumbled together. *Everything's all right,* Paul said, sounding breathless. *Thank you, officer.*

But everything was not all right. In the background, Bailey could hear Billy Ray weeping. She felt sick.

You think about what I said. Paul's voice was flat. Calm. Cruel. *I'll be back. You think about if you really want to be locked up for the rest of your life because your "friend"*— the word was vicious—*fucked your sister and duped you into getting rid of his little bastard by murdering them both.*

Bailey twisted her hands together, not daring to look at Steve. She was shaken and angry and ashamed. "He should have gone to the police."

Steve didn't say anything.

"Or Billy Ray's lawyer." She knew she was reaching, but she wanted—too late—to do something that would help the situation. That would excuse her own part in it. "I mean, he might have had grounds for a new trial."

"That would have helped book sales." Steve's tone was dry.

"It would have helped Billy Ray!"

"Unless he was killed to prevent him from giving Ellis a name."

She twisted in the chair to face him. "But then why was Paul killed? If he didn't know who Billy Ray's 'friend' was . . ."

"Maybe our mystery killer was afraid he'd figure it out."

Bailey exhaled. That made sense. "You need to tell Chief Clegg. Once he sees the interview—"

"I can't."

"I'll make a copy of the file."

"It doesn't matter." Steve's face was set. His eyes were like stones. "The Dawler case is closed. Sherman is going to the DA tomorrow to request Ellis's death be ruled a suicide. According to Clegg, it's over. I'm done. I go to him with new evidence now, and I can kiss my job good-bye."

TWENTY

BAILEY didn't believe him. Steve wouldn't drop the investigation. He was too good a cop. And too honest a man.

"Then what are you doing here?" she asked.

"Because you're in danger whether the chief wants to admit it or not." His face was gaunt, his tone harsh. "Whether he wants me to investigate or not."

Warmth enveloped her heart and weighted her chest. He was doing this for her. Risking his career, his future, his daughter's well-being for *her*.

"Why doesn't he want you to investigate?"

Steve paced, only to be brought up short by the bed. "I got the notes of the responding officer today. Not police reports, not case summaries, but the actual notes from the officer who canvassed the neighborhood. And two things stuck out. One, no attempt was made to follow up on the anonymous caller who reported the murders of Billy Ray's family. And two, a vehicle was spotted in the Dawlers' driveway not ten minutes before the call came in."

"Billy Ray's friend," Bailey whispered.

Steve's expression closed. "I don't think so."

But she was reluctant to give up on a lead or hope. "Did the officer get a license number?"

"No."

"Then how do you know? Maybe—"

"The neighbor described the vehicle as a blue Dodge Diplomat four-door sedan. He particularly remembered it because it looked like an unmarked police car." Steve met her gaze. "Right down to the prisoner cage and the light on the dash."

Oh, shit. Bailey's stomach dropped. "Could the neighbor be wrong about the time? If the police had already arrived on the scene . . ."

"The first car on the scene was a black-and-white. Apparently, the neighbor liked to keep track of the action next door. He claims he was watching TV when he saw headlights and looked out the window. The responding officer was interested enough in the guy's story to check the TV listings for that night. His story checks out."

"Maybe the officer in the car—the unmarked car—was simply patrolling his friendly neighborhood whorehouse."

"And maybe he was a patron. Or a witness. We can't know because the investigating detective didn't follow up."

Bailey had a very bad feeling about this. "Who was the investigating detective?"

But she knew. She had read the police reports.

Steve's face was bleak. The muscle worked in his jaw. "Walter Clegg."

"Okay," she said carefully. "I can see you wouldn't be stupid enough to confront him on that one. But—"

"Wrong. I am exactly that stupid. I drove to his house on a Sunday afternoon and demanded—hell, I practically begged him for an explanation."

"And?"

"He told me to drop it." Bitterness flattened his voice. "The crime was reported. The criminal was caught. The case is closed. Nothing I can do."

"There must be something."

He paced the strip of carpet between the dresser and the bed. "Not without getting the court involved. Which would take a hell of a lot more evidence than we have now."

"But Paul's murder—"

"Is Sherman's case. The best I can do is try to convince him to keep it open a little longer."

"Will he listen?"

"To what? All I've got is an interview with a dead convict and a hunch. If I could give him a name . . ." Steve shrugged. "Then maybe."

Bailey sat with her hands folded and her mind racing. In books, the identity of the bad guy always seemed obvious to her. But even Paul hadn't figured out the name of the "friend" who got Billy Ray drunk and his sister pregnant. Who had played on the troubled teen's outsider status until he was willing to commit murder.

"Everybody knew Paul was seeing Billy Ray to get him to talk," she said slowly. "Maybe somebody else tried to reach him to shut him up."

Steve shoved his hands into his pockets. "I'll go to the prison tomorrow to check the visitors' record."

"Why wait until tomorrow?"

"The records office doesn't open until Monday morning at eight o'clock."

"Will they let you see the records?"

"I'm still a cop," Steve said evenly. "Clegg hasn't taken my shield."

Yet.

The unspoken word dropped between them like a stone.

"I can't do this," she said in panic. "This could cost you your job. I don't want to be responsible for screwing up your life."

"You're not responsible for my choices." His eyes were steady on hers. "Someone I trust told me that."

Emotion tightened her chest. She could barely breathe. "Chief Clegg ordered you not to get involved."

Steve advanced on her. "Too late. I'm already involved. With you."

"Then your timing sucks."

"Bailey." Just the sound of her name in his deep drawl brought her heart to her throat. "Teresa tried to teach me there is no good time or bad time for love. All we have is the time we're given. I wasn't ready to learn that then. But now . . . I don't want to lose this. I don't want to lose you."

"Oh," she cried, torn between hope and despair, "how can I think when you talk to me like that?"

Leaning over her chair, he drew her to her feet. "Maybe I don't want you to think. Maybe we both think too much."

He pressed a kiss to the ridge of her brow, to the corner of her eye, to the tip of her nose. He flattened her hand against his chest. Beneath the soft white cotton, she could see the shadow of his chest hair. His heart thudded under her palm, steady and strong.

"Let's just feel for a while."

She could feel *him,* hot and hard against her. Desire uncurled in her belly. He didn't mean . . . He didn't want . . . *Now?*

"You're out of your mind," she said breathlessly, as his mouth cruised the line of her jaw.

"Mmm." He nuzzled beneath her ear, and she sagged against him. "Go crazy with me, sugar."

She was crazy for him. She had fallen hopelessly for this tough, terse, intense cop, committed to his daughter and a dozen years her senior.

Maybe she was out of her mind, too. Because this didn't feel crazy. It felt . . . right. Better than anything had in a long time.

He brushed his lips over hers, tempting, teasing. She opened to him on a sigh. He kissed her again, slower, deeper, longer. Her fingers slid between the buttons of his shirt. His hot skin, his rough hair, filled her with delight. His big hands skated over her, stroking her back, rubbing her shoulders, kneading her behind. She'd never imagined she was the type of woman who could be appreciated for her body, but under his hands she felt beautiful. She was beautiful.

He molded her breasts while he lavished her with more slow, wet, devastating kisses. She floated on a current of sensation, tugged along by his expert touch. He nudged his thigh between both of hers, and she gasped.

She had wanted him before, but this was different. Everything was different now. She eased his buttons from their holes. He slipped her shirt straps down her shoulders. They uncovered one another, standing face-to-face with the last light of day edging the motel curtains. Her heart pounded in her chest. His breath rasped in her ears.

The air was humid, the room lost in shadow. It was like making love underground or under water. Each kiss spun them down another level. Each touch took them deeper, like water falling, flowing, seeking. They sank down onto the bed. He was open to her, unguarded, his heart and his eyes naked. She was open to him, languid, lifting, her body and her soul bare.

The room swam. Her heart filled to overflowing.

"Inside me," she whispered, holding him. Loving him.

"Let me . . ." He rolled away from her, breaking the connection.

She clutched at him. "Stay."

"I'll be back," he promised hoarsely.

She watched, wanting him so much, loving him so much, as he sheathed himself with a condom, resenting even that thinnest barrier that kept him from her.

She ran her hands over his broad, heavy shoulders, down his smooth back, wanting him with her, needing him inside her, thick and hard inside her, filling her with his passion and his strength.

"Now."

"Yes. Oh, God, Bailey."

He plunged to her and into her. She shuddered and he groaned. They met and moved together. His hands sought hers on either side of the pillow. Their fingers laced and linked. Their eyes caught and held.

"With me," he said through his teeth.

"Yes." *Always*.

Joined, connected, they tumbled together into the deep, into the dark, into the pulse beat at the heart of the world.

"I don't want to move," Bailey said.

She was sunk, mired with this man in this bed at this moment, their bodies plastered together, every nerve tingling and every muscle limp with satisfaction. She could stay this way forever.

He grunted. "I can't move. So that makes us even."

Even. Equal. Matched.

She snuggled closer. Except, of course, they couldn't stay like this forever. He had to get back to his daughter. To work. To his life. And she had to get back to . . .

There wasn't anything she was eager to go back to. She

wanted to look forward. Only now, when she envisioned her future, she saw Steve. Steve and Gabrielle. Bailey smiled. Steve and Gabrielle and Stokesville, which was a nice town, really, unless you didn't particularly want to stay the person you had been in high school for the rest of your life.

Her smile faded.

Steve threaded his fingers through her hair, smoothing it behind one ear. "You're thinking again."

"I know. Bad habit."

"I like it," he said, surprising her. "What are you thinking about?"

She opened her mouth and then closed it again. How could she tell him she was worrying about marrying him and spending the next fifty or so years in Stokesville when he hadn't even said the L word?

But she knew that was an excuse. After what they had shared, he didn't have to tell her. He cared for her. She felt it, in the marrow of her bones, in every cell and fiber.

She was simply afraid.

At her continued silence, his eyebrows raised. "It wasn't a trick question."

She flushed. "I was just thinking you probably need to get home soon. Gabrielle will be expecting you. You don't want to be late."

"Yeah. She's already sulking because I didn't bring her today. She wants to see you when all this is over."

"That's nice, because I want to see her," she said honestly. And then, even though she had told herself she didn't need the words, she heard herself ask, "What about you? Do you want to see me, too?"

His gaze narrowed on her face.

"Oh, yeah," he said softly. "I want."

She felt the muscles of her womb contract.

So he was late getting out the door after all.

"I'll call you," he said, as he slung on his shoulder holster and adjusted his jacket.

That awoke some old, bad memories. Bailey briefly felt like teenage Tanya getting the brush-off from her high school crush. But Bailey wasn't Tanya. And Steve wasn't like any other man she'd known. His job would always interrupt the daily rhythm of their lives, would always put him at risk. If they were going to be together, she had to get better at good-bye.

"Are you going to the prison in the morning?" she asked.

He nodded.

"Well, good luck with that."

He frowned. "I don't like leaving you alone."

"Don't worry. I told you, I don't intend to be the dumb dead girl."

He smiled reluctantly. "Glad to hear it. This guy is escalating. He's getting closer to his victims and he's apparently convinced he won't be caught. He worked on Billy Ray to kill Tanya, and he may have arranged for Billy Ray's death in prison. But he pulled the trigger on Ellis himself. He waltzed into your parents' house in broad daylight and attacked your father. You be careful."

"I will," she said, and thought about adding, *I love you.* But after all his warnings it sounded too final, as if she didn't believe she would see him again.

As if they wouldn't have another chance to say it.

And maybe a small part of her still wished he would say it first.

"You be careful, too," she said.

This time he didn't ask her why.

ON Monday morning at eight o'clock, the prison reminded Steve of the ant hills that erupted in his front yard every summer. Uniformed guards patrolled like worker ants, crossing the yard, marching purposefully through the corridors, while hordes teemed out of sight.

Leaning against the front counter of the main building, Steve missed the familiar weight of his gun. He had turned it in at the main gate. The lockbox key rested in his pocket.

He showed his shield to the female deputy on the other side of the glass. "Steve Burke, Stokesville PD. I'd like to see William Ray Dawler's visitor list for the past month."

The young woman examined his ID and then his face. She was pretty in a severe kind of way: no dangling earrings or long hair for an inmate to grab hold of.

"You'll have to ask the warden." She gave him another once-over. "I could place the call for you if you'd like."

"I'd appreciate that," he drawled.

The warden was genial and incurious. "Go talk to the ladies in Records. They'll take care of you."

The ladies in Records, bless their hearts, tried. But when they brought Steve the list of Billy Ray's visitors, he saw at once the only person to visit in the past thirty days was Paul Ellis.

Another dead end. Frustration balled in his gut.

He had been so sure Paul's killer would have attempted to reach Billy Ray. But then why wasn't he on the visitor list? All friends and family members at the prison needed an appointment. Only officers of the court, law enforcement personnel and attorneys, could come and go as they pleased.

Only officers of the court . . .

The hair rose on the back of Steve's neck. He spoke through the glass. "Could I see the professional log, too, please?"

Unlike the visitor lists for each individual inmate, the professional log consisted of a daily log sheet at the front counter where all officers of the court who visited the prison were required to sign in.

"Those are filed separately," the female deputy said.

"Is that a problem?"

"Not really." She smiled at him through the glass. "Wait here."

He waited, his impatience firmly in check.

Eventually the deputy returned with a stack of scrawled on sheets which she slid to him under the pass-through.

Steve raised his eyebrows at the size of the stack. "I might be a while."

"Take your time. Nobody here is going anywhere." She smiled at her little joke.

"Right. Thanks."

Each day's log recorded visitor's name, inmate's name, time in, time out, and the nature of the visitor's business. One day, one sheet, one line at a time, Steve studied the scribbled columns, searching for Billy Ray's name.

He didn't find it.

Occasionally he recognized another name: a cop pursuing a lead in an investigation, an attorney visiting a client. Macon Reynolds was there.

Steve frowned. What was an estate lawyer doing at the prison?

He studied the spidery signature—*Macon Reynolds III*—a prickling at the back of his neck and in the tips of his fingers. Last Tuesday afternoon, two days after the murder of Helen Ellis, her lawyer had paid a prison visit to a Clyde Miller.

He nudged the log sheet toward the window, tapping a finger on the relevant entry. "You know this guy?"

The deputy squinted through the glass. "Miller? Sure. He was just transferred to isolation."

Apprehension gripped Steve. "Why?"

"He killed that other inmate."

"Which other inmate?" he asked urgently.

The pretty deputy's face creased in confusion. "Why, the one you were asking about. Billy Ray Dawler."

TWENTY-ONE

MACON pulled his Lexus SUV into his reserved space in front of the law office at nine-thirty. He had a ten o'clock appointment with that little bitch Regan Poole, after which she would undoubtedly expect him to take her to lunch.

He might. He might not.

Her usefulness to him was over. The girl just proved Macon's general rule that once you stuck your dick in a woman, she became less interesting and more demanding. She was too conscious of what he owed her, too critical in bed. Hell, if he wanted that kind of attitude, he could fuck his wife.

He swung out onto the sidewalk—God, it was hot—pausing to admire the picture of Leann Edwards strolling up the street, a pharmacy bag in her hand. Two kids and twenty years hadn't robbed the bounce from her tight little cheerleader's body. He rather regretted missing his chance with her in high school. Back then, of course, good girls hadn't interested him. And by the time he finished law school, Leann was already married to that stick, Bryce.

He wouldn't miss his chance now.

He lengthened his steps to intercept her. "Leann. This is a pleasant surprise. What brings you into town?"

She waggled the bag at him. "I had to pick up a prescription for Mama. She's that upset about what happened to Daddy."

He arranged his face into a suitably grave expression. "I heard. How is your father?"

"Doctor says he'll be fine."

"That's good. You tell them I missed them in church yesterday. Your sister, too," he added casually. "How's she holding up?"

Leann rolled her eyes. "You know Bailey. She's making a big fuss over nothing."

Macon didn't know Bailey, but she hadn't struck him as the fussy type. She seemed quiet. Smart. Observant. All of which made her more dangerous to him.

"I guess that's natural," he said. "It can't be easy for her, being in that house all alone after your father was attacked like that."

"She's not staying in the house. She checked herself into a hotel."

Macon widened his eyes. "Really? Well, the Do Drop's nice."

"She's not at the Do Drop. She's at one of those nasty places out by the highway."

His pulse picked up. "Some of them aren't so bad. Which one?"

"Pineview? Pinecrest? I went to see her this morning, and all I can say is I'm glad I'm not staying there. Of course, it didn't help any that she has papers all over the room."

"Papers?" Macon asked carefully.

"Just something she's working on: The Lord knows what she's going to do with herself now that . . . you know, she doesn't have a job. She asked me to bring her my old yearbooks, of all things."

"Yearbooks." He could barely breathe. His blood drummed in his ears.

"All four of them. I thought it was funny, too."

Not funny. And now Leann would remember this conversation, would remember she told him about the hotel and the yearbook . . . *Shit*.

"Maybe she was bored," he suggested. "Staying by herself."

"She could have stayed with us. Although Mama's in the guest bedroom now, and I don't know what Bryce would have said, having my whole family staying with us as if they didn't have a perfectly good house not ten miles away."

He had to think. He had to.act. Quickly.

"I'm sure Bryce would go along with whatever you wanted, Leann. He's a lucky man."

She dimpled and didn't deny it. "Aren't you sweet to say so."

"I always thought you were the prettiest girl in high school."

"You did not. You never once looked my way. You thought I was just some skinny ass little Goody Two-Shoes."

Macon heard the hint of pique and smiled. He could use that. He could use her.

"Oh, I looked," he assured her. "But you were one of the good girls, and back then, well . . ." He smiled disarmingly. "I was always such a bad boy."

She laughed.

He took a step closer, careful not to touch her, careful

not to alarm her, enjoying the pretty pink flush of excitement in her cheeks and the guilty sparkle in her eye.

"Come be a little bad with me," he invited. "We could grab a cup of coffee."

She tapped her well-manicured foot in its expensive sandal. "Oh, I don't know. Bryce . . ."

"Would be welcome to join us, of course," Macon said promptly. He observed with satisfaction the disappointed downturn of her lips. "But I'm sure he wouldn't grudge me buying his lovely wife a cup of coffee. For old times' sake."

"We-ell." Leann smiled at him, confident in her ability to attract. Secure in the knowledge she would never, ever cross the line. "I guess for old times' sake . . ."

"My car's right here," Macon said, and swept her away.

THAT fucking bastard stood her up.

Regan narrowed her eyes at Macon's middle-aged office assistant. "What do you mean, he isn't in this morning? I had an appointment."

The woman consulted her desk calendar. "I see that. I don't know what could have kept him, but—"

"This really pisses me off."

"I'm sorry, Ms. Poole." The genuine sympathy in her eyes made everything worse. "I'll tell him you were unhappy."

"I'll tell him myself." She marched toward the door to his office.

The assistant stood. "You can't go in there."

Regan barged through, fully expecting to find Macon behind his desk.

Fuck. He wasn't there. His assistant wasn't lying about that, at least.

She appeared in the doorway, her pleasant, round face creased in worried lines. "You'll have to leave."

Regan tossed her hair. "Why?"

"This is Mr. Reynolds's office," she explained. Like Regan was stupid or something.

"But he's not using it now, is he?"

The woman pressed her dark red lips together. Regan could have told her a lighter shade would be more flattering to her skin tone, but she wasn't in a charitable mood. "If you'd like to wait, you can do so in the reception area."

Regan cocked her head. "With you? You really want me out there with you and all the firm's other clients, complaining about what an asshole your boss is? And how I can't wait to replace him with somebody who hasn't ridden his daddy's coattails all his life? Maybe somebody who, I don't know, actually knows how to spell barrister." The woman's eyes widened. "Yeah, I thought so," Regan said in satisfaction. "I'll wait in here."

"It's very irregular," the assistant complained.

"So is blowing off a really big client, but that doesn't seem to bother your stupid boss."

Her point won, Regan sank into Macon's large leather desk chair. She was sick of being dismissed. Ignored. Just the way her mother had ignored her, just the way her brother ignored her. Richie hadn't even returned her call last night.

Tears tightened her throat. Asshole. They were all assholes.

Bereft, bored, and at a loss, she looked for something to occupy the time until Macon showed up. All those big fat law books had to be just for show. The man she had gotten to know was hardly the world's biggest intellect. He probably stashed dirty magazines in his desk.

The thought cheered her. She opened a bottom drawer to reveal a box of thick, cream-colored stationery. Boring. But under it . . . Her lips curled. He had something hidden there. She tugged on a dark corner. A notebook. She pulled it out.

TANYA DAWLER. MY DIARY. KEEP OUT.

Now, why would he keep some girl's diary in his desk? Opening it at random, she began to read.

BAILEY lined her pencils in a row and flipped the yearbook open to the section with the seniors. If she was right—big "if"—all she had to do to identify the father of Tanya Dawler's baby was find a good-looking upperclassman with the name or nickname Trip. Which could be anyone with a "III" after his name.

Not that a name alone would be enough to win a conviction or even to reopen the case. But she might turn up an actual person for Steve to interview.

Margaret Allen, Evelyn Armstrong, Dawn Ayers . . .

The girls had big hair and fake pearls and velvet drapes pinned firmly between their shoulder blades by Georgina Stewart of Stewart Photography.

Reflexively, Bailey straightened her spine. Ten years after these pictures were taken she had worn the same pearls, endured the same pins and disparaging comments about her lack of bosom. She had hated it then. It was funny now.

The boys' photographs were funny, too, with their uncomfortable expressions and tuxedo-style dickies Velcroed around their throats.

Daniel Baldwin, Richard Bland, Jr., Steven Burke . . .

Steve.

Gosh, he looked young. All that *hair*. She smiled. How did he fit that under a football helmet? He looked out from the page with all the assurance of strength and youth, and her heart broke for him a little because his life hadn't turned out the way he must have planned. She thought of the experience that had etched lines across his forehead and the loss that carved brackets around his mouth. And yet . . . He was the same. Tougher, maybe. Improved with age. But she recognized his dark, level gaze, his firm lips, the confident set of his shoulders.

He'd left town shortly after graduation, just like her. Just like her, he was back.

But for different reasons. Steve had come home for his daughter. For Gabrielle. Bailey understood and respected his decision. But once their hearts healed, once they'd both made peace with their loss . . . what then? Was Stokesville enough for him and Gabrielle?

Was it enough for her?

She sighed and turned the page. *Andrew Carroll, Matthew Clark, Eugene Cotton* . . .

She was working her way through the M's (*McDonald, McKinney, Mitchell*) when someone knocked on the door.

Bailey raised her head with relief. It was almost ten. Could Steve be back from the prison already?

But when she checked through the peephole, she saw her sister standing there with her weight on one foot and a stricken expression in her eyes.

She jerked the door open. "Leann, what's wrong? Is it Daddy?"

Macon Reynolds III stepped in from the side, his jacket over his arm and his swathed hand pointed at Leann's head. "It's not Daddy. It's me." With his free hand, he pushed Leann toward the door. "Get in."

STEVE whipped his truck to the curb in front of the fire hydrant. No matter how disliked he was in the department, no cop would ticket another cop for a parking violation. Besides, right now he didn't give a good God damn.

He slammed the door of his truck, trying to quell the panic pounding in his chest. Bailey was fine. He was in time. He had a genuine lead at last, and Macon Reynolds didn't even realize he was under suspicion.

But an irrational urgency drove him.

A bell suspended above the law office door jangled as he entered.

A pale older woman with a slash of red lipstick looked up at the sound. "Good morning. May I help you?"

"Yes, ma'am." Steve flashed ID. "I'm here to see Macon Reynolds."

She glanced over her shoulder nervously. "I'm sorry, he's not in."

Steve followed the direction of her gaze to where an office door stood half open. "You don't mind if I see for myself."

"Well, really, I—"

He strode inside; stopped in surprise. Regan Poole curled in the big black leather chair behind the desk, her chin propped on one hand, a notebook in her lap.

"What are you doing here?" he demanded.

She stretched indolently, calling attention to the long line of her legs, the thrust of her breasts. "I could ask you the same thing."

Steve glanced around the empty office. "Where's Reynolds?"

"Wow, another good question."

He leveled a look at her.

Regan flushed. "I honestly don't know. Frankly, I don't care if I never see that bastard again."

"Then what are you doing here?"

"Catching up on my reading." She flashed the notebook at him.

Printed in bold, black letters on the purple cover were the words, TANYA DAWLER. MY DIARY. KEEP OUT.

Steve's heart hurtled into this throat. Cold sweat broke out under his arms and down his back. "Where did you get that?"

"In his desk. It's pathetic, really. He knocked her up, and she actually thought he loved her and was going to marry her and make her life all better." Regan laughed shortly. "I could have told her how that one turns out. What are you doing?"

He ignored her, already punching Bailey's preset number into the cell phone gripped in his hand.

Pause. Click. Ring.

Come on, sugar, he thought desperately. *Pick up.*

Ring. Ring.

BAILEY'S cell phone shrilled from her purse. *Ring. Ring. Ring.*

She knelt at her sister's feet, tying Leann's ankles to the chair legs with bras from her own overnight bag. A third bra secured Leann's hands behind her. Macon's handkerchief was stuffed in her mouth. Bailey's fingers fumbled. Her eyes swam with terrified tears. She could barely see the knots she was making. She tied them as loosely as she dared. Given enough time, Leann might be able to work herself free.

Too bad they'd both be dead before then.

Ring. Ring. Ring.

Bailey jerked. She turned her head to Macon, sitting on the edge of the mattress. With an effort she focused on his face, ignoring the muzzle of the gun, which stared at her like a third, blank eye. "I should probably answer that."

Macon sneered. "Do you think I'm stupid?"

Stupid. Sick. Psycho.

Bailey's heart pounded in her chest. She did her best to answer evenly. "I think you've been lucky. But your luck can't hold out forever. If I don't answer my phone, someone's going to guess something's wrong." *Please, God, let Steve guess something's wrong.*

"Or they'll think you're in the shower." Macon smirked. He stood, looming over them both. Leann shrank. "Where are the tapes?"

Bailey's mouth dried. "What tapes?"

"Don't play dumb. Everybody always says what a bright girl you are. I want the interview tapes."

"I don't know what you're talking about."

"You will," he promised. "Of course, by then it may be too late for your sister."

Leann whimpered.

It was too late anyway. He couldn't afford to let either of them live now. But maybe Leann hadn't realized that yet. Bailey hoped not.

She didn't say anything.

Macon waved the gun. "Over there."

Bailey scuttled to the dresser on her knees. If she could distract his attention from Leann, maybe they had a chance. If Leann could get her hands free . . . If Bailey could stall him long enough . . . Sooner or later, Steve would come looking for her. She just had to keep them alive until then.

Macon watched her cross the floor, his gun pointed unwaveringly at her head. "That's good."

She stopped.

Casually, he reached across his body with his free hand and backhanded Leann across her face, snapping her head against the chair.

Bailey's cry merged with her sister's scream, a high,

thin sound from behind the gag. Above her distended mouth, Leann's eyes were wide and terrified, the left one already rapidly swelling shut.

After one horrified look, Bailey fixed her gaze on Macon, willing him to look at her. To focus on her.

"Oh, *those* tapes," she said.

He chuckled, smoothing his hair. His hand trembled slightly. His knuckles were red. "Now she remembers," he mocked.

"I was confused before." She didn't have to pretend to produce that quaver in her voice. She would beg, she would cry, she would do whatever it took to stay alive.

Whatever happened, she vowed fiercely, Steve would never have to question her will to fight.

"The interviews aren't actually on cassette tapes," she explained. "They're computer files. Like music downloads," she added when he frowned.

"I don't believe you." He raised his hand again.

Leann cringed.

"Stop! I'll show you," Bailey said desperately. Her muscles ached with tension. Her hands shook with fear. "If you'd listen . . . it will only take a minute."

He considered her thoughtfully. In the silence, her phone trilled again, three short rings before voice mail routed the call. Bailey held her breath.

"This computer?" Macon asked finally.

She exhaled. "The interviews aren't . . . um . . . actually on the computer. They're stored on a flash drive in my purse. I'll just . . ." She reached cautiously for her purse on the floor by the bed.

He kicked her in the side, so swiftly she didn't see it coming, so hard the pain detonated along her ribs and forced the air from her lungs. White pain. Red light. Her mind went blank.

She lay with her cheek pressed to the carpet and tried to breathe while above her Leann moaned.

Not Leann, Bailey realized gradually. The moans were hers.

"I told you not to answer the phone," Macon chided.

"No . . . phone," Bailey gasped. "Just . . . flash drive."

Every breath stabbed like a knife. Had that bastard broken her ribs?

"You have to ask." He plucked her cell phone from its pocket and dangled her purse above the floor, smiling at her like a fifth-grade bully spotting his victim across the playground. "Nicely."

She hated him more than she had hated anyone in her life. Which was good. Hate made her strong.

"Please," she whispered.

Please don't let him open my purse.

Please don't let him look inside.

Please let Steve come soon.

Please.

Macon let the bag drop.

Bailey crawled forward, her sides aching, and dragged her purse to her by its strap. With shaking hands, she pawed through the contents. Tissues, Tic Tacs, condoms, mace . . . Her heart hammered against her ribs. She panted with fear and triumph. Curling her fingers, she withdrew the flash drive and the mace together.

"Got it."

RACING toward the motel—lights, no sirens—Steve prayed, as he hadn't prayed since Teresa was first diagnosed with cancer, negotiating with God.

Please let me get there on time.

Please let Bailey be all right.

Please strike that fucking bastard with lightning.

And finally, breathlessly, hopelessly, just . . . *Please*.

If Macon was holding Bailey hostage . . . Steve's heart shuddered.

Fuck the chief's notions of jurisdiction. He needed a SWAT team. He'd already broadcast to the dispatcher requesting all available backup. Every cop in radio range, from the Stokesville PD to the county sheriff to the state patrol, knew a crisis situation was brewing at the Pinecrest Motor Lodge.

Bailey had told him he wasn't responsible for his wife's choices or her death. But if he lost Bailey, it would be his fault. It would be because he hadn't been smart enough or quick enough to save her.

He had survived losing Teresa. He wasn't sure he could survive loving and losing Bailey.

He should have told her.

After all his big talk about living in the moment, he had wasted too many moments with her.

He only prayed he'd get another chance. *Please*.

TWENTY-TWO

EVERY breath hurt.

Bailey stared at the computer keyboard. Her vision blurred. Her head swam. She pressed her thighs together, squeezing the tiny canister of mace between them. She couldn't use it. She didn't dare. Macon wasn't close enough.

So she would fight him with every other weapon at her disposal. With trembling hands, she depressed a few keys, closed and opened windows, searching through PLAY and RECORD.

On the other side of the room, Macon moved restlessly, his gun at the ready. "You said this would only take a minute."

Every minute she delayed was another minute she could live. Another minute for Steve to find them. *All we have is the time we're given,* he'd told her. The words took on a terrible significance now.

Once she played the audio file, there was no going back. Macon would kill her.

Who was she kidding? He was going to kill her anyway. And Leann.

Above her makeshift gag, her sister's eyes begged her to help her, to save her. *Brainy Bailey. If you're so smart, think of something. Do something.*

Right.

Bailey licked dry lips. "This is the interview." She clicked to start it, praying the computer could perform two functions at once.

Macon listened just long enough to identify both voices before he ordered, "Delete it."

"It's not that bad," Bailey said. *Time,* she thought. *Keep him talking.* "It might actually help you. Billy Ray never gave Paul a name. I don't think he even knew you were the father of Tanya's child."

"Until Ellis told him." Macon shook his head. "Twenty years that dumb fuck kept his mouth shut. And your boss couldn't leave it alone."

Bailey's heart hammered. "So you killed Billy Ray before he could talk."

"I didn't kill him. I wouldn't dirty my hands with him. Dawler trash." He smiled, a small, mean smile that made her shudder. "I had someone else do it."

Bailey swallowed. "Who? How?"

"Some other dumb fuck doing eight-to-ten for armed robbery. A client of my father's, with a pregnant girlfriend. I told him I'd take care of them if he'd take care of Billy Ray."

She was horrified. "You killed his girlfriend?"

Macon looked amused. "No, I gave her money. It was only *my* pregnant girlfriend I found it necessary to dispose of."

Tanya. Poor Tanya.

"Did you kill her?" Bailey asked.

"I didn't have to. I provided the alcohol and the . . .

inspiration, would you say? Billy Ray really did the rest."

"He murdered his sister. He murdered his mother and his grandmother. For you."

"For himself. I had nothing to do with Tammy and Shirley's deaths." Macon shrugged. "Although I can't say I was sorry they were gone."

Bailey racked her brain for something else to keep him talking. "Did you kill Helen?"

Macon appeared genuinely surprised by the question. "Hell, no. The old bitch was worth more to me alive than dead." He smiled. "I can't bill every client one hundred and fifty dollars an hour for a lunchtime fuck."

Leann made a small, choking noise.

Bailey felt sick. "Then, why? If you didn't kill them, if you didn't kill Helen . . . What did it matter what Billy Ray said or what Paul wrote? You're a lawyer, for God's sake. All you were guilty of was getting some underaged girl pregnant and supplying alcohol to a minor. Even if the publicity surrounding the book forced a case to court, a jury would never convict you. You'd never serve time."

"You're supposed to be so smart. It was never about going to jail. It was about being trapped in this bumfuck town with no way out. That little bitch threatened to go to my father, did you know that? I was graduating in another year. I was already looking at colleges. And she was babbling about love and the baby and our future. As if I would actually contemplate a future with the town slut and her bastard. I wasn't going to stay here and go to community college and listen to my father prate about responsibility and obligation for the rest of my life. I had the chance to be somebody. You of all people should understand that. I have plans. I wasn't going to let my life be ruined by some two-bit whore. Or some two-bit writer."

"So you killed him. You killed Paul to protect your reputation."

"That's right. And now I'll kill you. I'll even have to kill your pretty sister. Poor Leann." He stroked her cheek and then her breast. She whimpered and strained away. Tears streaked her face above the gag.

Bailey clenched her hands in her lap.

"I'll try to make it up to you. Would you like that? One last fuck before you die." He raised his head and smiled at Bailey. "I'll kill you first. Unless you want to watch."

Bailey's stomach twisted into knots. She lifted her chin. "I'll pass, thanks. Whatever you have probably isn't worth looking at, anyway."

His face changed, the smooth surface cracking to reveal the teeming ugliness underneath. He strode toward her. "I'll show you what I've got."

She sat frightened, frozen, on the end of the bed. Cold sweat slithered down her back and glued her thighs together.

He reached her and grabbed her hair.

She raised her hand and sprayed the mace directly into his face.

"Aaargh!" He howled and spun away, clutching the gun, clawing at his eyes.

Bolting from the bed, Bailey pushed past him and threw open the heavy metal security door, adrenaline pumping through her system, every muscle tensing, every instinct shrieking at her to run.

Leann.

She couldn't leave Leann.

She stumbled back into the room, dropped to her knees, and fumbled with the elastic binding her sister's legs to the chair. Frustration robbed her of breath. Of strength. She couldn't do it. She would never get her untied in time.

Macon struggled to his feet, rubbing his face and cursing.

Grabbing the chair, Bailey tipped it on two legs and backed toward the door, dragging her sister after her across the worn carpet. Pain stabbed her side. She gasped and tugged.

"You bitch!" Macon roared. "You fucking bitches! I'll fucking kill you!"

Bailey bumped into something solid. She cried out in despair.

Warm arms swept her out of the way.

And a cold, familiar voice rang over her head. Steve's voice. "Police! Freeze! Drop your weapon."

He was here. She was safe. She sagged in relief.

"Fucking bitches!" Macon sobbed, pointing his wavering gun in the direction of Steve's voice.

The gunshot cracked, explosive, echoing in the small room. Bailey screamed. Her heart shattered. *Oh, God, was he hit? Was Steve hit?*

She opened her eyes and saw the blood bloom on Macon's shoulder like a flower. His arm fell uselessly to his side. His gun tumbled to the floor. He crumpled, sobbing and choking.

Steve stood over him like the angel of death, his gun pointed straight at the lawyer's head. "Don't move," he said, still in that cold, deadly voice. His cop voice. "Or I'll shoot."

On her knees in the doorway, Bailey heard the rising wail of sirens. It was over.

Police rushed the door. Bodies pushed past her. Uniforms, brown, black, blue. She blinked. She recognized Wayne Lewis, pink-eared with excitement, and the tall black sergeant, what was his name? Law enforcement personnel crowded the room.

Officer Marge Conner bent and touched her arm. "Honey? You all right?"

Bailey worked enough moisture into her mouth to answer. "My sister . . ."

Conner followed the direction of her gaze to Leann, still strapped into the chair. "I got her."

Steve turned and saw her on her knees. Leaving the knot of officers around Macon, he pulled her to her feet, supporting her, his face hard and his eyes anxious. He stroked the hair back from her face, his hands trembling.

"Are you all right?" he demanded. "Did he hurt you?"

Mutely, she shook her head, and then winced when he pulled her against him and held her close. That was okay. She needed him to hold her. She rested her head against his broad chest, absorbing his strength, listening to the staccato rhythm of his heart. He'd been frightened. For her. Ignoring the pain of her ribs, she tightened her arms around him.

"I know my rights," Macon's voice rose sharply. "I want an attorney."

Bailey shuddered.

Steve stiffened protectively. "He can hire a hundred attorneys. He won't get out of this one, I swear."

"I know." Raising her head, she smiled at him. "I recorded him."

Steve's eyes narrowed. "You what?"

"The laptop you brought me has a built-in microphone. I got almost everything. His confession, his threats against me and Leann . . . I recorded it all."

He stared at her a long time before an answering smile tugged the corner of his mouth. "Think you're pretty smart, huh?"

She grinned. "Well . . . yes."

"So do I."

He pulled her close again. Knees shaking, ribs aching, she leaned against his chest. It was all over.

And it was just beginning.

EPILOGUE

THERE was nothing clearer or more beautiful than the December sky at night. Peace wrapped the house. The sky pulsed with stars.

Bailey stood on the porch of Steve's mother's house and tipped her head back against his broad shoulder, enjoying the warmth of his arms. Above them, the thin crescent moon hung on the bare winter branches of the oak in the front yard.

Earlier that evening, they had attended Christmas Eve mass at Saint Mildred's with Gabrielle. The candlelit church was filled with half-remembered faces. The traditional carols and beautiful words of the liturgy had seemed familiar and strange, comforting and challenging, all at once.

Not unlike Bailey's relationship with Steve's daughter, actually.

Or her life these past six months.

"Watching for Santa?" Steve murmured in her ear.

She smiled and turned in his arms. "Could be. I have been a very good girl this year."

"The DA would certainly agree with you."

"I'm just glad he isn't going to charge me with killing Helen Ellis."

Steve shook his head. "Never happen. He knows you're innocent."

"You mean, you convinced him."

"*You* did. You and your tape against Reynolds. You're the DA's star witness, sugar."

"Leann is."

"Yeah, you just saved her life."

"After I endangered it in the first place. You're the one who came to the rescue." She batted her eyelashes. "My hero."

Steve grunted. "Save it for your books," he said. But he was smiling.

"My books." She savored the words. "I can hardly believe Paragon wants to buy a sequel."

"You said it yourself, honey," Steve drawled.

She looked at him in quick question.

"You're good."

She laughed and linked her arms around his neck. "Yes, but I was thinking more along the lines of 'I finally brought a nice Southern boy home to meet my mother.'"

His mouth quirked. "That's good?"

She nodded. "Do I get my present now?"

"You can have anything you want," he promised. His eyes were lazy and warm. Her breath quickened in anticipation. "What did you have in mind?"

"Come inside by the fire," she invited, "and I'll show you."

A garland wrapped the staircase banister in the hall. Clusters of candles and bowls of potpourri scented the house with cinnamon and vanilla. Stockings were hung by the chimney with care. There was even a plate of cookies by the tree.

"Just in case Santa's hungry," Gabrielle had said earlier, with a sidelong look at her father.

Yearning caught Bailey unaware, like the residual ache along her ribs. She wanted this. Wanted them. She wasn't afraid to go after what she wanted any longer.

But what they needed counted, too.

"And what do *you* want for Christmas?" she asked brightly.

Steve raised his eyebrows at her tone. Tugging her down beside him on the couch, he twined his fingers with hers. "Besides you?"

She ignored the thrum of pleasure his words gave her. "Besides me."

"Well." His thumb rubbed the back of her hand. "I intended to tell you—I still have a job, if I want one. Our new police chief made an official offer. Once my probation period is up, he wants me on the force."

After Macon Reynolds's arrest, Chief Clegg had quietly resigned. Steve had explained it to Bailey. Twenty years ago, Walt Clegg had been a client of Billy Ray and Tanya's mother, Tammy. Arriving for a late-night appointment, Clegg had stumbled upon the murder scene. Rather than confess the reason for his presence at the house, he had retreated from the scene and placed an anonymous call reporting the crime. Clegg's resignation allowed him to keep his pension and his reputation. And Sergeant Darian Jackson, after three months as acting chief, had been hired to take his place.

"That's wonderful," Bailey said, ignoring the slight pang she felt at his news. Steve deserved this job. If it was what he wanted. . . . "You must be very happy."

He looked at her, his face serious. "I haven't said yes yet."

Her mouth went dry. Her heart pounded in her chest. "Why not?"

"I've had another offer."

She moistened her lips. "Another . . ."

"My old captain called from D.C.," he explained. "There's an opening in Homicide. They want me back."

"Oh," Bailey said faintly. "Wow."

She sat there, absorbing the news. Good news, she thought. Steve was too good of a cop to devote his days to chasing vandals at the high school and writing barking dog citations. She didn't worry his job would take him away from her. After the past five months, there was no question in her mind she would continue to see him. But how often? And would she visit D.C. as his girlfriend? Or as something more?

Was it too soon to expect something more?

Steve wasn't like Paul, she reminded herself. He wouldn't ask her to leave her life behind and offer her nothing in return.

And she had changed, too. It wasn't as if she was sitting around waiting for a marriage proposal. She had a book contract now, and a deadline. Not to mention her family's support.

You can have anything you want, Steve had said.

Maybe, she thought. But her dreams this year wouldn't quite fit into a Christmas stocking.

"What are you going to do?" she asked.

He reached for the plate of cookies. She smiled. Typical guy move, going for the food when the talk turned emotional.

"That depends," he said.

She nestled into the space created by his outstretched arm. "On what?"

He shifted her to reach into his pocket and then handed her the cookie plate. Tucked between a gingerbread man and a coconut macaroon sat a black velvet ring box. "On you."

Bailey's vision blurred. She blinked.

The box was still there.

"Here." He opened it, revealing a delicate gold basket setting supporting a flashing diamond. She couldn't speak. Couldn't move. Couldn't breathe. "The setting was my grandmother's. Do you like it?"

Emotion flooded her chest and filled her eyes. "I love it." The words escaped on a sob.

I love you.

Steve cupped her face and kissed her, with sweetness and heat. They kissed for a very long time while the fire burned and her future glowed as bright and weighted with promise as the Christmas tree.

"So," he drawled at last. "Are you going to wear it?"

Bailey drew back a little and scowled at him. "Oh, no, you don't. You have to say it. You have to say the words."

He smiled crookedly and gave her everything she wanted. "I love you, Bailey. I want to spend the rest of my life with you. For richer or poorer, in sickness and health, the whole damn deal. Gabrielle loves you. My mother loves you. *I* love you." He exhaled. "Did I say that?"

She smiled at him through her tears, her heart more full than she would have believed possible. "You mentioned it, yes."

"Good. So." He took her hands. His were warm and strong and not particularly steady. "Will you marry me?"

The resolution in his gaze, the slight trembling of his hands, shook her heart and steadied her nerves.

"Yes," she said. "Absolutely. I love you, too."

He slid the ring onto her finger. It fit. Naturally. Steve

was a detail man. With a sigh, she settled her head on his shoulder, feeling his heart beat under her palm.

In the hall, the clock chimed midnight.

Bailey closed her eyes, smiling. *Home at last.*